GH00580088

A Bronx Summer

Frances Brouser

A Bronx Summer

Frances Browner

LIMERICK WRITERS' CENTRE
PUBLISHING

Copyright © Frances Browner 2023

First published in Ireland by

The Limerick Writers' Centre
c/o The Umbrella Project, 78 O'Connell St., Limerick

www.limerickwriterscentre.com
www.facebook.com/limerickwriterscentre

All rights reserved

1 3 5 7 9 10 8 6 4 2

No part of this publication may be reproduced or transmitted in any form or by any means, electronic or mechanical without permission in writing from the publisher, except by a reviewer who may quote brief passages in a review.

Book and Cover Design: Lotte Bender (www.pamalottestudios.com)
Managing Editor: Dominic Taylor

This is a work of fiction. Names, characters, businesses, places, events, locales, and incidents are either the products of the author's imagination or used in a fictitious manner. Any resemblance to actual persons, living or dead, or actual events is purely coincidental.

ISBN 978-1-7392070-7-6

Available as an e-book at www.smashwords.com/limerickwriterscentre
Print copy: www.limerickwriterscentre.com

ACIP catalogue number for this publication is available from The British Library

This is dedicated to my parents:
Sadie & Con Browner
who were my first storytellers.

ACKNOWLEDGEMENTS

I would like to thank Dominic Taylor and Limerick Writers' Centre for once again publishing my work. Editors, Liza Costello, and Bernadette Kearns (Book Nanny) for polishing this novel, which has been a labour of love for many years now. Proofreaders – Monica Keane, Una Halligan, Audrey Sadlier, Lucia Browne, Alice Keegan, and Audrey O'Carroll who are also my students, and my teachers. David Butler, author, who was my mentor, on the National Mentorship Programme 2020, under the auspices of the Arts Council, and for an Agility Award from the Arts Council in 2022. I am also grateful to Offaly Arts for a writing residency this summer, 2023, in Brendan House, Birr, where I put the finishing touches to the manuscript, and to their host, Rosalind Fanning, who looked after me so wonderfully. And last but not least to my brother, Gerry, for photocopying and huge thanks to everyone who has supported my work over the years.

CHAPTER ONE

"I've something to tell you." Liam's grin was lopsided. "Meet me over the holidays?"

"Tell me now." Kaye's gaze was level with his heart, his forest green blazer. He should wear blue. A woman would sort that.

"Not here," he said, his hand sweeping the ballroom.

A lone balloon drifted across the dancefloor. Miss Doolin from Loans was swaying to Slade, her tights around her neck. The manager was sipping fruit punch *poitín* from a soup ladle. Miss Kane from Securities spraying every man in sight with her new bottle of *Ma Griffe*; Olivia and Bren slow dancing.

Olivia and Bren slow dancing? How had she missed that?

This would be Kaye's last official Christmas party with the Bank. She had dreamt about it since the first day she'd entered that imposing institution; ever since she'd walked through the wide, wooden doors of the tall, grey building at the top of Main Street, opposite the Town Hall. A young seventeen-year-old trapped in a tweed suit. She had hoped they'd place in her in a branch down the country, in the Midlands near her cousin, Chrissie, and Auntie May. Instead, they'd landed her in Bray. Hardly the escape she had hoped for.

Then, she met Liam. And started hoping for something else altogether.

On arrival at the party, everyone had been given a card bearing a name from a well-known couple. When the band announced the 'partners' dance, Liam came striding towards her holding up his SONNY sign, grinning at her CHER one. Kaye was certain he had found out what hers was and had asked for its match. They waltzed to *So this is Christmas*, tried to jive to *Merry Christmas Everyone*, and joined a circle for *I'm dreaming of a White Christmas*.

She was convinced then that this was it, this was the night. And he was about to tell her.

"We'll go somewhere quiet." She clutched her clutch bag and made for the door, rushing then through the foyer of the Royal Hotel. There would be no more missed opportunities. She'd been collecting them lately like stamps or seashells.

"How's college?" he asked, as they walked across the carpark.

"Fine," she said.

She sounded calm, but once inside the car, her shaking hand betrayed her, as she tried to light a cigarette. Tried to exhale the smoke away from his face; to think of something smart to say; to act confident. Confidence was an aphrodisiac, Olivia, her friend since she was seven, was always saying.

Liam clenched the steering wheel.

She started to panic. Had he found someone else? Was that it? He never had any girlfriends. It was what had kept her going, the fact that there was no one else, and he so tall and blonde and athletic, not your typical Irishman.

He sighed. Such a long sigh. Was he sick? Dying? About to declare his undying love for her? Say he was sorry for all the times he'd been a cad (his word) cruel, inconsiderate, unkind? He buried his head in his hands; fingers raking his long wheaten hair.

"What is it?" Kaye couldn't wait any longer. "Just tell me."

Because it had been four years of waiting, of hoping he'd come into the Bank and stride up to her cubbyhole, of searching for his corn-coloured head around the town. Four years of lifts home, of wondering whether he'd kiss her or not; four years of dinner dances, parties, even a corporate breakfast in the Burlington Hotel once; any occasion where he needed a partner. His absence in between left her floundering, like a parachuter seeking solid ground; wondering what she had done wrong.

Sometimes, she felt like she was number twenty on his list. 'That's because the first nineteen are himself,' Chrissie would say.

"I think ..." His head was in his hands again.

"Think what?" She went to light another cigarette, but her cerise pink bag had fallen to the floor. She felt for it with her foot. The rain drizzled on the windscreen, the wipers tapping out her thoughts. Was he impotent? Infertile? Sterile? Had Olivia been right about the mumps? Or did he have a woman? That was it, he had found someone else. Or a child? Did he have a child from his past?

"I don't want you to waste any more time, so ... oh!"

Suddenly, he sprung upright, still holding on to the steering wheel. The car started to sway.

Kaye grabbed hold of his sleeve. "What's that?" She cried.

Then she heard a laugh, a cackle, saw Bren's face in the windscreen, his hand slapping the bonnet, howling "yoo hoo."

"C'mon Bren." Someone laughed. A girl. "Let's go."

Kaye swung around, saw Olivia running down Main Street, Bren leaping into the air behind her. "What the hell is going on?" She exclaimed.

"I have no idea." Liam sat for a while, his breathing heavy, beads of sweat on his forehead. Then, he turned the ignition. "I'll take you home now."

"But, no! What about?"

"It can wait for some other time." He accelerated out of the carpark.

The party would be winding down. Miss Doolin waltzing with the manager, her tights now around his neck. Miss Kane nursing her empty perfume bottle. 'What's with the Ma Griffe?' Kaye had asked her once. 'It means my clutches,' Miss Kane had said. 'I always wanted to have a man in my clutches.' The spongy skin at her throat had quivered. 'Tell Liam how you feel,' she whispered. 'Don't end up like me.'

In silence, they drove onto the Dargle Road, through Old Conna, past Woodbrook Golf Club, before circling the green at Seafield, stopping at Number 16.

"Sorry about that," Liam said. "I ... "

"You can tell me now ... if you like ... if you want to, that is." Kaye tried not to come across too pushy.

"No," he said. "I'll give you a ring sometime, arrange to meet."

In her bedroom, she undressed, pulled back the *Pierrot* duvet, and was about to get into bed when, without intending to, she flicked open the venetian blinds. His car was still parked outside, his head on the steering wheel.

She sat there for what seemed like ages, not moving, not taking her eyes off him, out there under the streetlamp, until eventually, he lifted his head, revved up the car, and drove away. And she was overcome with an immense sense of fear and foreboding that whatever it was, she was not going to be able to help him.

Chapter Two

"What was all that about?" Kaye phoned Olivia the next day.

"Nothin'," she said.

"What were you and Bren even doing there?" Kaye persisted.

"We were coming home from the Harbour and thought it would be a laugh to gatecrash the party. Surprise ye. It was Bren's idea to follow ye outside." Olivia giggled.

A rare chance to be alone with Liam, destroyed by her two friends.

"Well, it wasn't funny for me," Kaye told her.

"We didn't mean anything by it," Olivia replied. "What were ye talkin' about anyhow? Ye looked deep in conversation."

"Nothin'."

For the next two weeks, the only time Kaye didn't have a pen in her hand was on the walk up to UCD from the DART station in Booterstown; the only time in her day she wasn't reading, underlining, making notes. Lectures and tutorials were attended, essays and teaching hours completed. The pupils gave her chocolates, and a bottle of wine. They'd never been known to do that before, Olivia, who was the school secretary, told her. Now, she had something to aim for - pass her exams, get her Diploma in Higher Education, and become a teacher. 'You don't want to be a two-bit typist all your life,' Liam had said to her. 'You could do much better.'

Auntie May would say the same. 'I always thought you'd be someone.' Did no one want Kaye as she was? 'Well, you're not a lump of shite.' Chrissie consoled her.

Liam's friends remarked that she was the only woman they ever saw him with. And only on important occasions. 'I'm with an escort agency.' She would joke with them. 'And Liam always picks me.' One of them once exclaimed, 'Gosh, you must be good.'

Every now and then, her mind flashed back to that night in the Royal. What had he been going to tell her? He must trust her; that was some consolation. But was it enough?

"I'm going to America," said Chrissie.

"What for?" She huddled into the telephone kiosk, hugging her coat. Their dog, Lucky, at her feet. A packet of purple *Silk Cut* in her fist. "You have a job?"

"Ever hear of ad-ven-ture? I could do with some, and so could you."

"Ya must be joking, what would I be doing in America."

"You could work as a waitress. Make loads of tips. Get off with a big American hunk. Get over yer man."

"I don't want to get over him. I'm going to become a teacher to impress him." There, she'd said it, aloud. "To make Mam happy too." She added quickly. "It nearly killed her when I resigned from the bank. I can't disappoint her again."

Kaye didn't mention that Liam had something to tell her. She couldn't bear all the awful scenarios Chrissie was capable of coming up with.

The Butlers had kept to their Christmas traditions long after Santa stopped coming. Hot ham sandwiches after Midnight Mass, cocktail sausages for breakfast the next morning, surprises under the tree, and the plum pudding soaked in whiskey, their father lighting a match until it burst into a blue flame.

"Happy Christmas." She repeated, making appropriate sounds when opening the presents, trying to laugh at the cracker jokes, donning the paper hat. Liam's voice, his sighs, his head buried in his hands were still whirling around her brain.

"What could it be?" Trish wondered.

Kaye had told her sister after dinner, the two of them alone in the kitchen with a box of *Roses* and a bottle of *Black Tower*, compliments of her pupils.

Trish put down her glass, looked at her. "We always knew there was something holding him back."

"Yeah," Kaye said, then thought for a while. "His father was very strict," she continued. "Making him go to boarding school, where he wet the bed every night. The Brothers would hang his sheets over the railings for the lads to see, their laughter ringing in his ears. But his father wouldn't let him leave, wouldn't let him come home."

"Ah the poor thing, I wonder was he abused by one of them?"

"Oh, you're so dramatic, Trish."

"Well, why don't you just ask him straight out what it is. Hear what he has to say, and then get on with your life."

But that implies he wouldn't be part of that life.

"Ya think?"

"I know. Then let him go."

"I can't."

Later, she got the urge to pick up the big, black telephone and dial his number, something she'd never done before. "Happy Christmas," she said when she heard his voice, relieved he had answered and not his mother, or one of his siblings.

"Happy Christmas to you too. Was Santie good?"

"Oh yes, I'm dyin' for some fresh air though, fancy a walk?"

Where did that come from?

"Yes," he said, without hesitation, "I'm getting cabin fever myself. I'll be over in five."

She waited at the gate, the first member of her family ever to leave the house on Christmas Day. In the car, their knees were touching, as he drove up the Burma Road. From where they walked to the top of Killiney Hill, chatting nonstop. There was an eerie silence about the place that made it more intimate. The perfect setting for their first outing as friends, real friends now. Maybe a couple one day?

"Did you do anything exciting since?" She asked him, knowing full well he hadn't.

"Yes," he said. "I went to a nightclub the other night."

"A nightclub?"

Kaye had never heard him mention anything remotely like a nightclub before.

"Yeah, the Cage it's called. In Dublin." He sounded excited.

Kaye had never heard of the Cage either, but that didn't mean it didn't exist.

"Oh, what was it like?"

"Good … good music … we danced a bit, met loads of new people."

She gazed down at Dun Laoghaire harbour, at the two piers embracing the Bay, at Dalkey Island and Howth Head in the distance.

"Oh, that's nice," she managed to say eventually. "Who did you go with?"

"My friend, Danny."

Danny? She'd never heard of him either. But she'd better not ask any more questions. People were always telling her not to ask so many questions. You get more information when you don't show any interest, they said.

Liam probably had this whole other world she knew nothing about. Of course a good-looking man like him would have a social life.

"Sounds great," she said.

And her thinking he had some terrible problem that she could help him with; that would make him fall in love with her. When was she going to learn?

"I'd better get home." She checked her watch. "Our family board game starts soon."

"Yes, let's go, it's getting dark."

She made small talk, kept things light, not wanting him to notice her disappointment.

"Thanks for that." He seemed more subdued when he dropped her off.

Kaye and Bren had been badminton partners for three years. They'd both spontaneously thrown their racquets in the air when they won their first match. The opposition said it hadn't made them feel any better. On their first night back after the Christmas break, they were practicing their drop shots, clears, smash shots, while talking about Liam. And Olivia.

"They looked very cosy the other night in the *Silver Tassie*." Bren was waiting for Kaye to serve. "Heads together."

"Heads together?"

"Yes. Deep in conversation, they were."

That's what Olivia had said about Kaye and Liam. The night outside the Royal. That they had looked deep in conversation. But not heads together.

"She was all about him too." Bren was still bouncing on his feet in front of the net. "Flirting to beat the band."

Kaye hoped Liam hadn't been telling Olivia his secret. She wanted to be first.

"Well, what about the two of you?" She teased him, finally letting go of the shuttlecock. "Slow dancing at the party, and then disrupting my chat with him."

"That was all her doing, trust me." Bren smashed it. "And it looked like she was moving in on him New Year's Eve too. Seems like she always wants what you have, Katie."

"Don't be so ridiculous." Kaye said, as they walked off the court.

She hadn't been aware that Olivia and Liam had met up over Christmas. Twice. Kaye hadn't gone out at all; half-hoping Liam would ring her, like he'd said he would.

"Why didn't you tell me?" She confronted Olivia when they were out walking in Herbert Park the next day.

"Because it was none of your business," Olivia said.

CHAPTER THREE

On a dark and sombre January evening, the phone rang, and Kaye slouched into the hall to answer it.

"D'ya fancy a quick pint?" Liam's voice was as warm as the kitchen she had just left. She hadn't seen him since Christmas Day.

"Now?" She tried to sound casual even though she was shivering. From the cold or excitement, she didn't know. Excitement, more than likely.

"Why not?" He sounded enthusiastic. "There's nothing like a teatime pint, is there?"

"I suppose not." She stubbed out the cigarette she had been smoking so as he wouldn't smell it from her breath. "Where will I meet you?"

"I'll come over," he said.

Her arm was already through a jacket that had been hanging over the banisters.

"See ya, Mam." She yelled into the kitchen, banged the door behind her and began the short walk to the end of the Avenue. Had he missed her; changed his mind; decided she was the one? An ongoing daydream for Kaye.

She walked slowly so as not to be red-faced and breathless. She couldn't wait to climb into the car, sit beside him, feel his breath, hear his voice, touch him maybe when fastening her seatbelt. It would be easier to talk when they weren't facing one another; when there was no eye contact. She couldn't be bossy, or prissy, or judgemental for the next few hours. She had to make the most of it, whatever it was. He stopped the car when he saw her and she sat into the front seat, her black corduroy skirt sliding up her leg.

"All set?" He turned on the ignition, flicking the key back and forth a few times.

"Yep," she said.

There was a splutter, the engine staggered, stumbled and then died.

Not a sound. He tried again, and again, but there wasn't a jig out of it, as her father would say. "What's going on?" His knuckles were white, as he gripped the steering wheel in the ten past two position.

"Don't ask me." She fidgeted with the buttons of her jacket, tugged at the sleeves, pressing her bottom into the seat, urging the car forward. "Was it alright up to this?"

"It was grand." He released the gearstick and clasped his hands on his lap. "There's nothing I can do now. I'll have to go home and get the brother to tow it."

No, no, not now. What about our drink, our cosy chat in the pub, you telling me you loved me? Our teatime pint? You and me together like a real couple?

She couldn't trudge home now, trek up the Avenue, into the house she had just left, after nothing, nothing happening.

"How's Danny?" She tried to stall things a little longer.

"Alright."

"Good." She took a deep breath. "So, what is it you have to tell me?"

He grasped the steering wheel again. "Just that … all we can be is friends now … For a while, I thought we could be something else. Part of me wanted it. Part of me couldn't …"

Part of him wanted it.

"Isn't that what we are?" She tried to make her voice sound normal. "Friends?"

"No, you're still holding out for more and I don't want you to. I'm unable to reciprocate your feelings right now."

"So, that's what you were going to tell me the night of the party? That's what you dragged me out for tonight? To tell me you just want to be friends?"

"Sort of."

She was suddenly tired of it all. Tired of always being there when he needed her. Tired of going for pints, walks, cups of coffee, whenever he wanted. Tired of his bestowing and withholding affection. She couldn't touch him, kiss him, caress him, run her fingers through his hair, lock him in an embrace, or even a hug whenever she felt like it. He hadn't contacted her once since Christmas, to ask how she was, to ask her how the teaching was going. "No," she heard herself whisper. "I don't think I can be your friend anymore."

The evening commuters scurried past. Rush hour traffic crept by the parked car.

His face crumpled.

She was not going along with what he wanted for the first time since she'd met him. She was putting herself first.

"I'm sorry," he said.

"Me too."

I did the right thing. She walked home along the Avenue. One minute she felt strong, resilient. *I'll get over it.* Next she faltered, knees trembling, feet leaden. *How am I going to get through?* A block of cement weighed down on her chest; the emptiness seeping into her veins and coursing through her body; filling up the space where her heart used to be.

Right now, he had said. He couldn't return her feelings RIGHT NOW. Did that imply there was hope for the future?

Pat Kenny was signing off his radio programme, the steam hissing from the pots in the kitchen, her father ruffling his newspaper, her mother calling "dinner", Trish and Gary scampering out of the sitting room. Twenty minutes was all it had taken, she noted on the grandfather clock. She trudged up the stairs and slipped under her *Pierrot* duvet and, this time, surrendered to the grief.

"Your mother said she never heard anything like the wailing." Olivia arrived early next morning. "It was as if someone was dead, she said. What happened?"

"He just wants to be friends."

"So?"

"I said I couldn't."

"What did you do that for?" Olivia flopped down on the bed. "Our social life is all wrapped up in his. The craic, the banter, the sessions. You can't just give it up."

"Oh, I know, I know." She started rocking back and forth.

Olivia lit two cigarettes, handed her one.

Mam brought them tea on a tray, muttering about fish in the sea and they didn't break the mould when they made him, then backed out of the room.

"You'd think you were dyin' of a deadly disease." Olivia scoffed.

"Well, a broken heart is a sort of an illness," Kaye said. "Remember the arm bands you made us wear when Morgan got married?"

"Oh, stop it," Olivia jumped up. "Look, think long and hard about this. If you're no longer friends with Liam, you'll lose other friends too, maybe even me."

"Gee thanks."

She still didn't know if Liam had confided in Olivia or not and for the first time since they'd met, she wasn't able to ask.

They'd been friends since the Butlers had moved to Dublin from Kilcoughlan and Kaye had to start school all over again. It was attached to a House, where children from broken homes lived, including Olivia. They were in the same class but didn't speak until one day they met in the House – Kaye needing a hat for sodality, Olivia a dry pair of knickers. 'I have a kidney infection,' she told her, and Kaye had been fascinated. Later, they linked arms down to the Church and from then on, Olivia was allowed out to Butlers on Sundays. Even when her Ma took her home for good, Olivia still went on drives with them to Brittas Bay and Glendalough, and the Pantomime at Christmas.

At last, Kaye had a friend.

The next five months were spent trying to drum Hamlet into disinterested fifth years. "Drum is not the right word," the Inspector said. "You should relate the play to their lives. Compare Bray to Denmark. Bring the sea and the yacht club into it." Kaye didn't bother reminding him that these teenagers were never going to be inside a yacht club.

"We know where he lives," they told her. "We'll throw stones at his window, Miss."

"Leave his windows alone," she pleaded with them.

"Don't mind him, Miss, we think you're a great teacher. Shakespeare's a thicko."

"Who's NB, Miss, is that your boyfriend?" One of them pointed at the initials she'd scrawled in the margins of her book.

Yet, she still only managed to get a D in teaching practice.

In the meantime, she missed the Friday night sessions and was not included in the annual Pitch 'n Putt league between the Bank, County Council and Technical College.

"It would be too awkward," Olivia told her.

The loss was like an ache.

There weren't even nights in Dublin with Chrissie to look forward to. When her cousin got a job in the Telephone Exchange and a flat in Drumcondra, Kaye often joined her and her colleagues on nights out to the Ace of Clubs, the Revolution and Doctor Zhivago's, *where love stories begin,* the ad said.

When Chrissie first started talking about America, Kaye hadn't believed she would really go. Next thing, she was applying for a holiday visa and giving in her notice at work, deciding on a departure date and booking her flight. Kaye's world was shrinking.

She took to getting off the DART in Dun Laoghaire for a walk on the pier. She'd arranged to meet Liam there once. He'd been sitting on the cinema wall when she got there, eating an apple, and had teased her for being late. A good sign, Chrissie said. Men always made fun of girls they fancied. Together, they had walked to the end of the East Pier and sat on a blue bench watching lobster pots bobbing on lace-edged waves.

'I can feel your heartbeat.' She'd rested her head against the thin fabric of his shirt.

'It would be worse if you couldn't.' He'd whispered.

Every week, she replayed the memory, until one day in May, there he was, walking towards her, smiling shyly, muttering "hi". Only then did it dawn on her that had been her reason for going there all along. The piers like two arms hugged the waters, turquoise and teal, behind him; the swans' beaks touched, their long necks forming a heart. Her face burning, she stepped aside to let him pass. He stepped too. She stepped back, so did he.

"Sorry," he said.

"Sorry." She walked away.

Sorry.

Her hair was falling out in tufts, and she was putting on weight. Everyone else lost weight after a crisis, Kaye put it on. Comfort food, Trish called it. A few days after seeing Liam on the pier, she wrote him a letter, pouring everything onto the page. How he'd used her, then discarded her like an old boot; had made her believe there was something, when there was nothing; had led her on at the beginning, then left her in the end. She told him not to reply; that she never wanted to hear from him again. Then regretted it as soon as the envelope dropped into the post box.

On the last day of term, the Dean of Education announced that only eleven percent of them would find full-time employment. One in eleven. "Look at the person to the left and right." His voice boomed through the auditorium. "They'll be emigrating." He pointed to people at random, "you and you and you." He kept indicating. "Fifty-seven thousand left last year. In cycles of thirty years Ireland has been drained of its youth, the twenties, fifties and now the eighties. When they're gone, the rest of us can turn out the lights."

Kaye shuddered.

And her after giving up her job.

CHAPTER FOUR

She wandered into the Harbour Bar one Friday night and they were all there, playing their various instruments – Liam on mandolin, Bren trying the guitar, Olivia on the fiddle and tin whistle, along with a piano accordionist, and some banjo, and ukulele players. Kaye didn't play an instrument, but she sang. Her voice was her instrument, Liam used to say, but Kaye never felt it was good enough.

Someone called for a song.

I am a rambling Irishman, she began.

"A lovely immigrant song," Liam said when she'd finished.

"Yeah, I'm off to America."

He looked at her, didn't speak for a moment, finally managed, "Good for you."

Olivia tilted her head, regarded her sideways, frowning.

Bren's mouth opened and closed again.

"To New York, to join Chrissie." The words tumbled out.

New York, New York, the others started singing, and Kaye danced around them.

What was she thinking?

"Just for the summer." She added, starting to lose her nerve.

It turned out to be the best night she'd had in a long time. She could've been there all along, she realised, could've stayed friends with Liam, like they'd always been. Nothing needed to have changed, at all. If only she'd been more patient, it might have worked out. But just for the summer was a good idea. Maybe he'd miss her. Then she'd come back tanned, and thin, and full of confidence, looking so sensational he wouldn't be able to resist her.

"I'm glad you decided to come." Chrissie gushed into the phone. "You'll love it here."

"I will?" Kaye still couldn't believe she'd made the call.

"We'll have a laugh, and you'll make a fortune. The tips are amazing."

"I will?" She couldn't tell Chrissie the real reason. She couldn't tell anyone.

"And you can stay here, Mo won't mind."

"Ok. Let me think about it." She pretended. There'd be no thinking about it. She had to go, now.

"You think too much already. Oh, and Kaye."

"Yeah?"

"Bring some *Tayto* and *Sure* deodorant."

"*Sure*? Deodorant? Don't they have it over there?"

"They do, but it's brutal. OK?"

"OK."

She looped a curl around her ear and sank into the velour seat of the telephone table, the only sound the tick-tick-tick of the grandfather clock. What had she just done?

"So, you're going?" Trish bounced down the stairs.

"I think so. For the summer."

"Great!" Trish clapped her hands. "I'll be able visit on my way home."

"Oh yeah, I forgot about that."

Trish had got herself a J1 student visa and a job in a summer camp in San Diego. It hadn't dawned on Kaye to apply for one at the time. She'd hadn't had the slightest interest.

"Should I take the bull by the horns as Mam would say?"

"Grab him by the balls," said Trish.

"September 18th," she told the man in Global Travel on Abbey Street when he asked for a return date. This had not been part of the plan, she counted out two hundred pounds onto the desk. Not part of the plan at all.

When she rang to say when she was arriving, it was Mo who answered.

"It's hard enough get a job here," she told Kaye. "And you work your ass off for those tips."

"Oh," was all Kaye could say.

"Make sure you have an invitation from someone over here, to a wedding or something."

"What for?"

"To prove to Immigration you're not staying. Chrissie brought a camogie stick and pretended she was coming over to play a game."

"She did?" Kaye stifled a laugh. No way could she picture Chrissie in camogie gear.

"And whatever you do, don't attract attention on the subway."

"Ok."

Kaye hung up. What had she let herself in for?

Olivia asked them to help her move into a house she was renting in Shankill. There had been a strange man in her Ma's flat when they arrived, but Olivia didn't introduce them. After they dropped the boxes on the floor of her new home, the three of them crammed into the small sitting room for *Carlsbergs* and bars of *Club Milks*.

"Here's to friendship." Liam raised a bottle, and Kaye's heart sank into her shoes. If only she was staying, she could try being his friend again.

It was a warm evening, no clouds in the sky, the Sugar Loaf purple in the distance, birds chirruping outside and the DART rumbling by. Kaye wanted the day to last forever. To bottle it, Bren would say, bottle it. The conversation got around to children and Kaye hinted that it wouldn't bother her too much if she couldn't have any.

"I hope to have a hundred." Olivia declared and the three of them laughed.

"Well, you won't fit them in here, that's for sure." Liam stretched out on the carpet. He was wearing a white football jersey and jeans. "Is it because you've no brothers and sisters?"

"Maybe," Olivia said.

Kaye held her breath, she had never discussed Olivia's family situation with her.

"I'll probably never have a child." He jumped up and the girls looked at each other.

Kaye thought he was going to tell them about the mumps. Instead, he lunged at her in an awkward hug. "I'd better go. Safe journey." He then turned to Olivia, "See you tomorrow," and made a hasty escape out the door.

"Tomorrow?" Kaye looked at her.

"Yes, he's helping me with the heavier stuff." Olivia kept her head down.

"Oh."

They were obviously spending more time together than she'd realised. It could've been her, could've been her. She wished she was staying, wished she was staying. She had handled it all wrong. September. September. She'd start all over again in September.

"Was that your father earlier?" She asked Olivia. The words had always been unspoken between them, a territory they'd never ventured into.

"Nah, that's an uncle. Da's in London. That's where Ma met him. He left when I was two and she came home, put me into the House, came to see me whenever she could. But I was fine. The nuns were nice."

"That's good."

"But, in school, the teachers were mean, the pupils too. We were the odd ones out."

"Like me." Kaye had been called a culchie by her new Dublin classmates.

"Oh, you weren't as odd as we were. You had a normal family. Anyhow," Olivia stretched up her arms and yawned, "we survived and came out the other end."

"You did." Kaye grabbed her bag and jacket.

"The babies were the worst," Olivia followed her to the door.

"Babies?"

"In the House. At first, they'd be smiling and chuckling and gurgling, kicking their tiny feet. Within days, there wouldn't be a sound out of them. The silence was deafening."

Kaye trudged step by step to the DART station, feeling as awful as she possibly could.

Bren insisted on buying her a drink to celebrate the end of the season, and her going-away. They were hunched over a low table, racquets and shuttlecocks strewn on the floor, the air reeking with cigarettes and stale beer and the cackle of teammates. "You'd never know when I'll see you again." He clinked her glass.

"I'll be back before you know it." She took a mouthful of beer. "Were you ever in The Cage?"

"Whoa, where did that come from?" He put down his glass. "I wandered into it once. Why?"

"What was it like?"

"Grand, a nice place, nice people, great music. I just had the one drink and left."

"Why?"

"Ah, it wasn't for me. Why do you want to know?"

"Liam said he was there one night. I was just wondering."

"Oh," said Bren. "That reminds me, I saw himself and Olivia in the Harbour Bar."

"So," she shrugged. "They're always at the sessions."

"No, this was midweek, on their own." He pulled on a cigarette.

She felt a thump to her gut. For the millionth time, she wondered if Liam had confided in Olivia? They did seem to have become very friendly.

"Ah, sure they're friends." She tried to keep it light.

"Oh, I'd say she'd like it to be more than that."

She packed her rucksack with shorts and tops, and flipflops and capri pants, because it was all casual over there, Mo had said.

"Don't mind her." Trish stuffed in a fuchsia silk dress. "In case you have a date or something. Americans are always going on dates."

She also brought a black skirt for waitressing, and a peach one for interviews, and the six packets of *Taytos* Gary brought home from the pub.

"Crisps for Crispy." He tossed them onto her lap, and Kaye regretted nearly hitting him with a hurley when they were small.

The next morning, her mother tried to kiss her goodbye. Mam had only ever kissed her once before, and that was on her First Holy Communion Day when it had kinda caught her on the nose, as she turned away. "It's only for the summer." Kaye stumbled out the door, her rucksack on her back, the dog yapping at her heels, and rushed towards Olivia's car. Mam was still standing on the doorstep, waving, as they rounded the corner onto Seafield Road.

Olivia also attempted to kiss her when she dropped her off at the station, Olivia who hated kissing women. She'd never given Kaye a hug or an affectionate peck before.

"It's only for the summer." Kaye opened the car door before she got too close.

"You'd never know." Olivia's sleek, black hair swished around her shoulders.

Kaye used to iron hers but had despaired of ever getting it that straight. Nor would she ever be as thin as Olivia who was now handing her an envelope.

Kaye recognized the familiar scrawl. "What's this?" she asked.

Olivia shrugged. "I don't want to get involved. Just grieve and get over it. Move on."

"Should I wear a black arm band?"

Olivia rattled the gearstick. "Don't be so smart."

"What's going on?" Kaye asked.

"I don't know. Like I said, I don't want to get involved. He's my friend too."

Kaye watched the red Mini Minor disappear into a cluster of trees at the end of Railway Road, then hoisted her rucksack onto her back and ambled over to the station.

But I was your friend first.

CHAPTER FIVE

The first thing that hit her was the heat. The revolving doors of JFK spun her slam into a wall of heat, petrol fumes, and snarling traffic. Kaye dumped Auntie Lou's bogus wedding invitation into a nearby bin and a letter from the Technical College to say that Miss Katherine Butler would return to teach there in September. Immigration had been terrifying, although if they'd deported her, so what? 'Have a nice day' the official had waved her on. Have a nice life. She stepped into a swarm of pedestrians. Feck it, she'd left the *Taytos* underneath her seat on the plane. Chrissie would kill her. She'd spun a fancy for Gary lately. Even though they were first cousins, Kaye liked to point out. Didn't they need a dispensation from the Pope or something? Then again, Chrissie fancied everyone, whereas Kaye; Kaye could only keep her eye on one at a time.

Squinting at the buses lining the pavement, she took the one marked SUBWAY. It wound around a myriad of roadways, with blocks of glass and chrome glittering in the sunshine, and signposts for what seemed like every airline in the world. She figured out how to buy a token, shuffled onto the A train, and heeding Mo's advice, pretended to study a map on the wall. Making changes at West 4th and 59th streets, she finally settled on the Number 1 Uptown, hurtling towards 242nd Street. Did that mean there were one hundred and eighty-three more stops?

The carriage rattled from side to side, reeking of mouthwash, cologne, and spicy cigarettes, heaving with hip-hop, reggae, rap. Buskers strummed guitars, banged drums, jingled coffee cups. A man with no legs sailed by on a skateboard, using his hands as oars. A quartet sang *When Irish Eyes Are Smiling*. Was she that obvious? Her legs were glued to the Fanta-orange plastic seat, her arms and thighs stuck to the arms and thighs each side of her.

So different from the DART that morning, rolling through sleepy seafront stations. The Dublin Area Rapid Transport, modelled on the BART in San Francisco, had replaced the old brown train of her childhood. What would it be called in Frankfurt had been Bren's joke at the time. Or Warsaw? Torremolinos?

She plucked Liam's letter out of her bag. She couldn't wait to show it to Chrissie, to hear what she made of it. I'M SORRY IF I HURT YOU. He'd written. I'VE BUILT A WALL AROUND MY HEART. WHEN YOU'RE TAKEN UP WITH YOUR OWN PROBLEMS, IT'S HARD TO SEE WHEN SOMEONE ELSE IS HURTING. Yeah, real hard when you're not even looking. AND I FEEL MORE COMFORTABLE WITH OLIVIA BECAUSE SHE'S NOT INVOLVED LIKE YOU ARE. The words caught in her chest. She couldn't breathe. The pain coursing through her.

During a summer in Cape Cod, he'd visited Manhattan, taken a quick look at the subway, he said, then legged it on up to the street again. Kaye pictured his gangly frame loping the tunnels, his lanky limbs manoeuvring the turnstiles, his furrowed brow as he navigated this underground bedlam. Then the train wormed its way up into the open air.

Block after block of brownstone buildings met her gaze, black stairways zig-zagging the walls, lines of washing suspended between them. People loitered at doorways, lolled against cars, gyrated to boom-boxes the size of suitcases. A girl in a pink dress sat in a window, a chunky pink telephone clamped to her shiny black curls, its chord looping out onto the ledge. Women in hair rollers chatted in doorways. This was not what Auntie Lou's long-ago photographs had depicted. Not how Chrissie had described it. Not at all what Kaye had been expecting.

Chrissie was working late, so it was Mo she'd be meeting first, after she collected the keys to the apartment in some pub. When all she wanted was a cup of tea, a bath, and not to meet anyone until she had a chance to do herself up. Her capris and crochet top that had been ironed and clean that morning, were now creased and grubby looking.

The train screeched into 242nd street; they hadn't stopped at every street, after all. Struggling down the rusted steel steps of the station, she wondered why the tracks were now up in the air? A group of men were kicking cans, shouting, 'Taxi, taxi. You want taxi, Miss?' Well, if she did, she'd bloody well ask for one. She tiptoed over bird droppings, the sweat sticking to her and picked her way through the rubbish cascading out of kerbside bins. Shouldering open the battered brown door of the Terminal Bar, she kicked her rucksack in before her. *This cannot be it*, she rubbed her eyes; *this cannot be it.*

It took a moment to adjust to the darkness and eventually she was able to make out a circular counter, faded paper shamrocks on grubby cream walls, green paint flaking from the ceiling, a lone customer bent over a pint of Guinness, watching television, from which came the excited voice of an Irish commentator, a cheering crowd.

A barman emerged out of the shadows, as tall as a tree and as willowy; his mousy hair curling around the collar of his white cotton shirt. Legs all the way up to his elbows.

"Hi there." He flicked a beermat on the counter. "What can I get you?"

"I'm here to collect the keys of Crisp, eh, Chrissie, Christine's apartment," she told him.

He retrieved them from the cash register, held out his hand without smiling.

"Nick's the name, and you are?"

"Kaye."

She clasped his hand, wishing she'd put on some make-up, dampened her hair, flattened the frizz, had a chance to run to the loo first.

"Katherine? Kathleen?"

"Katherine."

"Take a seat, K for Katherine." He gestured at a stool. His eyes were a light chestnut colour. "You look like you could do with a cold beer."

Fumbling in her purse, she wondered what she did look like? The barstool swivelled, as she sat onto a leathery seat that had clumps of wool, cotton, and coiled springs oozing out of it. "A *Bud*, please," she said, the only American beer she could think of.

"You got it." He placed a bottle on the counter and spun away.

The beer tasted bitter, as it swirled to the back of her throat and trickled into her tummy. She realised she hadn't eaten anything since the plane. Maybe she should grab something before Chrissie arrived. But then Nick returned with another beer. She reached for her purse again and tweaked out a ten.

"Keep your money, pet." He pressed the note into her palm, folding her fingers over it. He sounded American, but pet was an Irish sort of a thing to say. "Wait until you're working. That is, I presume you'll be looking for a job?"

"I suppose," she said. "In a few days maybe." She didn't want to seem desperate.

Look mysterious, Olivia would say. A sure man magnet.

The Fields of Athenry started to blare from somewhere. Humming along, she tried to act like she was used to sitting at a bar by herself. A few GAA jerseys wandered in, the television was turned up full volume, the digital clock above the till blinked 6.00. Her watch said eleven. She'd go as soon as her drink was finished.

"Here's Sil." Nick was back, tilting his head at a black curly haired fella, with a black moustache, who was ambling in. He looked like one of the taxi drivers from outside.

"Give the girl a drink." He sat beside Kaye, tossing a twenty on the counter.

"I really should go." Kaye attempted to swivel off the swivel stool. "The girls will be wondering where I am."

"What girls?"

"Chrissie and Mo?"

"Those two? There's not a fear of it." He insisted. "Sure they'll be stopping in soon."

"Oh, Ok."

Jaysus!

It was rude to refuse, was Olivia's motto; never say no to a drink or a dance was Chrissie's. So, she sat there chatting to Sil, watching the drinks pile up on the counter. Three more barmen joined Nick, and a band started up in an adjacent room. The jukebox flipped over to Madonna, the TV to basketball, and the air reverberated with the ping of football machines. Tanned, freckled faces flooded in, clapping hands, and shouting '*Alright!*' in flat Irish accents.

"Another?" She eyed the nearly empty bottle twirling in Sil's fingers.

"Don't mind if I do," he said.

Shite.

"So, you're the cousin?" He addressed the beer handles on the bar in front of him.

"Yep," she said.

"We used to live near one another, down the country, then my family moved to Dublin when I was seven."

"And do you have a man at home?" Sil smiled at her now, his eyes black as tar.

Jaysus!

"Em, sort of." Kaye rubbed her arms, shivering. "This place is freezing."

"Well, you either do or you don't."

"I did, I don't really anymore." Kaye couldn't stop herself. She wanted to have a story, like everyone else. "I think my friend might be after him."

"Oh, forget about them so." Sil looked at her. "Start a new leaf."

At least he hadn't told her to move on.

"Ya think so?" She screwed up her eyes.

"Of course." He looked away again. "A fine-looking woman like you? Hey, Romeo," he roared at Nick. "Call the girls, and turn down the AC."

"I'm on it!" Nick picked up the telephone. So he had their number.

Sil started chatting to an Irish girl the other side of him who was upset over a Claddagh ring she'd lost the night before. He teased her about whose bed she had woken up in, whose bedroom it was left in. Kaye envied them their banter, their ease with each other; the way they flirted without worrying about the consequences.

"You're to hold on." Nick's hand was on her shoulder. "Mo's on her way."

"And Chrissie?"

"No idea." He took his hand away. "So, I suppose you're looking for a man too?" He leaned in, flecks of amber in the chestnut eyes.

Jaysus!

"Em, no, I have one actually, at home."

"Really? So, what are you doin' here then?"

"I just wanted to get away for the summer." She squirmed around in her seat. What had possessed her to lie?

"Oh, forget about him." Nick straightened up. "Stay here, start a new chapter."

As he walked away, his back muscles rippled against his shirt. What did he know about her chapters?

"He's a bit of a lad." It was Sil, back to her again. "All the girls fall for him."

"Well, I won't."

"You'll be grand here." Sil spurted out. "And isn't it better than sittin' on your arse at home, waitin' for the dole to open?'

Kaye supposed it was, although she'd never been on the dole in her life.

"It's hard being illegal though." He addressed the beer handles again. "Afraid to go home, in case I don't get back in. Afraid to leave my apartment, my new stereo system."

Kaye was trying to imagine not going home because of a stereo when a pixie face, framed by brown wispy hair, popped in between them, slapped a clump of dollars on the counter and turned to her. "You must be Kaye."

"Hey Mo," Sil said.

"Oh, hello." Kaye sat up straight and looked around. "Where's Chrissie?"

"She's delayed downtown."

"But it's nearly eleven, isn't it closing time soon?" Kaye fiddled with her watch.

"Nah, not until four. Now, who's for a drink? And, have ya got a cigarette?"

"Eh, no, I gave them up, but I'd love some peanuts or crisps." Kaye's eyes were blurring. She could see two glasses on the counter now where there should be only her one.

Mo grabbed Sil's packet "I'll have one of these. Hey Nick, what's up?"

"Hey there." Nick cruised by, blowing a kiss. "Who's bustin' your chops?"

"Just breakin' balls, that's all." Mo strutted off up the bar. She hadn't asked Kaye about home, her flight, nothing. As if Kaye was in the Terminal every Saturday night, with Sil.

And where was Chrissie? She could see two cigarettes between her fingers now and couldn't make out which one to pull on. She had intended giving them up, but what the heck.

"Can I have a soda water?" she asked Nick.

"Club Soda, coming up." He filled a glass with ice and fizzy soda from a pump. "Not able for the pace, eh, Katherine?" He leaned in again, his tealeaf eyes close to hers.

"No, just thirsty, that's all." She tried to smile but it came out in a yawn.

"Can I take you home?" Sil's moustache was scratching her cheek.

"I'd better, I suppose." Mo was back, feeding her the soda water through a straw.

"You'd better," Nick said.

Kaye wanted to explain that she wasn't always like this. That she wasn't drunk, just tired, that's all; that she hadn't slept in nearly a day; hadn't eaten in ages. But Mo helped her off the stool, and steered her outside, without giving her a chance to say goodbye.

"Mind yourself," she heard Nick call after her. Like something her mother would say.

The footpath was wedged, the air heavy with heat, throbbing music, Taxi, Taxi.

"Hey, Andy," Mo roared at a sallow-skinned boy with long black hair.

"Hey." He took Kaye's arms and lowered her into a white car. Sil slid in beside her. Where did he come from? Mo sat in front. Up a wide street, the car swerved and zoomed into traffic lights, headlights, neon lights, all the while Mo chatted non-stop to the driver. How did she know the bloomin' taxi driver? Sil kept falling into Kaye; she kept elbowing him away until the cab stopped in front of a tall brown building, like the ones she'd seen from the train.

"Bye, Andy." Mo jumped out, pulled Kaye and her rucksack out of the back seat, and banged the door.

"Can I come in, Kaye?" Sil scraped at the window with his fingers.

"For a cuppa?"

Mo looked at her, one eye arched.

"Don't look at me." Kaye struggled to pick up her rucksack. "No." She started to stumble away. "Say no. Tell him we've no milk."

Mo caught Kaye by the arm and shoved her up three steps to a glass door.

"I wouldn't encroach on anyone's territory this quick, if I were you." She whispered.

CHAPTER SIX

When she woke the next morning on a lumpy, hot couch, her head felt like a cement block. When she tried to turn it, left and right, the pain knifed through her. For a while, she lay there in the silent, unfamiliar room, until it felt possible to ease herself up onto her elbows, squinting her eyes open. It took a minute or so before she dared lower her feet to the floor and then the dizziness came, so she had to wait, before making her way carefully over to the barred window, the air muggy, the heat a shawl. She was sweating in places she didn't know she could sweat.

There were two brownstone buildings each side of her, with the same black stairs snaking the walls and wide glass doors creaking every time someone went in or out. DELI flashed in neon above a shop on the corner. Spanish music wafted from the street, where people sat on chairs, their voices chiming like bells. Opposite was a row of houses - peach, blue, lemon, lime, like the *Iced Caramel* sweets she used to love as a child. Sirens squealed, horns beeped, voices roared, music blared, dogs barked.

So this was the Bronx.

Before last night, she'd imagined it a street, a block, or a few blocks maybe. Judging from the drive home, it was much bigger than that.

At least there were dogs.

From the L-shaped hallway she could see into two bedrooms - one empty, two beds in the other, a double and a single, but no Chrissie, or Mo.

She managed a shower without fainting, though as soon as she was out and had pulled on a top and shorts, she was perspiring again. The sitting-room, with its high ceilings and wooden floors led straight into the kitchen. In a tank-size fridge, she found *Coconut Creams* and *Cadbury's* chocolate. Feck it, the *Taytos*, the girls would've loved *Taytos*. She filled the kettle and had to light the gas cooker with a match;

couldn't find tea, only teabags.

A sliver of sun slanted in the window, snagging the dust. It didn't feel like a Sunday, not like at home where she'd be sitting in an armchair, hunkered over a newspaper open on the kitchen floor; roast beef sizzling in the oven; peas and raspberry jelly in twin glass bowls on the sideboard; a Begnets' match in the afternoon, afterwards the club bar.

Before she left, Chrissie had imagined herself in an apartment like Rhoda, the TV character they both loved, with a doorman like Carlton.

"Hello." Mo was in the door and down the hall, tugging at her nurse's hat, yanking open the buttons of her white uniform.

"Hi." Kaye jumped up. The packet of biscuits rolled off the table, onto the floor.

"Oh Lord, I'm pooped." Mo fell onto a chair. "I sure wasn't in the mood for changin' bedpans today. Pass me a soda?"

"Em, yeah." Kaye opened the fridge door. "Soda?"

"Coke. Coke. Gimme the *Coca-Cola*." Mo pointed at a giant bottle.

"D'ya have ta wear tights? Even in summer?" Kaye handed Mo the bottle.

"Yeah." Mo took a gulp. "They're gross in this heat." She placed the bottle on the table and proceeded to peel off her thick, black tights. "How's the head?"

"Grand," said Kaye. "It's me tummy that's squeamish and these tea bags are no help."

"Ah, you get used to them. Wanna send out for a Chinese?"

"Send out?"

"Yeah." Mo rooted in a drawer, tossed her a KING WOK leaflet. "They'll deliver."

"Deliver?"

"Animal fat and pure MSG. Just what the doctor ordered. Perfect hangover food."

Gary's cure was another drink: the hair of the dog, he called it. For Trish, it was *Lucozade*.

"Em," Kaye perused the page. "I'll have Beef 'n' Broccoli?"

"Sesame chicken for me." Mo unhooked a cream telephone off the wall, dialled a number and called out the order.

"Now, I'm going to call Jim." She headed for the hall. "You can get the bill, and don't forget to tip the delivery guy."

"Of course." Kaye looked around for her bag. "Who's Jim?"

"My boyfriend at home." Mo disappeared again and could soon be heard chattering in the bedroom.

Two phones? Kaye made another cup of tea, sat down at the kitchen table to sip it. Didn't Mo have a boyfriend here? Two phones and two boyfriends. At least she hadn't mentioned 'encroaching' or 'territory.'

A buzzer sounded in the hall.

"Press the button," Mo roared.

Button. Button. Kaye found a button on the wall beside the hall door. "Oh! Yes, the button." Like the one in Rhoda, after all. "KING WOK DELIVERY," a voice boomed.

"Press the button again," Mo cried. "No, not you, Jim," she giggled. "To let him in."

Kaye pressed the button again and by the time she opened the door, a young fella was stomping up the stairs clutching a brown paper bag. She handed him a twenty and for the first time in her life, said, "Keep the change."

"I'd eat a horse and follow it with a jockey." Mo reappeared zipping up a pair of khaki shorts. "Wanna beer?"

"Ya must be jokin'."

"We might as well get started. Sunday's a big night in the Bronx. Everyone goes out."

"Even Chrissie?"

"Even Chrissie, Chrissie, Chrissie. Don't worry, Chrissie will be there."

"Oh, ok." Kaye tugged at the ring and severed off the top of the beer can, still holding back from asking where her cousin had been all this time. "So, d'ya like it here?"

"Sure." Mo opened the food cartons. "The money's awesome." She divided clouds of white fluffy rice onto two plates and topped them with chicken and beef. "But it's hard work. Twelve-hour shifts without a break, taking care of an old lady who sleeps half the time."

"Would you not prefer a hospital?"

"Yeah, but I'd have to do the State Board exams, and they take ages. I keep putting them off, thinking I'm going home."

Home. Like Sil. Both thinking they're going home. Like they're only here on a temporary basis. Ireland was still home.

"But you're legal here, right? You were born here."

"Conceived." Mo mopped sauce from her plate with the end of an egg roll. "And, what's with all the questions?" She tapped her nose with a pointy red nail.

"Oh sorry," Kaye said. "And about last night ..."

"Don't." Mo held up her hand. "It's Chris you should be apologising to, she and Sil have a thing. And Nick's just a charmer, it's part of his job."

"Oh, I know that. And I won't be going after Sil. You see, I think my friend is after a fella I like at home."

"No need to explain, now let's get going." Mo cleared the rubbish into a bin.

But Kaye wanted to explain. "Should I change?" She eyed Mo's shorts, the blue jersey.

"Nah. Nobody dresses up here. I'll call a cab. Oh, and, by the way, you don't have to analyse every word I say, ok?"

"Ok."

CHAPTER SEVEN

"Gimme five," Chrissie cried.

"Wha'?" Kaye saw a hand sway in front of her.

"You're supposed to hit me back, thick head." Chrissie lifted her hand again, her copper bob swishing against her chubby cheeks. "You're supposed to say, 'high five'."

"Oh, ok, high five." Kaye slapped her palm, eyed her up and down; the WOMEN ON THE VERGE OF A NERVOUS BREAKDOWN T-shirt; baseball cap turned back to front, the runners with no socks. Chrissie, who'd had a charge card for Switzer's department store and wore Michael Mortell suits to work, who had her hair highlighted every six weeks and got a facial every two, who had always been so athletic looking, Kaye had envied her.

"Ya go so fat!" Kaye said and wanted to immediately cut off her tongue.

"Ah, isn't it bedder to have it than to be lookin' for it." Chrissie wasn't a bit perturbed and gave another slap at Kaye's raised hand.

"How's Katherine today?" Nick appeared. "Back for more punishment, eh?"

Her face on fire, Kaye pointed at Chrissie's *Amstel*. "I'll have one of them."

"On me." He knocked on the counter and was gone.

"What does he mean by more punishment?"

"She conked out here last night." Mo whispered, as if Kaye couldn't hear.

"Alright!" Chrissie cried. "Imagine?" She leaned into Mo. "Makin' a show of us in front of our new friends?"

"Stop it!" Kaye put her head in her hands.

"And she was all over Nick like a rash." Mo continued. "Sil too on the way home. Wanted to bring him in for tea."

Kaye couldn't tell if Mo was joking. "I did not! I was just being friendly, trying to fit in, that's all. I'd never go after someone else's man. I'm mad about Liam." She looked at Chrissie. "You know that."

"Ah, shud up, she was only slaggin', only messin'." Chrissie's eyes widened. "And as for that other eejit, forget about him, you're going to have a ball here, an absolute ball."

"Really?" Kaye looked around. She certainly couldn't imagine that in this dark, dingy place, with the sad Irish music.

"And everyone fancies Nick. You will too."

"I will not!"

"What's that?" His long legs strode towards them again.

"Nothin', nothin'," Chrissie and Mo chorused.

Nick fanned three beer mats onto the counter. "You have a drink coming with Pete."

"Tell him he's a darlin', and I'll take care of him lader."

"Is that a promise now, Chris?" Nick winked at Kaye.

Jaysus!

"I'll go over and say hello," Mo said.

"First." Chrissie raised her glass. "Let's drink to the summer."

"The summer." They clinked bottles and Mo wandered off.

The summer. How was she even going to last the summer? At the thoughts of more beer, Kaye's stomach turned.

"I can't believe it." Chrissie pinched her arm. "I can't believe you're really here."

"I can't believe it meself."

The place was starting to fill up, getting even more packed than the night before, with people pushing into the bar, crushing those lucky enough to have a stool. The jukebox had been cranked up, and the TV. There were no tables and chairs, like in a pub at home, where the only sounds would be chatting and laughter. This was no place for a cosy chat with a friend. Nick shot by and winked again.

"What d'ya think?" Chrissie nudged her.

"Grand, but I thought you were with Sil?"

"Ah, sure I can have my eye on two at a time, can't I. So, you met Sil last night?"

"Yeah," Kaye tried to sound like she hardly remembered. "Where were you anyhow?"

"Oh, out with the gang from work, just for one. But there's no such thing as one, is there? We Irish wouldn't dream of going home before the pub closes, which means four o'clock over here. I stayed with one of the guys, in his place."

"Right."

"Nothing happened. It wasn't like that." Chrissie's face clouded with guilt; a look Kaye knew so well.

"Oh, I know it wasn't. I was just surprised you weren't here to welcome me, that's all."

"Ah, I knew you wouldn't mind, and was sure you'd be grand here. It was handier for me getting to work this morning. I don't usually work weekends, but I took the extra shifts, for the money, then one thing led to another."

"And, what about Sil? Are goin' with him or wha'?"

"Sorta." Chrissie flicked her hair. "Mo's dating his roommate, so it's handy."

"But I thought she had a boyfriend at home? Jim?"

"She hasn't seen him in years. All's fair in love and war, you know."

"Olivia used to say that too."

"Don't mind that one."

"I got a letter, from Liam, here d'ya want to see it?" Kaye took it from her pocket, thrust it quickly into Chrissie's hands.

Her blue marble eyes scanned the pages. "A wall's a good idea," she said. "A massive, great big wall to protect you from him." She bunched the lined pages into a ball and tossed them on the counter.

Kaye had never considered that the wall might be protecting her.

"Don't think about him," Chrissie said. "For the next three months, you're not to think at all." She tapped Kaye's temple. "Find someone new to date."

As if it was that easy. Kaye swivelled into the sea of Irish faces. She'd never given them a thought before. Unemployment, factories closing, multi-nationals pulling out, the collapse of the building trade were mere newspaper headlines. Gary had been idle since he'd finished his engineering degree, his bulk visible through the blotched glass of the sitting-room door every day, playing Patience, watching TV, reading the newspaper. Several of her father's colleagues had been let go. Kaye's classmates were off to Turkey and Hong Kong.

"They're too young!"

"Who?" Chrissie disentangled herself from a boy who was trying to get a drink.

"They're only children." Kaye's hand swept the bar. "They should be at home, dancing in the local disco, still living with their parents."

"They'll be grand." Chrissie slithered off her stool. "I'll be back in a minute."

Mo reappeared. "It's like musical chairs here," Kaye said to her. "Where's Chrissie?"

"Over on Pete's side." Mo was gone again.

Next thing, Nick was in front of her. "Missing your guy at home?"

"Yeah, I am actually. I wish I was back there with him."

"Well, you're here now, so you may as well make the most of it."

Jaysus.

He sounded pissed off with her. Who cares? It was true, she didn't want to be here. She wanted to be back in Ireland, sitting in the Harbour Bar beside Liam, having a nice chat. Not all this craziness. She was too tired, and lonely, and disappointed.

"HEY, WIMP, GET OVER HERE! This is the new recruit I was tellin' you about." Chrissie was roaring her way back.

A bald head appeared through the opening beside the cash register. His shovel hands grasped Kaye's. "Sorry for your troubles." His round face beamed.

"Ya ain't seen nothin' yet," Chrissie said. "This is the funniest girl to hit the Bronx."

Kaye groaned.

"Another party animal, eh?" Pete grinned at her. "I've a bottle of *Heineken* in the freezer with your name on it," he said to Chrissie.

"No, Pete, no." Mo was back. "No *Heineken* for her tonight."

"Why not?" Kaye tried to perk up. "What's wrong with *Heineken?*"

"Oh! So, you haven't heard about her wee allergy to the haitches?"

"SHUT UP, WIMP!"

"*Heineken* and *Hennessey* make her do peculiar things in the most peculiar places." Pete propped his elbows on the counter. "Like sleeping in the jacks one night."

Chrissie banged her bottle on the counter. "Give's an *Amstel* and take a hike."

Pete topped three more beers and retreated to his corner, shoulders heaving.

"Be friendly with the bartenders," Mo told Kaye. "They're good to know."

Kaye wanted to say she had tried that and then was accused of flirting with them.

"They're great for finding jobs and places to live," Mo continued. "For some people, it's their only contact when they get here."

"Really?"

"Yeah," said Mo. "I was staying with my uncle in New Jersey when I met Pete in Gaelic Park one Sunday. He told me about 4D and found me a roommate; even brought us shopping for beds. Drove us home from Fordham Road, the mattresses strapped to the roof of his van."

"Oh, that was nice of him."

"Yes. So, make sure you always tip the bartenders."

"I will."

The girls had settled into the scene so easily; leaving their money on the counter, buying drinks for other people at the bar, and collecting beer mats to trade in for those bought for them. There was no round system like at home. "These are all buybacks," Chrissie explained. "Every third drink is free, sometimes fourth and fifth, if it's from Nick."

"And does everyone really fancy him?"

"Oh, yeah, he's the best. Can have anyone he wants. Plays hard to get though."

Like Liam.

Even if she did fancy Nick, she'd never tell anyone. She'd never let him know. She'd never get him anyhow. Olivia said she gave out all the wrong signals. 'It's not a crime to like someone, you know,' she said one morning after a booze-up. At the end of the night, Kaye and Liam had been swaying close together and Olivia kept playing the piano. Kept playing even when the barman lifted her off the stool and tried to close the piano lid on her fingers.

"Ye looked so happy, I didn't want to stop," she told Kaye.

Would she do that now?

"What's so special about Nick anyhow?" She asked Mo.

"Well, he's from here and he knows all the right spots downtown," Mo said.

"Does he ever bring yis to any of these places?"

"Oh, yeah. He took us to U2 in the Meadowlands. A bartender's a great catch. They can get any woman they want because they make so much money, they make a flipping' fortune."

Kaye scanned the bar, mesmerised by it all. "Where's Chrissie now?"

"Oh, on one of her Vincent DePaul rounds; she has to talk to every oddball in the bar."

"She does? She never used to. And listen I wasn't after Sil last night, Nick neither."

"Well, it looked awful like it to me." Mo walked away, leaving Kaye wondering what she was doing in the Terminal Bar on Broadway, instead of Begnet's bar in Bray?

"Were ya in Begs' lately?" Chrissie was back, yelling above the din.

"I was there Thursday night for badminton. Had a drink with Bren after."

"So, does he still fancy ya?"

"Nah, but he said he'll miss my frilly knickers at the net."

Mo returned with a fella in a tattered leather jacket and wiry John Lennon glasses whom she introduced as Seanie. The boyfriend.

"Nice meetin' ya." He shook Kaye's hand with his sweaty one. "I suppose you're on the prowl for a man too?" He winked at the others. "I heard ya brought Sil home last night?"

Shouldn't he be slagging Chrissie about Sil? Kaye could feel her face flame.

"He's ragin'." Chrissie made a grab at his glasses. "'Cos he's not gettin' any himself."

Seanie ducked out of her way. "It's the ones talkin' about it that are not gettin' it."

Chrissie boxed him on the chest. "If yer referrin' to me, ya got that wrong."

"That's enough." Mo separated them. "We're going to The Short Stop for breakfast."

"Breakfast?" Kaye checked her watch.

"Yes," said Seanie. "Greasy eggs and bacon twenty-four hours a day. Wanna come?"

"We're going home to fry up the rashers and sausages Kaye brought." Chrissie rubbed her hands together, chortling, her chest bursting through the WOMEN ON THE VERGE caption. "And *Taytos*." She picked a strand of hair off her lip gloss. "I'd kill for a bag of *Taytos*."

"Oh no." Kaye buried her head in her hands. "I left them on the plane."

"What?" Chrissie rolled her eyes to the paint-peeling ceiling. "Ya bloody eejit!"

"Well." Seanie draped an arm around Mo. "Sorry we can't stay, but I'd ate a young Christian Brother this minute. Catch yis later." They strolled, arm-in-arm, out the door.

"Is all fair in love?" Kaye looked after them. "Why string Jim along, if she has Seanie?"

"Mo has to have a man. There's room in our hearts for more than one, you know?"

"How about Liam feeling more comfortable with Olivia, because she's not involved?"

"Fuck him."

"I wish I could." Kaye quickly put her hand to her mouth.

"All ride!" Chrissie caught it in a high-five. "And don't be tellin' everyone your story," she said. "Find a real love, instead."

"And when did you get to be so wise?"

Before they left, she folded a few dollar bills under her glass and waved at Nick to make sure he saw it. Then Chrissie leaned over the counter and threw her arms around his neck, knocking Liam's balled-up letter to the floor. Kaye tried to rescue it, but someone kicked it away.

"Have a good night, Katherine." Nick called over Chrissie's shoulder.

"Thanks," she said, "I will."

The street was wedged again with people drinking beer and eating giant slices of pizza. Taxi drivers didn't know whether to wait for the girls or grab the passengers straggling down the subway stairs.

"Chrissie, the letter! It's inside on the floor."

"So what?" Chrissie beckoned at Andy. "Take it as an omen and move on."

"I sure am moving on now." Kaye opened the taxi door and sank into the back seat.

"No Sil tonight?" Andy peered in the rearview mirror at Kaye, as he drove.

"Nah." Chrissie waved him away, "probably got stuck in Gaelic Park."

"If this is Broadway, where are all the musicals?" Kaye wondered.

"Down on 42nd Street, on Times Square, this is the longest street in the world, you know," Chrissie said proudly, as if she'd lived there all her life.

When they got to the apartment block, Andy looked at her through the mirror again. "Got milk tonight, Katee?"

"What are ya talkin' aboud?" Chrissie stuffed her hand into her shorts pocket and retrieved a bunch of bills. "Five dollies?"

"No money, Mamasita," he said. "I celebrate the first night my bonitas together."

"I'm not your mama." Chrissie kissed him on the cheek. "But yer good craic."

"This is a great country." Kaye clomped up the stairs. "I've hardly spent a penny yet."

"That's about to change real soon." Chrissie opened the door. "Jaysus!" She jumped.

Mo was sitting at the kitchen table. "What happened to breakfast?" Kaye asked.

"Ah, I decided to have left-over Chinese, and celebrate our first night together in 4D."

Chrissie lay her head on Kaye's shoulder. "Isn't this nice, just us girls?"

"It is," Kaye said, although she would've preferred if it was just the two of them. "Oh, I can't believe I left the letter in the Terminal."

"What letter?" Mo wanted to know.

"From Liam, my fella at home."

"He's not your fella." Chrissie banged her fist on the table. "He's a prick and he doesn't deserve you. Now, I don't want to hear his name anymore. You've wasted far too much time already. It's time to MOVE ON!" Chrissie rose from her chair and stomped out of the room.

"We'd better get to bed." Mo gathered up the cups and put them in the sink.

"We'd better." Kaye sighed, reeling from Chrissie's outburst. "D'ya think I'll get a job?" She followed Mo down to the bathroom, trying to act normal.

"You have to. Chris didn't start looking for a week. I was afraid I'd never see the rent."

"Sure, I spent the first three days sunbathin'," said Chrissie from the toilet.

Kaye fled to the bedroom, not able for such intimacy. The girls trooped in, stripping off their clothes. "How come we're all in here when there's another bedroom?"

"It's safer this way." Chrissie patted a place and Kaye reluctantly got in beside her.

"Don't forget your breast examinations," Mo said from the other bed.

"Wouldn't mind someone examinin' them now." Chrissie snuggled into Kaye.

"Anyone we know?" Kaye asked, trying to act as if nothing had happened. She was here for another three months after all; she'd have to get on with the girls. She pulled away a little from Chrissie and fought back the tears. Things were not turning out, as she'd hoped.

"Night, night everyone."

"Night Chrissie."

"Night Mo."

"Night Kaye."

"Night Kaye."

"Night Kaye."

"Ah, jaysus, yer no craic."

CHAPTER EIGHT

The first thing Kaye saw when she opened her eyes was Chrissie's arm flapping over her face in an attempt to turn off the alarm clock.

Six am, it flashed. Six am.

"What possessed me to work the breakfast shift on a Monday?" Chrissie poked her in the ribs. "Rub me back?"

"No."

Kaye still wanted to talk about Liam, but Chrissie had made it clear she didn't want to hear. Which means there was no one to talk to about him. She watched her leap to the floor and open the blinds.

"What a beautiful, sun shining day."

"OK, OK." Mo groaned. "Save the running commentary."

"I'd a lovely sleep." Chrissie stretched her arms in the air and bent over to tip her toes. "Now I'm gonna jump in the shower and then I'll feel really great."

"And don't forget to tell us what you do in the toilet, while you're at it."

The shower started to swish, and Chrissie's singing filled the hall, *As I leave behind Néidín,* while outside a truck roared – did they ever stop - and sirens screeched.

Chrissie returned, wrapped in a towel, dragging a comb through her wet hair. Kaye was tempted to comment again on how much weight she'd put on but remembered how awful she'd felt after the last time.

"Anyone for tea?" asked Chrissie.

Mo pulled a pillow over her head. "Can a girl not get a lie-in, for Chrissake. And by the way, you look like Phyllis Diller."

"Who?" Chrissie screwed up her face, then started lathering body lotion into her arms and legs, the towel now dangling between her thumb and forefinger.

"How about a toasted English?" She asked.

"A wha'?" Kaye's face was still in the pillow.

"An English muffin." Mo sighed. "Don't they have them at home by now?"

"Oh, yeah," said Kaye turning over, "in Marks and Sparks. I'll have one of them."

"With budder, or on the side?"

"Wha'?"

"Just bring the blooming breakfast without a song and dance." Mo swung her legs out of the bed and hit the floor with a thud. "I have to pee."

"OK, OK." Chrissie disappeared into the hall singing, *Without the Fanfare*.

After they'd had their breakfast, and Chrissie had left for work amid a flurry of keys, shoes, aprons, deodorant, bags, Mo turned to Kaye.

"Right. What's got into you?"

Kaye looked back at her, bewildered.

"You're annoyed with Chrissie for shutting you up last night, when you were talking about your guy."

"No, I'm not."

"She's just sick of hearing about him, is all."

"I haven't been going on about him *that* much."

The sun blazed into the bedroom. Outside, doors slammed, and horns beeped.

Mo landed beside her on the bed. "Try me."

Kaye looked at her. As far as she could tell, Mo wasn't having a laugh. "Really?"

"Shoot. When did you meet him?"

"When did I meet him? Let me think. It was four years ago. In February. A dull day."

"Jeez, let me grab my cigarettes if you're going to be getting all poetic on me." Mo reached for a packet of *Marlboro* on the locker and lit two – one for her, one for Kaye.

Kaye took a drag. And then started to talk. She started even further back; told her all about the commercial course she'd taken after the Leaving Cert, and everyone being disappointed with her for not going to university. How she'd felt so grown up taking the train into town every day and her typing and shorthand speeds increasing every week without having to study. How when she went for the job in the bank that Easter, she'd passed with flying colours: aptitude test, group discussion and interview. Then they'd stuck her in the branch out in Bray. How the teacher who ran the commercial college was so ecstatic with her for getting the job, she'd insisted Kaye sit for the typing teacher's diploma too.

Mo snapped her fingers. "Ok, ok, let's get to the guy."

He'd strode into the bank one day, all arms and legs, wearing a green tracksuit and anorak, the Viking hair tied back with a rubber band, a gear bag slung over his shoulder and a football under his arm. Kaye had been in the job a year by then and was bored. But that wasn't why he'd caught her eye. It was because he was gorgeous.

And slowly, it dawned on her that the commercial course, getting the boring job, and being stuck out in Bray had all led to that moment, when he walked through the door.

"Oh," said Mo. "I suppose you think it was your destiny."

"There's no need to be sarcastic."

"Oh, I don't believe all that malarkey. Anyhow, keep going, you have me hooked."

After asking around, she discovered he was the new sports liaison officer with the county council. Liam, his name was. As luck would have it, he started coming along to the folk sessions in the Harbour Bar. The very first night, he bought Kaye a drink! A vodka and lime, her usual. She sang her heart out to get his attention. Olivia reckoned a girl should show off her assets, as quickly as possible. Singing wasn't what she meant, but it was all Kaye had. And maybe it worked because, towards the end of the night, he offered her a lift home, leaning in so close she could smell his apple shampoo. She didn't have to be asked twice. And then in the car, driving up Seapoint Road and onto the Dublin Road, his fingers brushed against hers, anytime he changed gears. That would have been enough for her, but when he pulled over.

"I'm going to stop you there," said Mo. "Or we'll be in bed all day. Shower, change and we'll go get some supplies. You can pick up when we're *en route*."

Outside, the sun burnt the backs of their necks. Steam puffed from a grate, with the scent of fabric softener. They passed a deli, a church, and a school. Imagine teaching in that school?

"We'll take this street," said Mo. "It's safer because of the cop station.

So, anyhow, did he kiss you or what."

"Oh yes!"

Mo raised her eyebrows, but Kaye kept on talking. "First, he sort of pulled my head back, but in a gentle kind of way. Then he put his lips on mine."

"Any tongue action?"

"Don't be disgusting."

"Well?"

"No, not then."

Mo frowned.

"But he did ask for my number."

"Did he call?"

"Well, no." There had been days of waiting, making sure to always sound either light and cheery when she answered the phone, or slow and provocative. Olivia had said men don't like it when you're down. "He did even better than that." She added. "He called to the house!"

"Wow. Keen."

"That's what my sister, Trish, said. I was just sitting there on the rocking chair reading the Situations Vacant in the *Evening Press*."

Mo snorted. "Classy."

"I didn't know he was going to arrive in the door." Kaye was indignant. "Anyhow, in he came and asked if I'd go to a reception thingy in Dublin Castle."

"Nice."

"I mean, he didn't exactly bend over backwards asking me. Said I could come if I liked, if I wanted to. But you know how Irish men are."

"Oh, I know."

They'd arrived at Foodtown. A huge-looking place. Kaye remembered her Auntie Lou telling her that when she came to the States, she'd been afraid to go into a supermarket at first, in case she couldn't find her way out. Mo released a trolley and led the way, through the sliding doors, to its lovely, air-conditioned coolness.

"So, you went to the Castle, I take it," she said, as they browsed the aisles.

"Of course I went. All dressed up. Even got a new pair of ankle boots. He was in an olive-green suit. It was gorgeous there. Marble staircase, glass chandeliers, alabaster ceiling; frosty waiters going around with trays of wine in crystal goblets. And we talked all night."

"Got on well."

"For the most part. He was a bit snooty about me doing a typing course instead of a degree. Called me a two-bit typist."

"Dickhead!"

"Ah, he's not. Anyhow, we had another kiss that night. A real one this time."

"Woohoo. So you started seeing each other then. Going out?"

"Yeah. Well, sort of. Not exactly."

Mo was raising her eyebrows again. They were at the till now, unloading the trolley.

"I'd see him Friday nights, like. In the Harbour Bar. Sometimes he gave me a lift home. Sometimes not. Sometimes kissed me goodnight, sometimes not."

"How did you stick it?" said Mo. "I'd have put him on the back boiler."

Kaye had an image of Liam stuck in a pot on her mother's cooker. "Well, I did at times, and I did go out with other people, but then he'd ask me to a dinner dance, or a party and I'd be mad about him all over again. You know what men are like. When they think they can't have you, they're all keen." Kaye didn't believe this, she was just quoting Chrissie, and Olivia.

Back outside in the heat, Mo put her sunglasses on. "If you want my honest opinion, it just sounds like he wasn't that interested."

"Really?" She tried to be offhand, but just couldn't believe Mo had said that. "So, why ask me to all those dos and things?"

"Some men are like that. String women along until someone else shows up. Wasters."

"Not Liam." Kaye began. "He never had anyone else … and … I love him."

"You only think you do." Mo pointed at a sign on a window across the street. BROADWAY DINER. OPENING SOON. "You might get work there," she said. "Wanna go ask?"

"No, I don't. I mean, not now. Maybe tomorrow."

"Well, don't leave it too long." We can't be supporting you forever, you know."

"You won't be supporting me." Kaye was tired of it all.

Sharing her story usually made her feel warm and fuzzy, this time she felt foolish.

Celtic House was another dark and dingy pub with sad Irish ballads, more run-down than the Terminal, if that was possible, its barman blond and stocky.

"Keep your greasy paws off of him." Chrissie told her. "He's mine."

"You can have him." Kaye prized a twenty-dollar bill out of her shorts' pocket and put it on the counter, still not convinced it wouldn't be snatched. All the notes looked the same. At home, a fiver or tenner were a different colour to a twenty or a one-pound note.

"You could have him too," said Chrissie, "with your personality and brains."

"Men don't want brains, and I haven't been able to get anyone I wanted so far." Kaye hadn't meant it to come out so sharp. She saw Chrissie and Mo exchange glances.

"Here come Nick and Pete." Mo hissed. "Hey guys, come and join us."

"Don't mind if we do." Nick ambled over and grabbed a stool, sat in between Chrissie and Kaye, placed a wad of notes on the counter. "This calls for a shot." He nodded at Blondie.

"It's the party animals." Pete rubbed his hands. "*Slippery Nipples* all round?"

"Alright!" Chrissie gave him a high five.

Kaye tried to light a cigarette, tried to ignore Nick's knee touching hers.

Blondie lined up six miniature glasses and filled them with a blue liquid that they had to tip to their lips and drink in one gulp. After that, was a round of *Peach Schnapps*.

"Let's have some *BJ's*." Pete slammed more money on the counter.

Blondie filled six more small glasses with *Bailey's* and another liqueur, topped with blobs of cream. Pete held Kaye's hands behind her back. She had to grip the glass with her lips and tip back her head. The liquid rushed down her throat, and into her gullet. When she straightened her head again, the glass was stuck to her mouth. Pete had to slap her on the back and out it popped to cheers and applause.

"You intrigue me." Kaye told Nick, who looked perplexed. "You seem coooold and alooooof, then all ffffriendly." She swivelled on the swivel stool.

"I do? And you figured that out in a couple of nights?"

"Yep." Kaye kept swivelling.

The girls were nodding furiously behind his back. Indicating to Kaye to zip her lips. "Let's have some *Alabama Slammers*." They called to the barman.

"Why do they caaall you a bit of a lllaaad?" Kaye ignored them.

"Who does?"

"Everybody."

She knocked back another shot. Lights, faces, mirrors whizzed by. She kept swivelling. "Oh, and did you fffind me llletter? Ffffffrom me bbboyfriend?" She hit the tiled floor, shorts and top drenched in grenadine.

"Boyfriend? You don't have a boyfriend?" It was Mo.

"I know. I know." Kaye tried to sit up.

"So, stop going on about it."

"I will. I will." She flopped back on the floor again.

"Ah, Kate, c'mon."

Two strong arms yanked her up, pulled her out into the hot air, and deposited her onto a car seat. Lights, noise, traffic flashed by, as she lay on her side, one cheek resting on the cool leather.

Shite. She'd left her money on the counter and hadn't bought a round. *Shite.*

CHAPTER NINE

This was more like it. They exited at 59th Street and Lexington Avenue. This was what she'd been waiting for.

Kaye arched her back to look at the sky; the sun warming her face, as she gazed at the towers of glass swaying towards it. Cars bobbed by in a yellow stream of taxis, cyclists whizzing in and out.

She stomped off in the direction of Bloomingdale's.

"This way." Mo turned her around. "We're going to 56th Street, remember?"

All Kaye knew was that Chrissie had called the apartment that morning, while she was still asleep, and told Mo there was a job going in another branch of Burger Heaven. Kaye was to meet someone called George at 11 o'clock, and wear something nice, Chrissie had said.

As if she wouldn't?

"She's not annoyed with me, then?" She'd tentatively asked Mo.

"Annoyed?"

"After makin' a show of her last night?"

"You made a show of yourself." Mo had told her.

Jaysus!

She'd been a bag of nerves coming down on the subway, afraid to meet Mo's eyes, and wondering if the reason Mo was accompanying her was to make sure Kaye turned up at all?

"Here we are!" Mo now announced.

The big brown sign that said BURGER HEAVEN in yellow letters made Kaye's stomach flutter. She was about to lie through her teeth.

"I know I won't get it."

She looked in the window where a bronze weighing scales held an onion on one tray and a bunch of parsley on the other. Underneath were the words: EAT YOUR ONIONS SPARSELY AND TAKE A SPRIG OF PARSLEY.

"You'd better." Mo nudged her through the glass door, a bell chiming their arrival.

A man in a grey dicky bow and waistcoat approached them holding out a menu.

"I'm here for an interview," she told him.

"Interview?" His eyebrows converged in a V above his nose, as he sleeked back his greasy, black hair with a bony, girlish hand. He looked like Uriah Heep in David Copperfield.

"For a job?" she said.

"Oh! You need George." He pointed the menu towards the back of the restaurant, to where a man was talking on a telephone.

"Thanks."

Walking towards him, Kaye tried to appear relaxed, even as she caught sight of herself in the mirror-lined walls, her backside in the peach pencil skirt, her face, sweaty and red.

She had to get this job, no matter what.

"Katherine Butler," she said to the man, George, when his call had ended, holding out her hand and making herself smile.

"Who?" He picked up the phone again.

"I'm here for an interview."

"Interview?"

"Yeah, about a job. Chrissie–Chris from 49th Street arranged it."

"Have you any experience?"

"Em ... yeah."

"Can you work tomorrow lunch?"

"Em ... I think so."

"You either can or you can't." He heaved a huge sigh.

"I can."

"Be here at ten, in black and white."

"Ok."

"George here." He barked into the phone.

Kaye turned, made her way back through the restaurant, afraid to breathe in case he changed his mind. A young woman with yellow spirally hair sat at the cash register. Another with plaits like black ropes said "Hi" from behind the counter. Uriah Heep gave her a watery grin. Two older ladies sauntered by with plates along their arms, as Kaye's boobs wobbled, and her heels jabbed the tiled floor. She all but fell out the door.

"Jaysus!"

"What wrong now?" Mo rolled her eyes.

"I got the job." Kaye told her. "Starting tomorrow, lunch."

"Well, that's a relief." Mo steered her towards a pedestrian crossing.

"Walk, don't walk," Kaye started to sing, her heart now lighter. "This must be where Bob Geldoff got the idea. Let's get a coffee, me nerves are shattered; that was the maddest interview I was ever on. As for dressing up."

"We could go up to Chris."

"Ooh, I don't know?"

"You have to face her sooner, or later."

Mo dragged her by the arm across Madison Avenue. The lights blinked: WALK DON'T WALK. Kaye started singing again, half-heartedly, *I don't like Mondays.* "I won't like Wednesdays this week."

"The streets are numbered." Mo explained. 'We're now heading downtown."

Downtown. Wasn't that a song? They took 50th Street and turned onto Park Avenue.

Park Avenue. When they were fourteen, she and Olivia had read *79 Park Avenue* by Harold Robbins, underlining the dirty bits, hiding it under the mattress, her mother wondering why they were spending so much time in the bedroom. The real Park Avenue was shops, street traders, food vans, smells, and colours: a concrete madness, and all man-made too. Whoever would've thought a cement landscape would take her breath away.

Fifth Avenue. Where five million people trod every day, Liam had told her. And Ireland's population only three and a half. They passed St. Patrick's Cathedral where the Kennedys went to Mass and turned onto 49th Street, kept walking until they saw the familiar brown sign, BURGER HEAVEN in large yellow letters, like the one she'd just left.

It didn't take long to spot Chrissie, there at the hostess desk, cradling a phone between her ear and shoulder.

Kaye avoided her, followed Mo, took a stool beside her at the counter, picked up a menu and pretended to study it.

"Well?" Chrissie shouted over. "Did ya get the job or not?"

"I got it."

The phone shrilled. Chrissie scribbled on a notepad, roared into a microphone, and packed cartons of food into brown paper bags.

"Have ya got a uniform?"

"I brought a black skirt like you told me, and flat black shoes I got in Dunnes."

"They'll do, for now. TUNA WHISKEY DOWN. GAC BAC WITH TOMMY. Until you get sneakers. HELLO, BURGER HEAVEN. Everyone wears them here, even with suits and fur coats. Fur coats and no knickers. SORRY SIR, CAN I HELP YOU?"

Kaye had to laugh.

"You can borrow one of my shirts, if you don't dirty it, but you'll have to buy your own," said Mo.

"I will."

"I've an extra apron you can have." Chrissie hung up the phone.

"Thanks." Kaye chanced a smile.

Chrissie grimaced back at her.

Mo clapped her hands. "Can a gal get a cup of coffee?" She clicked her fingers. "And a slice of All-American apple pie."

"Certainly, madam, would you like it *à la mode*?" Chrissie heaped a slice onto a plate.

"It's far from *à la mode* I was reared, but sure I'll have it anyway."

"How about you?" Chrissie looked at Kaye.

"The same," she said.

"You sure?" said Mo. "You're gonna be piling on the weight."

Jaysus!

"Oh, and by the way, cuz." Chrissie roared into the microphone.

"Yeah?"

"Stop swivelling on that stool, or you'll land on your arse like last night."

Mo snorted. Some of the customers hooted and shouted, "Alright!" Others clapped, as Chrissie held up her thumb.

Kaye gulped, stopped swivelling, felt her face flame up, her heartbeat race faster. What would she do if the girls asked her to leave? She'd have to go home and face everyone and tell them what happened. Liam especially. How would she explain to him that it hadn't worked out? Hardly make her more appealing to him. She'd have to be more careful with her words, slow down on the drinking, think before she spoke. Thank God for the job, thank God.

Now to keep it.

"Are yis ready?" Chrissie banged down her pen and pad and tugged at her apron. "Ouda here!" She stuffed a wad of bills in her bag and yelled, "Ah ride!"

"What does that mean, 'ah ride'?" Kaye tried to make conversation.

"Are you for real?" Chrissie said and Kaye didn't know if she meant it, or not.

They all squeezed through the glass door onto Fifth Avenue.

"Will we go for a walk in Central Park?" said Mo. "Get the train from Columbus Circle?"

"Sounds like an awful lot of walkin' to me,'" said Chrissie.

"Yes, let's." Kaye was anxious to walk off the pie.

She strolled on ahead while the girls lagged behind, chattering. Like when Olivia would get friendly with one of the other girls in the class and leave Kaye out. She stalled outside FAO Schwarz, pretending to be interested in the window, allowing them to catch up with her. "The biggest toyshop in the world." They chanted and kept walking, laughing as they went. Kaye peeked into the lobby of the Plaza Hotel, again feigning interest, before crossing the road and joining them in the park.

Central Park, people scurrying by. Skating. Jogging. The city whirring like a machine beyond the trees, the skyscrapers a reminder of where they were, as if they were put there for that reason. The grass crunched under her feet – unlike the grass at home, which was usually wet, and dewy.

Home. Now seemed so far away.

They strolled through the gates onto 59th Street.

Kaye stepped out onto the road, where her foot was nearly amputated by a cab.

"Wait for the WALK sign." Chrissie yelled at her.

Kaye simulated a hum, as they browsed sidewalk stalls.

"Not that stupid song again." Mo held up a pair of earrings. "What do you think?"

"Nah," said Chrissie. "What song?"

"Boomtown Rats." Kaye took a white embroidered blouse off a rail. "How about this?"

"You'd look like a gypsy." Mo sniggered, and Kaye put it back.

"No, you need something plainer for work." Chrissie delved into her bag. "I have tokens for the subway," she said, handing them one apiece. "Let's get ouda here."

Musicians busked at the bottom of an escalator. Stalls displayed jewellery and trinkets; kiosks sold newspapers, magazines, cigarettes, sweets. The place stank of heat, fumes, sweat, musk.

On the train, Kaye eased off her sandals and wanted to prop her feet on the opposite seat between Chrissie and Mo but dared not. "What am I going to do tomorrow?" She suddenly blurted out, rubbing her head with her hands.

"I'll go over the menu with you later," said Chrissie.

"That means we're not going out?" Mo elbowed her in the side.

"I'm not," said Kaye. "If you don't mind … I'll stay home … Get sorted." She couldn't bear the sight of another drink. And she didn't want to see Nick. And she had work the next morning.

Work!

At 242nd Street, taxi drivers cluttered the bottom of the steps.

"Andy, Andy." They trooped towards a black car. Does he have a different one for every day?

"You ok after last night?" Andy asked Kaye.

"Em, yeah. Why?"

"I take you home, you very tired. You sleep the whole way."

"Oh. Do I owe you for the fare?"

"No. It's ok, Mr. Nick, he want to fix me up, but I say no, I bring you home."

Jaysus!

"But you give me very nice kiss, its ok."

"My God." Mo rolled her eyes.

"Slut." Chrissie nudged her. "Hey, Andy, how come ya never give me a free ride?"

"Stop, stop." Andy shook his head. "You girls too funny. You can have ride anytime."

"Be careful," said Mo. "You know what she means by ride."

"Ha, ha. Don't worry, I know. I have Irish girlfriend; I know these things."

"If you ever get fed up with her, give me a shout," said Chrissie. "I spend a bloody fortune on cabs, so I do. Now, first, take us to South Broadway for pizza. And then swing by the beer distributors for a six-pack."

Kaye threw a twenty into Chrissie's lap, for the food and the beer. Chrissie tossed it back. Over her shoulder, she saw Nick at the Terminal door, watching the car roar away.

"That's where you'll get off the bus tomorrow," Mo pointed to a bus shelter across from the pizzeria. "And make this another landmark," she said when they stopped at the beer distributor's, an off-licence it looked like to Kaye.

As they trooped up the stairs of the apartment building, the door to 2B opened. "What are yis up ta?" A girl said, a mess of wavy hair, her eyes like beads behind bottle-bottom glasses.

"We're having pizza, Izzy, c'mon up," said Chrissie.

"Bring your own beer," yelled Mo.

On the floor, backs propped against the wall, they ate pizza, and drank beer like real Americans. The table was soon strewn with crusts and beer cans, the tape recorder turned up, Maura O'Connell singing, *If You Love Me, Really Love Me.*

"I'd love someone to sing that at my wedding," Chrissie sighed.

"Were ya ever nearly married?" Izzy asked her.

"Yeah, once."

"Go 'way." Izzy moved closer. "What happened?"

"He went off to Saudi Arabia and came back with another woman."

"You're not serious, girl?" Izzy's beady eyes popped. "I'd die if Tim did that to me."

"Goin' out with him seven years, I was." Chrissie crossed her legs and nestled a beer between her thighs. "Since I was nineteen. Since I started working in Dublin. He took me on a holiday to Lanzarote and I was made up. Thought he was a real man of the world. Thought he was loaded too. Then, he went to Saudi to make money. For our future. I met him on Grafton Street before Christmas, with his arm around this one. He told me she was a workmate."

Kaye recalled late-night phone calls, Chrissie upset, not distraught though, like Kaye would have been. She envied Chrissie. She'd had seven years. Whereas what had Kaye except splintered dreams, a loss of hope and a fantasy never fulfilled? The pain had been the same, for she grieved the loss of what might have been.

"He called up to the house a few nights later and asked if I needed any money. So, I said I did, and he gave me a blank cheque. I filled it out for five hundred pounds; spent it in Switzer's, in the January sales."

"Ya did not!" Izzy's face twisted into a thousand creases.

"I'll always associate it with Bewley's coffee and carol-singing,"

Chrissie sighed.

Kaye associated hers with the salt sea air, swans in the Harbour, folk songs, and the strain of a banjo or mandolin. Liam's green blazer and blue eyes.

"And I haven't looked back since." Chrissie raised her can. "Let's toast the bastard!"

"The bastard." They stood up and tipped cans, sang along with Maura O'Connell, ended in perfect harmony, curtsied, fell back on the floor again, panting, their faces pink.

"So, what d'ya work at?" Kaye asked Izzy when she'd caught her breath.

"I'm a medical receptionist up on Riverdale Avenue, for the summer. Doctor Fingers is his name, I thought he was pulling me leg."

"With his fingers?" said Chrissie. "Finger this, sez you."

"How did ya get that job?" Kaye asked her.

"I used to be their nanny when his kids were younger. I still mind them at weekends. The extra few bob is handy. This summer I'm fillin' in for his receptionist, who's had a baby."

"What do you do in the winter?"

"I teach in a Catholic School. They don't pay much, but it's safer than a public school. I tutor in the evenings for extra money." She struggled onto her feet.

Kaye would like to have heard more about the teaching.

"Well, I'm off," Izzy said.

"Is that the smell?" Chrissie tugged her T-shirt out of her shorts, escorting Izzy out the door and onto the landing. "And, if you ever get tired of Tim, send him up to me."

"Never." Izzy's voice echoed the stairwell. "I'll never tire of him, nor him of me. Known him since I was sixteen. Getting married in September. Ye'll all be at the wedding?"

"Sure." Chrissie banged the door closed and slumped against it. "You and your questions," she said to Kaye. "We got her life story, and invited to her weddin', all in one go."

"Do yis not like her?"

"Herself and Tim are two cute hoors, if you ask me." Chrissie slid onto the floor again.

"No, they're not." Mo jumped up. "They're nice. We're just jealous because they have it all sewn up, whereas we, we're still arsing around."

She's right.

"Now, I'm going to bed." Mo stretched. "Because I actually have to work tomorrow."

"And me and Kaye have to get down to business." Chrissie pulled a menu out of her bag and proceeded to explain the ways eggs and burgers were cooked; the various kinds of toast and salad dressings there were.

"You have to learn the abbreviations," she said. "For instance, 'tuna whiskey down' is a tuna sandwich on toasted rye bread. 'Whiskey' is rye, 'down' is toast. After you call in the order, take them their drinks. When the bell rings, collect their food at the hatch. When they're finished eating, clear the dishes, tot up the check. Wipe the table and reset. Ya have to be quick, that's how you make your money. Now, take my order, write it down and call it out."

They practised until Chrissie started to yawn. Kaye had been hoping for a chat, but Chrissie tore up the orders and announced bed.

Kaye retired to the vacant room where a single bed had been placed by the Super. She'd have preferred to be sharing with Chrissie but had been afraid to suggest it. Anyhow, she was relieved that the day had gone so well, after the catastrophe of the night before.

"Can you give me that twenty now?" Chrissie's head reappeared around the door.

"Of course." Kaye reached for her bag and handed her a twenty-dollar bill.

Chrissie had never asked her for money before.

CHAPTER TEN

She edged open the glass door, grimacing at the dreaded bell, more nervous than the day before. The curly blonde approached with menus, then realising it was Kaye, introduced herself as Tina, the hostess. The nerves increased as Tina hurried her towards George, who was talking on the telephone again, and he had a delivery boy escort her upstairs to her 'station' where her workmate was Melissa with the plaits.

"Is that like K, as in after J and before L in the alphabet?" Melissa asked.

Kaye had to think for a second, then said, "yes, yes it is!"

"Cool," Melissa cried, "I'll be Em then. Now, let's start the side work."

"Side work?"

"Yeah. Fill up the salt and peppers and sugar shakers. Shine the silverware, top up the relish and pickle containers and marry the ketchup."

"Marry?"

"Combine two bottles and screw 'em."

Uriah Heep, who was Bernard, appeared with a plastic bucket of ketchup and a funnel, through which she had to refill the empty bottles. Soon, red sauce was spilling down the sides of the bucket, the bottles, blotching her hands and apron. It took a whole packet of paper napkins to clean it up.

As soon as the clock struck twelve, people streamed in off the street and piled up the stairs, depositing briefcases, and shopping bags in the aisles. Kaye took a deep breath and approached Table Two. What was she supposed to say?

"New Yorker medium, mayo on the side, Diet Coke." The man handed her back the menu without looking at it.

She wrote in her notepad and ran down to the hatch where George knocked her head off a microphone to call it out. Her voice boomed through the restaurant, her first order.

"How can ya speak so fast without getting your lips in a mess?" The chef roared.

"Easy Fernando, easy." Melissa sauntered by. "Be nice to the Irish girl."

Table Two devoured his burger, drained his drink, flicked two dollars on the table and was gone. Her first tip: two dollars. She didn't pick it up immediately in case it would seem greedy; in case she came across too eager. Not that anyone would have noticed. There was another customer to take his place and she was off again.

"Toast, toast," cried George a while later, as he eyed a mountain of toast piling up on the counter. "Who owns the fricking toast?"

"Not me." Kaye galloped away.

"Toast, toast, girl." He screamed after her. "Are you giving out toast with the eggs?"

"Not unless they order it."

"Ya gotta give 'em toast. Were you ever in a diner that didn't give toast with the eggs?"

Kaye had never been in a diner, full stop.

"Some of these are mine." Melissa stacked plates along her arm, nodded at Kaye to do the same, and they scurried upstairs, wandering the aisles, jumping over bags, calling, "Toast, toast, who needs toast?" Kaye plonked a plate in front of a lady eating dessert. "On the house," she implored, "please take it." The lady ate it, with her brownie sundae.

Melissa could chat to her tables and still get things done. How does she listen to such crap? All some people wanted to do was talk.

"What a cute accent!" They exclaimed, as Kaye hurried past. "Where are you from?"

Dublin. Wicklow. Kilcoughlan. Kaye alternated. She never knew where she was from.

Every time she caught sight of herself in the mirrored walls - which she walked into several times – she saw the two rosy cheeks and two panda eyes. Her feet so swollen, the new shoes like boats, her insteps bloating over them. Like the nuns years ago in the House. Her apron pockets were bulging too, from tips, which she was now swiping, regardless of whether the customer was gone or not. She had to turn those tables.

"Are we havin' fun yet?" Melissa ambled by, balancing three plates on one arm.

Kaye didn't have time to reply. Table Two was scribbling an imaginary check in the air; Table Three pointing at their coffee cups; Table Four waiting to order, but the bell was ringing, ringing, summoning her to the hatch. Customers were still gushing in, clogging the stairs, getting in her way. "How long is the wait?" they wanted to know. She totted a check in her head for Table Four and still had to wipe down Table Six.

"This table's dirty, Miss," one of its occupants howled at her.

Through gritted teeth, she muttered, "Don't I fecking know it."

"Is feck a curse word?" Melissa was at the hatch.

"Sure sounds like a cuss to me." Fernando flipped over burgers on the grill.

Cuss? Kaye scampered back up the stairs.

"Would you like something to drink?"

She was getting the gist of it.

"No, just water."

And what are you going to do with that?

"Are ya ready to order?" Smile.

"Can you give us more time?" Smile.

"Sure, faith and begorrah Brigid, we'll be ordering now." Smile.

Things eased up after two o'clock. The queue of expectant faces was gone from the stairs. She had time to tell them where she was from, how long she'd been here, how it was her first day.

"Good job!" they said.

After three hours, she was able to exhale.

"Now, we have to do our side work," Melissa explained when the CLOSED sign was placed on the bottom step. Downstairs would remain open until nine that night.

"Again?"

"Yeah, break everything down. The salt, the sugar, the pickle, and relish containers. Then we wash out coffee pots and marry the ketchup."

"Am I going to spend my time in this place performing wedding ceremonies on bottles of tomato sauce?"

"You're funny." Melissa had a lazy laugh. "When we're done, we can order lunch."

Food?

All of a sudden she was starving. She hadn't thought she'd be capable of eating after watching people stuff their faces all morning, but she ordered a burger and took it to a shiny red Formica table. Propped her feet on a chair and emptied the contents of her apron pocket into her lap. Sixty dollars in nickels, dimes, and dollar bills.

Melissa and Fernando sat at the back, chatting, and laughing.

On her way up 57th Street later, she told Liam in her head about Burger Heaven, the customers, Melissa and Uriah Heep, the apartment, the Terminal and Andy, their cab driver. How she loved Manhattan and wasn't afraid of the subway. She could tell him in a card, but would he be interested? Had he ever been?

In the Coliseum bookstore, she bought two books of Ibsen and Shaw's plays instead. Studying Literature had given her more pleasure than anything ever had before, more than loving Liam, maybe. She bought the embroidered blouse from the stall at Columbus Circle, so what if she looked like a gypsy? Better than being under compliment to Mo, and it was more feminine than a man's shirt. The vendor wrapped it in tissue paper. Her mother would be proud; she was always advising her daughters to be stylish, even at work.

The girls were drinking tea at the big table in the sitting-room, the fan whirring, *No Frontiers* on the tape recorder. She flopped down beside them. "Wow, what a day," she said. "Those customers can be so demanding."

"You have to be nice to them." Mo told her. "You have to work those tips."

"Oh, I did. I smiled all day." Kaye clasped a cup and plonked her one-shoe-size-bigger fat feet on a nearby chair. "But as long as they get their food, shouldn't that be enough?"

"No," said Chrissie. "They want you to ask them how they are, tell them how you are, laugh at their jokes, tell them one back. You have to listen to their life stories and tell them yours – about how poor you are at home, and they'll throw the money at ya."

"Oh, money, it's all about money here." Kaye scoffed at them. "When I'm in a restaurant, I don't want to know the waitress's name, I don't tell her mine. I just want her to give me my food."

"That's you," said Mo. "Everyone is not like you."

"Isn't that a pity?" Kaye crossed her feet on the chair. Why was she being like this? The day had gone better than expected. She'd actually enjoyed it. Why couldn't she admit that to the girls. "Have they no lives?"

"Maybe not," said Mo. "The counter in a diner is a social gathering. Like a bar."

"I have great craic with me customers," said Chrissie.

"I'm sure you do."

"One man comes in every morning and wants me to serve him," Chrissie continued. "He's got pots of money, and I'm always tellin' him to give me some; that he'd never miss it. He loves the slaggin'. I'm the first person he talks to every morning; maybe the only person all day."

"I see them in The Short Stop every morning on my way home from work," said Mo. "The same people sit in the same seat and order the same thing every day. When the waitress sees them coming, she puts in their order and has their drink on the table when they get to their seat. It makes them feel important."

"Huh. I'm not here to make people feel important."

"Why not?" said Chrissie. "What's so wrong with making a customer's day? You'll have to lighten up. I'm always tellin' ya that."

"And it is your job," Mo said.

On Friday, Bernard walked out in the middle of lunch. Everyone was speculating over who'd get his station, the best one in the house, right inside the door.

Kaye didn't take any part in the discussion. She hadn't a notion of getting the job, even though she'd been making a real effort to chat to the customers. She'd decided she was going to get the hang of this waitressing. Be like Chrissie and make a fuss of everyone, not for the money, but for herself, to feel good about what she was doing.

"You wanna full-time job?" George asked her, as she was about to leave.

"Em, I dunno. Didn't I make a lot of mistakes?"

"Maybe." George shrugged. "But you never screw up on your checks."

Money again. That was all that mattered. Violet and Rose couldn't function unless they had a calculator. Couldn't figure out eight and a half percent tax in their heads, even on a check under twenty dollars. Couldn't multiply by eight and round off the answer to the nearest whole number. Maybe they could; it just never occurred to them.

George gave her a form to fill up and her hands shook writing down a false social security number - a different variation of Mo's — three digits, dash two, dash four. She stalled over the address section, then made one up.

"I was made permanent." She burst into 4D.

"Ya'd think ya were in the bloody Civil Service," Chrissie guffawed.

"Good," Mo said. "The more money you make the better. I don't want you sponging."

"Why are you always on about me sponging." Kaye untied her apron.

"I've been stung before," said Mo. "I just don't want it to happen again."

"Well, I won't be here long enough."

"This is cause for celebration," Chrissie said. "Bags be first in the shower." She tottered into the hall. "It's Friday night, after all."

"Call a cab." Mo fled after her. "Tell them to give us twenty minutes."

Kaye sat in front of a mirror that she'd found on the sidewalk with its corner chipped off. Smeared foundation on her face, hummed along to Dolores Keane. "No slippery nipples for me," she roared down to the girls.

"Are ya lonely in here, all by yourself?" Chrissie popped her head around the door.

"Nah," she said, even though she was, in a way, more left out than anything. "How was Nick the other night? Did he say anything?"

"About what?" Chrissie bunched up her forehead.

"About me fallin' on the floor, sayin' things to him."

"Nah." Chrissie elbowed Kaye out of the way to get a look in the mirror. "He's used to bar talk."

Bar talk? So, that was it. She was just another drunk in the bar.

"I'm sorry if I made a show of you."

"No, ya didn't." Chrissie turned left and right to admire herself even more. "You're gonna have to stop takin' everything to heart." She smoothed her hair and left.

They still hadn't had a real chat, like they used to, huddled into an electric fire in Chrissie's cold flat, a packet of cigarettes and two mugs of tea, the leaves floating on top. Still, it was nice having built-in friends here in 4D, someone to go out with all the time. Not having to plan ahead. She'd better not do anything else that might mess things up.

A cab hooted its horn. Dolores Keane faded into a whisper.

"Turn out the lights and leave the tape in the recorder."

"For what?"

"For the robbers, ya thick."

"Hey girls, what's up?" Nick dealt out the beer mats the minute they entered the bar, held up a bottle of *Amstel* and three heads nodded back at him.

"You tell us," Chrissie said. "What is up?"

"You're incorrigible, Chris." He shook his head and winked at Kaye.

"Encourageable, ya got that right." Chrissie held up her hand for a high-five.

Kaye sipped her beer. She was starting to acquire a taste for it and might try *Coors Lite* next. Beer wasn't as potent as vodka, but it was fattening.

"So, are you working yet?" It was Nick.

"Yes," she told him, mortified, remembering their last meeting. "I'm a ... waitress, downtown, and have been ... made permanent."

"Permanent, no less. I didn't know there was such a thing around here." He knocked on the counter and was gone.

Thank God!

The crowd was starting to thicken, a rock band was warming up, the jukebox cranking and a group of young lads dancing around it. Others were pulling on the football machine, the Americans screaming at the television. A few older Irishmen were curved over the counter, staring into their drinks; their faces craggy from the sun, lips pinched from smoking. A faint glimmer of a smile crossed their cheeks when they turned to look at the younger lads, but when they returned to their beer glasses and overflowing ashtrays, there was a sadness in their eyes.

"They cash their pay cheques on Friday." Mo followed her gaze. "Then drink all night."

"God. That's awful. Why don't they just go home? To Ireland, I mean."

"They're here too long. And anyhow, what's there to go back to?"

"There's loads to go back to." Kaye was adamant. Then remembered. Be nice. "Where's Chrissie gone?"

"She's around. Can't sit still."

"She's changed."

"Everyone does, here. You will too, hopefully." Mo rambled off too.

Kaye hopped off her stool and made for the loo, saw Sil in the crowd, but no sign of Chrissie. One of the cubicle doors was closed, but there was no sound coming from it. She washed her hands and left.

The band was singing a song she'd never heard before. *Where the Streets have no Name.* Must be about Manhattan.

Nick scuttled around, picking up glasses, stacking them one on top of the other into a tier under his left arm, the tendons pulsing through his skin. If she chanced that in Burger Heaven, they'd topple to the floor. Then, he was in front of her, holding out his hand. "Oh." The band had started, *Forever and Ever Amen.* He twirled her around in a jive. Like a real country lad, his hand strong, leading her, swirling her under his arms. Not too cool, after all.

"Thank you." She was panting by the time the song stopped.

"No, thank you." He bowed. "Not bad for a bit of a lad?"

Her jaws burned. "I'm so sorry."

"Don't worry about it." He moved away. "I'm used to it."

His head, above the crowd, disappeared through the back door.

"Be careful," Sil brushed by her. "He's living a lie. Ask him about the wife and kid."

"What?" She sat down, gulped her beer, tried to get breathing back to normal. Waited a while, and then Chrissie came through the door.

"Where were you?" she asked her.

"Outside."

"With Nick?"

"No, why would I be with Nick."

But Kaye knew she was lying.

CHAPTER ELEVEN

On Sunday morning they had breakfast in the Riverdale Diner, a must before Gaelic Park, seemingly. Cups of coffee were served the minute they sat down.

"I love it," said Chrissie.

"Me too," said Kaye. "This is one of the few things I do like about America."

Chrissie and Mo glanced at one another. This time, they didn't even try to be subtle.

"What about the money" Chrissie stirred in lashings of sugar. "Ya wouldn't have made that much in three days back home."

"Suppose not." Kaye had to agree. "But I didn't come for the money."

"What did ya come for then?"

"Ad–ven–ture, remember?"

"I'm feeling the sarcasm." Mo remarked.

"I wasn't being sarcastic."

"D'ya know how to be anything else?" Chrissie snapped her fingers for the waitress. "Admit it. You came for the money like the rest of us."

Kaye's whole body clamped up. Why was Chrissie being like this?

They gave the girl their order and Kaye watched her write OE for over easy; M for medium; SCR for scrambled. Of course, Chrissie had several extra orders, butter on the side, bacon extra crispy, no onions in the home fries. Mo wanted one egg, a bran muffin instead of toast, no sides; Kaye's only request was that the sausages be well done.

"Far from all that you were reared." She tried to tease them, to ease the tension.

"The way we were reared wasn't always best for us." Mo lit a cigarette.

"Oh it wasn't that bad." Kaye was getting fed up with them, and wished she'd stayed in Van Cortlandt Park instead. She could do with a bit of sunbathing.

"The squeaky door gets the oil." Chrissie crumpled up her napkin.

"That's one thing I've learnt over here. Anyhow." She dropped it on her empty plate. "Let's go. Tipperary's on first and I wanna see my man running onto the field."

"Which one?" Kaye asked.

"Blondie, of course. I wanna make sure he has the legs to go with that gorgeous chest."

"How d'ya keep track of them all?" Kaye munched her last mouthful of toast.

"Easy." Chrissie licked her fingers and made an imaginary calculation in the air. "It depends on where I am at the time – the Terminal, Characters, Celtic House, Hennessy's, Gaelic Park, the Terminal again; the Short Stop, if I'm stuck – I have a rag in every bush."

"And they have a rag in your bush too." Mo snorted into her napkin.

Chrissie looked at her in mock surprise. "And I thought you were a good Catholic girl."

"Sorry, I couldn't resist. Now, are we right?" Mo stood up. "I want to see the game too, and it's because my dad is from Tipperary; not because of some bartender's legs."

"Yeah, right." Chrissie picked up the bill. "You're all just as horny as me; just better at hiding it." She threw a twenty-dollar bill on the table.

Kaye threw a ten at her. "We'll chip in."

Chrissie threw the ten back. It landed on Kaye's lap; she tossed it onto the table. Chrissie picked it up and stuffed it in Kaye's bag. "Stop it," she said.

Kaye was about to say she'd pay into Gaelic Park but was too rattled to argue further..

"There's no point." Mo shrugged. "She always pays. Then, she's always broke."

"That's Crispy." Kaye told her. "Except for the being broke part. What's up with her anyhow? She seems to be annoyed with me for some reason."

"Oh, the two of you are too close, I think. You bounce off one another."

"Really?" Kaye didn't really know what Mo meant. "Where's she going now?"

"Isn't that Izzy and Tim?"

Chrissie had already marched up to their table. "What's up?"

"Well, lads," said Izzy. "Where are ye off to?"

"The Park, of course," said Chrissie. "Where else?"

"Well, some of us have to work." Izzy shook her head. "We're having dinner first."

"Divils for punishment girls." Tim smirked. "Did ye not get enough the other night?"

He was almost a hunk. He had the tan, the teeth, the black hair, and the broody blue eyes. But his lips were too thin, his nose, watery. He had just missed it.

"Depends on what you mean now, doesn't it?" Chrissie smiled at him. "Did ya not get enough of it yourself?"

"No, I didn't actually." He wiped his nose with the napkin.

"Well, next time you're stuck," said Chrissie. "Give's a shout."

"G'wan, Chris." Izzy whacked her on the arm. "You're an awful woman."

"Is the doctor's office open on a Sunday?" Kaye asked her.

"No. I'm mindin' a patient today. The extra money's handy; for the weddin' and all."

"Oh! Yeah," said Kaye. "The weddin'."

"Well, we'll be off," said Chrissie. "Don't wanna miss the match."

"I know what you're after," said Tim. "And it's not football."

"Whatever." Chrissie strutted off. "See yis, and mind that cold of yours, Timothy."

"What a jeer." Kaye helped herself to a handful of peppermints from a bowl beside the cash register. "What does she see in him?"

"You don't even know him." Mo was indignant. "Don't judge them until you've walked a mile in their shoes."

Jaysus!

"I'll ride him before he gets to the altar." Chrissie flounced out onto the street.

"What makes ya think he would?" Kaye tried to return the banter.

"Because they all would."

Chrissie had no reason to think such a thing. And what was between herself and Tim?

Spectators were jammed on planks of timber: men in tweed caps, cigarettes at the sides of their mouths. Another lot crammed behind the goalpost. More crushed into the bar, shoddy and run-down, complete with balding barstools. Burgers sizzled on a grill, underneath a striped canopy, the air heaved with heat. A band belted out *Take Me Home to Mayo'*. Couples waltzed around in circles. Some people had a bottle in each hand. At home, no one would dream of drinking during a match.

Chrissie handed Kaye a bottle of cider, as they headed towards the side-line.

"C'mon Tipperary," she roared at the blue-and-yellow jerseys.

It was like a regular Irish football pitch. Where was the big, American stadium? Some of Begnets' lads had played here. What had they thought of it?

At first, Kaye had gone to the hurling and football matches with her parents, to watch Gary playing. Then, she started hanging around afterwards and his friends wanted to know who she was chasing. She didn't tell them she had nothing better to do on a Sunday. She'd tried camogie but the girls kept tugging at her jersey and knocking her to the ground. It wasn't until she took up badminton that she became more immersed in the club. Converging on the pitch when the team won; joining in the singsong afterwards; heading off in a coach bus to away matches. Sundays were no longer boring after Kaye started following Begnet's.

Sundays didn't look boring here either. Out of the ocean of heads, she spotted a familiar face. The flame of orange hair? It had to be. She jostled through the crowd, still holding onto her cider. And indeed it was him - Billy, in knee-length shorts and a cut-off T-shirt. Last time she'd seen him was at his going-away party in Kilcoughlan. He used to drive a gold Ford Capri and was always good for a lift to a dance. Always the first to ask her and Chrissie up to jive, twirling the two of them under his arms at the same time.

"Be Jaysus, Katie, is it yourself?" He caught her by the waist and whirled her around nearly knocking a few bottles from a few fists. "Where did you come out of?"

"I'm here for the summer." Kaye steadied herself on the gravel.

"Be Janey, that's a good one. And are ya workin' like?"

"I'm waitressin' downtown. How about yourself?"

"In construction." He puffed out his chest. "Livin' over on Bainbridge. Ya'll have ta come over one night to the Roaring Twenties. It's mighty. Bring that Crispy one with ya."

Kaye took a swig of her cider. "I never dreamt I'd bump into you like this!"

"Did yer one not tell ya I was here of a Sunday?"

"No, she didn't."

"Lord, she's an awful woman."

"Did ya still like her?"

"Like her? I love her." Billy guffawed and Kaye thought that was lovely.

"D'ya miss home?" she asked him.

"Ya must be coddin'. What's there to miss?"

Kaye could think of several things, one in particular.

"Anyhow, enough about me," he said. "How about you? Any man in your life?"

"Nah, not really. Well, at home. But."

"At home!" His face creased up. "What good is that? A good-looking woman like you?" Billy whistled. "And you with all the lads in Kilcoughlan after ya. You were a fine bit o' stuff, Katie. Ya could've had yer fill of them." *Really?* "You'll surely find someone here." He scanned the crowd. "Wall-to-wall Irishmen. Unfortunately, I'm taken." He rocked back and forth in his flip-flops, eyed the shiny watch on his arm. "Better be getting' home to her soon."

"Is she Irish or American?"

"Oh, American." His chest swelled. "There's nothin' like an American woman for mindin' a man. They'd stand on their heads for ya."

"D'ya not miss the lads though?" She recalled Spanner, Soupy, Sweat, Beefy.

"They're here too, scattered over the Bronx and Yonkers and up as far as Westchester. The Bull has a place upstate. They're all doin' the finest and wouldn't go back if ya paid them. Sure, what is there to go back to?"

For some of them, there was nothing, she supposed. Most had been forced to leave because of unemployment. She thought of all the young men she had danced with, not so long ago, all gone now. "Well, it's Kilcoughlan's loss," she said. "And, as long as you're happy."

"Good for you." Kaye gave him a high-five.

When Billy left Ireland, Kaye had imagined him in a skyscraper, hanging out in nightclubs and fancy bars, working in Wall Street with a suit on him. That's all her imagination could conjure up at the time. Not Gaelic Park and North Broadway. Not the subway screeching on the elevated tracks above them, nor the clock on Manhattan College peeping out of the trees, and not the sea of Irish faces cheering for counties not their own.

She made her way back to the bar after promising to meet him in The Roaring Twenties. He could always be found there on a Friday night, cashing his pay cheque.

"You'll never guess who I met." She found Chrissie, eventually.

"Let me see." Chrissie put her finger on her chin. "Billy Bob?"

"How d'ya know?"

"Because he's here every week?"

"You never told me that. He's great gas. Would you not go back with him?"

"No."

"Are there no knots?"

"They all give me knots when I'm drunk, but there's no knots next mornin'."

"You used not be like that.

"Well, I am now, and you could be too. It just takes practice."

"D'ya know what Billy said. That I could've had anyone I wanted in Kilcoughlan."

"I knew that."

"I couldn't have Liam. And I wanted him."

"Not this again."

"What? I don't talk about him that much."

"You're like a broken record. It's getting to be a drag. Sure you never even went out with him. Not properly. And there's clearly somethin' wrong with him. Not you."

"What makes ya say that?"

"What full-blooded man would say no to a woman, not even for a court, like?"

Kaye didn't answer.

"Now, give's a loan of twenty and I'll go get us a drink."

CHAPTER TWELVE

Her footsteps pounded the footpath, a hamburger in each hand. Animal fat, just what the doctor ordered. It was still warm, the sun setting in a raspberry sky. Her clothes were creased and sweaty, her head dizzy.

No one talks sense in a pub, Bren used to say. What would he make of it here?

Tiptoeing over the bird droppings, that weekend in London came back to her. It was supposed to be good luck if they shit on you, a woman in Trafalgar Square told her. 'They can shit all over me,' Kaye responded to the woman's horror. 'It won't make any difference.'

Morgan had invited everyone from the Harbour to the afters of his wedding in the Summerhill in Enniskerry. It would've been a chance for Kaye to meet Liam, all dressed up, looking her best. Instead, Olivia had dragged her off to London to drown her sorrows, and Kaye ended up in Trafalgar Square dodging pigeons. One of her missed opportunities.

Characters looked grim with its lurking stragglers outside, and taxis shuttling in and out collecting, and depositing passengers. *All My Exes Live in Texas* boomed out of the jukebox, and as Kaye's eyes skimmed the bar, the only familiar face they landed on was Sil, holding an empty bottle, his face downcast.

"I hope they stay there." She slipped in beside him.

"Who?" His head jolted upright. "Oh! It's yerself, what's up?"

She beckoned the barman.

"Where's Chrissie?" she asked Sil. "She took a loan of a twenty to get us a drink and hasn't come back since."

"Em, I dunno, I was supposed to meet her here." He sighed. "So, what's up with you?"

"Nothin'. And you? You don't look so happy."

"Ah, I'm pissed off." He frowned. "Fed up with my job. Wish I was doing something more constructive than standing at a door. I have a degree, you know, I should be using it."

"Why don't you go home?"

"I will, but not for a while. I came with nothing. I'm not going back with nothing."

"And do you like the American women?"

"They're alright. Why?"

"Just wondering. Do men prefer them because they'd stand on their heads for ya?"

Sil smiled for the first time since she came in. "Yeah, they're nice. Eager to please."

"And what about sex? Are they better at it? And should we do it on the first night?"

"Me and you like?" He was having her on. She hoped.

"No. Girls in general. Should we do it the first night?"

"Not if you want to hear from him again." Sil's dark eyes flickered.

"Huh?"

"If you like him, don't do it; if you don't, then go for it."

"That doesn't make any sense. If I didn't like him, then why would I be doing it?"

"For the sex like."

"For the sex? Not for love? Ya see, I used to like this fella at home, and I never had sex with him, and I regret it now. But he never came onto me either. Is that strange?"

"It is a bit." Sil admitted.

"Yet, I don't know if I could sleep with just anyone," Kaye continued. "I have to like them. But I get the impression that they wouldn't be bothered with me over here otherwise."

"Not all of them. Some are willing to wait until the girl is ready. If they really like her."

"So, would you say Liam, my fella, didn't like me? That he would've tried, if he did?"

"Look, I don't know anything about your man. Every circumstance is different. Maybe ye just didn't click."

"Click, right, we have to click. Not go with the flow?"

"Well." Sil seemed unsure now. "Ya have to do that too. But if you click, you click; if you don't, you don't. But you must click first."

"If you do, you don't. If you don't, you do." Kaye was musing on all that when Chrissie sidled up to the bar.

"Not interruptin' I hope?" She stared at Sil, and he stared back. Her eyes were a darker blue than usual, her pupils like black beads.

"No," said Kaye. "Just talkin' about clickin'."

The look of longing on their faces, she'd never seen such raw lust before.

Chrissie's head tilted towards the door. Sil slid off his seat and followed her. And Kaye was left, again. Like when Olivia met that boyfriend and didn't tell her for six months. Everyone else in the class knew, except Kaye. That was the hard part. And now Olivia remaining friendly with Liam when Kaye no longer could. It wasn't that she'd wanted her taking sides. *Well, she did.* But Chrissie had never made her feel left out like that before.

Staggering out onto Broadway again, Kaye rounded the corner to the Terminal. At the door, she hesitated. But just for a moment.

Pete was behind the bar.

"Any of the girls around?" she asked him, knowing they weren't.

"They're gone long ago. Mo and Seanie popped in for one on her way to work, and I saw Chris and Sil speed away in a cab."

"Oh, I'll have one drink anyhow and then be off." She gestured at the bar.

"Grand job." He placed a bottle in front of her. "Many in the Park?"

"Packed."

"And ya didn't get a shift?"

"Who said I wanted one?" She asked, looking around for Nick, as she spoke. Not that she cared what he thought.

"Everyone wants the shift, Kate." Pete's round face was beaming.

"Maybe I didn't go with the flow?" she said. "Everyone keeps telling me that I need to do that more."

"Maybe ya left too early." Pete pointed at the clock above the register. "It's only now the lads will be galvanizing into action; the games are over, and their bellies are full. Twilight time, I call it. When I was single, it's only now I'd be gettin' around to chasin' a bit o' skirt."

"Really?"

"Really?" Nick appeared through the gap in the divider.

Jaysus!

Pete winked at her. "Meself and Kate are just havin' a chat."

"Oh, it's Kate now, is it? You look deep in thought."

"I'm just tired." Kaye yawned. "That's all." She slithered off the stool. "I'd better go home. It doesn't look like the girls are gonna show up."

She wasn't ready for Nick's views on shifting, yet.

"Oh, they're gone long ago." He linked her arm and escorted her to the door. "I was wondering where you'd got to. Figured you were still bouncing around Broadway."

"Yeah?" She looked down at her tee-shirt, saw the beer stains. *What am I like?*

"You take it easy now." He placed his hands on her shoulder and looked into her eyes. "You're a lovely woman, Kate, you know that?"

She turned away.

He lifted his hands, opened the door.

Pete yelled after her. "And as for going with the flow … Just lie on your back and float."

Andy was leaning against a silver car, it was this time. As soon as he saw Kaye stumbling towards him, he jumped up and opened the door for her.

"You shouldn't go out by yourself, you too nice."

"I didn't go out by myself." She slid into the front seat, for a change. "I was with the girls earlier. And there's loads of people around, it's grand."

"It's still dangerous," he said. "You cannot trust anyone, especially Mr. Nick."

"Why, what's wrong with him?"

"Just be careful, that's all." Andy drove into the night, into the familiar lights of Broadway, Van Cortlandt Park to their right. Had it only been that morning that she and the girls had passed there, on their way to the diner.

"Tell me about yer girlfriend."

"She Irish, she have other men, but that ok. I work a lot."

"How d'ya know she's got other men?"

"I leave her home all the time with them."

"And you don't mind?"

"It's natural, Katerina. You should know. Irish girls are hot."

Irish girls were not usually known for being hot. In Greece, the men had blessed themselves when they heard she and Olivia were Irish. In London a stand-up comic, upon hearing her accent, told the audience he'd never been that close to a nun before.

Irish girls seemed to take on a new persona in New York.

"What if I don't want to, the first night?"

"That's fine." Andy smiled. "But you have to put out the third."

"Put out. Third night." They had reached home. "I'll remember that." She handed him a five-dollar bill and jumped out of the car. "Ok, ta-ra. Thanks."

She skipped up the stairs. Nearly tripped over a body on the second floor.

"Iz locked me out. Sure, you won't tell anyone?" It was Tim.

"No, no. Me lips are sealed."

"You're a sound woman. Can I come up with ya?" He grinned. "To sit and chat, like?"

"Ya must be jokin'. I'm exhausted. And the girls will be wonderin' where I am."

He grabbed her by the ankle. "Am I doin' the right thing?"

"What d'ya mean?" She kept her eyes on her foot.

"Getting married." He released her, sniffled. "D'ya think I'm doin' the right thing?"

"Oh, yeah, you just have to go with the flow." She ran up the rest of the stairs.

The apartment was empty. She sat at the window. Children were still playing outside the DELI. The night throbbed with music and sirens. Worry beads clicked like castanets. Her plan to get Liam now felt like nothing more than pie in the sky.

One Valentine's Day, he had sent her a card. *Everybody thinks we already have,* on the cover. On the inside, *so why don't we?* She'd read it out to Olivia. 'I got one too,' she said.

A crescent moon hung on its side over the Iced Caramel houses, as if at any second its whole weight would come crashing down on them. She dialled the number for home, it was cheaper after midnight, to let them know she'd been made permanent.

"Good," said Mam, "because your dad's been let go."

CHAPTER THIRTEEN

She heard a key in the lock, then someone running the kettle. Kaye swung her feet onto the floor and plodded out to the kitchen. "Can a girl not get a wink of sleep around here?"

"Tea?" It was Mo.

"Yes, from my new teapot." Kaye produced the porcelain pot with bamboo handle she'd bought in the Chinese shop across the street from BURGER HEAVEN.

When it was brewed, she sat opposite from Mo, both sipping from their mugs.

"Do you think I go on too much about Liam?" She ventured to ask.

"Yes," Mo said. "You're wasting your energy, and everyone else's."

"What d'ya mean?"

"Nothin'."

The girls lapsed into an awkward silence. An articulated truck started to turn below on the street. The din was deafening.

"What's going on with Chrissie?" Kaye asked when things were quiet again.

"What do you mean?"

Kaye tried to think how to word it. Chrissie had always been so casual where men were concerned. Down the country, the local boys and girls were always more friendly with one another, going to co-ed school all the way up to sixth year, and Chrissie had three older brothers. Boys weren't a mystery to her; not like they were to Kaye. Still, she'd never been promiscuous. She'd never gone all the way with Billy, as far as Kaye knew.

"When did she start sleeping around?"

"I don't know, I thought you'd know that?"

"No, I don't?"

"Not that there's anything wrong with it. You should try it yourself." Mo got up from the table, took her tea into the living-room.

"My dad's been let go," Kaye told her, "I might have to go home earlier than planned."

"No prob," said Mo, now at the entrance into the hallway. "But you probably won't get your month's deposit back." She headed off down the hall to her bedroom.

Next thing, there was a rattle of the door, and Chrissie arrived in.

"What's wrong with you." She looked at Kaye. "You're like death warmed up."

"What d'ya think?" Kaye was holding her tummy now.

"D'ya want an *Advil?*" Chrissie popped two into her mouth.

"Nah. I'm not that bad. Guess what, Dad lost his job."

"Oh, no, that's terrible." Chrissie sat down beside her, looking genuinely concerned.

"I might have to go home."

"What on earth for?"

"I dunno." Kaye shrugged. "To help out, or somethin'?"

"Nonsense. You'll stay right here. You have a good job and are in a position to make a lot of money. You'd be mad to give it up. And I'm sure they don't expect you to."

"Probably not," said Kaye.

They sat there chatting, like they used to. Then Kaye had to dash down to the shower. She couldn't be late on her first day as a full-time waitress.

Liam used to ask her where she saw herself in five years' time and she couldn't answer. Didn't want to. Because the question implied that he wouldn't be part of that future. And she couldn't have contemplated that, then. She had never imagined New York though, had never ever seen herself here in the Bronx, of all places.

She had to keep to the shady side of the street when walking to the bus stop. At home, they wouldn't dream of avoiding the sun. Sixty degrees was a heatwave: she and Trish out in the back garden in their swimsuits, their father trying to mow the lawn around their blankets.

Commuters spilled in and out of the subway, the doors sliding open and closed. A voice announced the stations – Dyckman Street, Washington Heights, City College, Columbia University. Her head was pounding. She regretted not taking the *Advil*. At 96th Street, she crossed the platform for the Express. Next stop was 72nd, where she changed back to the local again for 59th and Columbus Circle. Ended up on the same train she'd started on.

As the sun bore down on 57th Street, Kaye admired the windows of Givenchy and Prada, shops she'd never be able to afford; passed Carnegie Hall, the Russian Tea Room, and Hard Rock Café. Vendors greeted her from behind fake Gucci watches and bags. The smell of mustard oozed out of hot dog and pretzel kiosks. And the tall buildings swayed so much, it looked like they were about to topple over.

At ten on the dot, she opened the glass doors. Tina was about to offer her a menu, then drew it back again.

"You marry me, Mama?" roared Fernando. "I give you three thousand dolla'."

Dodging a pat on the bottom from Perfecto, she dashed down the stairs to change. After a cup of Colombian roasted coffee and a toasted corn muffin with butter and grape jelly, she busied herself refilling containers, shining cutlery, and marrying ketchup. Soon, she was perched at her new station, right inside the door, notebook, and pen in hand.

"I make you the best waitress in town." George's suit was pinstripe grey, his shirt pristine white, his tie a regal red, and his face the ragged bronze of a Santorini fisherman. "As soon as a customer sits down, greet them, no matter how busy. When you can, take their order, call it in, bring their drinks. Take another order, call it in and pick up the food for the first one. When they finish eating, drop the check. Every time you pass a table, take something off. Have a rag ready to wipe it down and set for the next sitting. Bus those tables."

"Bus?"

He tied a damp dishtowel to her apron strings. "Clean your tables. Go."

He showed her how to hold two, three glasses in the palm of her hand; how to balance plates along her arm and suggested keeping straws and napkins in her pocket. For the next three hours, her feet pounded the tiled floor; her heart pounded in her embroidered blouse, her head pounded from dishes, glasses, cutlery, footsteps, the bell, cash register; voices ordering, whining, laughing, shouting, talking, talking. They never shut up talking.

Have a nice day. Tuna whiskey down. Where you from? GAC BAC with Tommy. Got any BLTs? No, only Lipton's. What a cute accent.

Dressing on the side. *On the side?* Deluxe all the way. *All the way?* Mayo? No, Dublin. I love your accent. I love yours. I don't have an accent. Oh, yes, you do My grandparents were from ...

Until Melissa whispered in her ear, "Are we having fun yet?"

"Fun? I'm having a nervous breakdown!"

"It's only a fricking burger." Melissa ambled away again. "Let them wait."

"I will." Kaye took the milkshake container from the machine too soon and the strawberry ice cream mixture spun out of control. Pink blobs dotted the counter, the floor, a couple of chairs and unsuspecting shoulders. Melissa appeared to help clean up. "Thanks a million." Kaye scuttled back to the hatch. "God help them if they ever have a crisis in their lives, they make such a big deal about a hamburger."

"You're welcome," said Melissa. "You watch my back and I'll watch yours."

"Ok, turn around."

"Why?"

"So, as I can watch your back?"

"You're funny, Kathy."

She felt guilty for thinking the job was beneath her. For not being nice to the customers; not listening to their stories and not telling them hers. Chrissie was right: they were providing her with a living, a good one. By the time she got to Table Six with a fresh milkshake, Kaye had managed to feel guilty about, just about everything.

At two thirty, Melissa suggested sharing a tuna melt and gravy fries. Because she was now working the full day, Kaye could take a break until three. Melissa worked evenings on the counter. They collapsed at an upstairs table, propped their feet on chairs and pulled clumps of dollar bills out of their pockets, ate, and counted their money at the same time.

"How do you keep so cool?" Kaye pushed away her empty plate.

"Oh, been doin' it since I was sixteen, I guess."

"Janey Mac."

"Who's she?"

"It's an expression. So, what did ya do at the weekend? Did ya have any craic at all?"

"I don't do that stuff."

"Well, I met a fella who told me I was lovely."

"Good for you." Melissa grinned. "You are a luvly woman."

"Do I talk like that?"

"I guess you do. Ok, time to go." Melissa pushed back her chair.

"Say a prayer I'm alright." Kaye blessed herself.

"I don't pray." Melissa chuckled.

In the afternoon, a hush descended on the restaurant. There was no wait for tables and more people sat at the counter. Kaye was glad of the lull. No Violet and Rose waving menus to attract prospective customers to the back, every time the door opened.

"I'm ouda here for now. Be back later." George was gruff, as usual. "Good job, Kathy," was all he said.

"Gimme five," said Melissa holding up her hand and Kaye smacked it, then made straight for the dessert stand and helped herself to a large slice of the strawberry shortcake.

"To feed my hangover," she told Melissa.

"It's also feeding your hips. You don't wanna ruin that cute little body of yours."

They could take another break at seven, but Melissa worked through it.

"I need the money," she told Kaye who ordered chicken and baked potato and sat at the counter.

"Now I know why people sit here," Kaye said. "It's not as forlorn as sitting at a table all by yourself. I'd never have done this at home."

"What's that?"

"Eaten in a restaurant alone."

A man in a blue suit and black briefcase barged through the glass doors, ignoring Tina's offer of a menu. He marched down the restaurant, stern-faced, his head in the air, stopping at a table where George was doing paperwork. Could he be from immigration?

Kaye felt a hand clamping her shoulder and was about to flee downstairs when she heard him ask, "Have you a WC?"

"Only what's on the menu." George didn't raise his head.

The man hesitated and walked out.

Kaye exhaled.

At nine o'clock, she hurried along Lexington Avenue, meandering among pedestrians, as far as Madison Avenue, where she bounded onto the Express Bus. Sinking into a seat, she peeled off her pop socks. A red ridge had formed under each knee like in Secondary school.

Kaye and Olivia were the class clowns, always getting into trouble, even hiding in a cupboard through one whole French class, the sweat near dripping off them, much to the amusement of their classmates. In sixth year, they'd decided not to bother studying for the Leaving Certificate, because they were going to travel the world when they left school. But Olivia never returned after the Christmas break. She had found a receptionist job in Bray Technical College; her Ma needed the money. And Kaye had felt forsaken – again.

Years later, it was Olivia who had then got her the hours teaching typing at night classes.

'It'll be a breeze,' she'd said. 'They're adults who want to learn.'

Kaye was dubious, but she hadn't yet used the teacher's diploma and it might give her a chance to see more of Liam. He coached basketball there on Wednesdays.

The first night, he strode into her classroom. 'A little bird told me I'd find you here.'

'Oh yeah?' She didn't know what else to say. Her real-life encounters with him never matched her daydreams.

'I was wondering if you were doing anything Friday night?'

'Huh?'

'Would you like to come to a dinner dance with me?'

'Em.'

'In the Glenview – for the football club, you might enjoy it.'

'OK.' No, she had never imagined this.

'Seven thirty?'

'Grand.'

He wrote on her notebook: FRI. 7.30.

'See you then.'

Without Olivia, there was no Liam.

Chapter fourteen

"Welcome to the Twilight Zone," Pete said, as he led them into the Shamrock.

Kaye couldn't get over how dark it was, with people mashed into one another, staring into space, tilting their glasses, hand to mouth, in slow motion. The only seats were a couple of stools against the bar, their occupants asleep, heads on the counter.

"Why would anyone want to come here?" Kaye grappled through the darkness. "Especially on the 4th of July."

"I love it!" Chrissie gasped.

"You would."

"It used be for bartenders." Pete handed them bottles of *Beck's*. "After their shifts."

"These are all bartenders?" Kaye swigged from her bottle.

"Used to be, I said. Now it's a free-for-all. Every Tom, Dick and Mary ends up here. Anyhow, relax and get them into ya. Ready for another?"

"I'm game," said Chrissie.

Kaye took in the sorry scene. Spotted Tim in a trance and was glad she hadn't told the others about meeting him on the stairs the previous week. She should've shared a cab home from the Terminal with Mo and Seanie. America's birthday my hat.

Suddenly, there was Nick pushing through the crowd.

"I'll have one more so," she shouted after Pete.

"Hi guys." Nick was smiling, faintly smiling. "Had a feeling I'd find you here." His shirt was unbuttoned at the collar, tie abandoned, revealing the start of a hairy chest.

"Didn't we tell ya we were comin'." Chrissie beamed. "Are ya followin' us?" She regarded him coyly.

Kaye couldn't think of a thing to say.

"Sure, am." He grinned. "Now, how about a beer?"

"Pete's gone to get one." Chrissie told him. "Hurry and you'll catch him."

Kaye watched his long legs, as they reached the bar in strides.

He was back in what seemed like seconds, with three more beers, so that now the girls had one in each hand.

"So how do you like this place?"

"Brilliant," said Chrissie. "Ya'd never see anything like this at home."

"Kate?" The green eyes bore into her, the amber bits glistening.

"Interesting." She hadn't the heart to tell him it was a dive, a right kip.

"It's interesting, all right. Excuse me while I get drinks for people." And off he went.

Kaye tried to light a cigarette whilst balancing two bottles between the fingers of one hand and striking a match with the other.

"A fine thing isn't he?" said Chrissie.

"Shouldn't you only have eyes for Sil?"

"No."

Kaye exhaled a puff of smoke, her eyes filled with tears. "Well, I'm a one-man woman."

"Don't even go there, and don't say you're gonna cry?"

"No, I'm not, ya eejit." Kaye coughed. "It's the smoke."

"Who's crying?" Nick returned. "And what's this about being a one-man woman?"

"Kaye is."

"Crying, or a one-man woman?"

"Both! But don't ask her why or you'll have to hear the whole story."

"She was complainin' earlier about the state of the place." Pete was back. "Don't hear her complainin' now with a fag in her mouth and two bottles of beer under her oxter."

"Will yis stop." Kaye was crying, from laughter. "As me mother would say, 'Who would yis laugh at, if I wasn't here'?"

Nick tipped one of her bottles with his. "You remind me of that comedienne, what's her name?" He clicked his fingers.

"Who?"

"Bette Midler?" said Pete.

"No." Nick was still clicking his fingers. "Tracey Ullman, that's it." He gave one last click. "You remind me of her."

"Never heard of her. What's she like?"

"She's lovely." He eyed her sideways before turning towards a group of lads wilting against a wall. Chrissie and Pete kept on talking, as if nothing had happened.

"Bartenders have to bounce around." Pete was explaining. "Buying drinks for customers who'd been tipping them all week."

The crowd grew thicker. Kaye was on her tippy toes, trying to get a good look around the place, and was thinking about going home when Chrissie prodded her and said, "Andy."

"Where?" She fell sideways.

"Just walked in the door. Andy, Andy, over here."

"Hi Andy."

"Hey guys." He smiled so much, his lips curled up at the corners, emphasising the dimple on his chin. "Let me buy you drink."

"No, let us buy you one," Chrissie insisted. "After all, it's not every day we see you out."

"Yeah, Andy." Kaye smoothed her hair behind her ears. "We never see you out."

"I go out all the time." He couldn't stop smiling. "After-hours and on weeknights."

"What'll ya have?" Chrissie asked him.

"Tia Maria on ice."

"Tia Maria, nice idea. I'll have one too." Kaye called after her. "So, Andy." She straightened up, smoothed her top over her shorts and smiled. He smiled back. They stood there smiling, until she said, "Fancy meeting you here?"

"Oh." He hesitated. Smiled again. "You fancy meeting me?"

"Yeah, she fancies you." Chrissie had returned with the drinks.

"I do not. I said fancy . . ."

"I told ya," said Chrissie. "She fancies you. So there. What d'ya think?"

"Katerina is very nice girl," Andy's black hair swished against Kaye's cheek, with a whiff of musk. "Don't I take her home all the time?"

Jaysus!

Kaye hadn't noticed his brown velvet eyes before, or the way his brow wrinkled above his nose. It was finished with the Irish girl, he told her, arching his eye. She was about to embark on her Liam story when Pete startled her with a pat on her shoulder.

"See ya," he said. "Have a nice night."

A nice night? Isn't it the morning? She stood on tippytoes again. Nick was probably off with some woman by now. Wouldn't take him long here. After all, he had customers to take care of. For all she knew it was Chrissie, who just then came out of the loo before slipping out the back door. Not even a goodbye from her. And sure enough, there was Nick emerging from the crowd, and following behind her. So, Kaye was good for a laugh, maybe, but other girls were good for other things.

"Would you like to come back to my place?" Andy's cushion lips closed in on hers.

"Em." She couldn't take her eyes off them.

"We could make coffee, listen to music or something?"

"Em, ok, that would be lovely."

The daylight blinded her eyes. Yet, she still managed to make out Chrissie and Nick in the window seat of the next-door diner. As Andy's Oldsmobile, it was called, swerved away from the kerb, she saw them wave. They sped through five or six more streets, then Andy braked.

He led her inside an apartment building, up the stairs, and into a room, there seemed to be just one room; placed her on a bed and unzipped his pants. His penis sprung out, purple and erect. He pulled on a condom. *Would it fit?* Parted her legs and lay on top of her. A plastic bag at the end of the bed became entangled in his shoes. The more he thrust, the more the bag rustled, the more the bed shook, the more the wardrobe creaked. Kaye kept her eyes shut until he stopped trashing, rolled onto his side, and fell asleep.

So much for not doing it the first night.

As soon as he started snoring, she crept out the door and down the stairs. Ran in the direction of Broadway and didn't stop until she reached home. Took the stairs in twos and dashed down the hall to her bedroom. Fell back on her bed. Slept fitfully because of the firecrackers going off outside. Firecrackers? Of course, it was the 4th of July.

Images flitted before her eyes - Andy's penis, Chrissie and Nick, heads together in the diner, heads together.

She awoke to the sun streaming in the window, the sheets saturated from sweat.

Chrissie smiling at her.

"Aren't you like the cat that got the cream?"

"What time is it?" Kaye groaned.

"Eight o'clock."

"Wha'? She jumped out of bed, pulled on a pair of shorts. "Oh, I'm gonna be late," she cried. "George will kill me. What am I gonna do?"

"It's Sunday, ya eejit. And it's eight o'clock at night."

"Oh God!" Kaye fell back onto the bed, her shorts at her ankles, and had a sudden flashback. Andy.

"So?" Chrissie asked her. "Did you go home with him?"

"I did. I did. Am I mad?"

"No! Did ya do it?"

"Yeah, I think so. Yeah, I did."

"What was it like?"

"Oh, I dunno." Kaye scurried to the bathroom, holding her tummy, got there just in time to puke into the toilet.

"Ugh." Chrissie had been after her. "What's that?"

"Tia Maria."

"Not such a nice idea, after all? Anyhow, ya had a good time, that's all that matters."

"I suppose." Kaye retched.

"Stand under the shower for a while, and I'll make us a cup of tea."

"Why?" Kaye stood up, holding her tummy, her head. "Do I smell?"

"No, ya eejit, it'll make ya feel better, that's all."

"And where have you been all day?"

"In Sil's."

"Sil's? Didn't I see you having breakfast with Nick?" Kaye stepped into the bath.

"Yep." Chrissie examined her IF YOU'RE LOADED, I'M SINGLE T-shirt. "And I musta had eggs. Cheese. And chips because there's ketchup here."

Kaye burped, the bile near sickening her. "I thought you were with him?"

"Nah." Chrissie toddled down the hall.

"And, did he say anything, about me goin' off with Andy?"

"Nah, just hoped you were alright, that's all. Kept callin' you spacey Tracey."

Kaye took her tea back to bed, drank it down, drew her knees up to her chest, and covered her head with the duvet to drown out the noise outside on the street. She slept until six the next morning and lay there until it was time to go to work.

All the way down to the city, Kaye kept seeing Andy's face. Smelling his musky scent. Hearing his grunting, the wardrobe creaking, the plastic bag rustling.

Jaysus!

She fled up 59th Street, the sweat pouring out of her. Sloped into work, head down.

"Here comes Miss Pink." Tina bellowed. "Pink shoes, pink shirt, earrings, lips."

"Don't forget the pink eyes," said Perfecto.

The smell from the coffee grinder was turning her stomach. Her hands and feet were swollen, her apron too tight. She slouched up the stairs, headed for the shake machine.

"Let me." Melissa grabbed the stainless-steel container from her. "You better sit."

"Thanks Mel. God, I'm dyin'."

"Again?" Melissa's brow lifted. "What'll it be? A black-and-white?"

She heaped vanilla ice cream and chocolate sauce into the container, placed it in the shake machine, poured the brown mixture into a tall glass and placed a cherry on top.

"Perfecto," Kaye said, sitting at the counter.

"Me, Mama?" said Perfecto.

"No, no." She waved him away. "The shake. The shake is perfect."

"Don't give me any tables." She shouted at Tina. "Make Violet and Rose happy."

"Be nice." Melissa tapped her hand. "They might need the money more than you."

Kaye moaned. "I'm sorry, it's just that I went home with Andy."

"Andy? Who's Andy?"

"What's goin' on with you Irish?" Tina said. "What's with all this drinking?"

Kaye bent over, held her head. "I'll have to stop. I can't go on. What am I doing here?"

"Just quit the alcohol some. What kind of air conditioner you got in that apartment?" Tina was sitting at her perch inside the door. "Smoking or no-smoking?"

"Just a fan."

"Are you crazy? Just a fan?"

"Excuse me?" said a customer. "I said NO smoking."

"Are you trying to kill yourselves?"

"I'll take smoking if you'd prefer," the bewildered customer said to Tina.

"One fan in this heat?" She addressed the line in general. "These Irish girls are crazy." Heads nodded in agreement. "You're dehydrated." She exclaimed. Eyes blinked. "Drink plenty of water." She guided waiting customers to their tables.

"We will." One of them replied, as Tina handed out menus.

Later in the morning, Kaye had to get sick again. Melissa held her head over the toilet. "I knew it, I knew you got laid."

Kaye's head jolted out of the bowl. "How did you know?"

"This." Melissa ruffled Kaye's hair. "You're having a good hair day."

"Oh!" Kaye straightened up. "I'm sick. How am I ever gonna take his cab again?"

"His cab? You mean you slept with the cab driver? Are you insane?"

"We know him." Kaye splashed water on her face. "We always take him home."

"And last night you took him literally?" Melissa chuckled all the way up the stairs.

Tina met them at the top. "Was it your first time in America?"

"It was actually." Kaye straightened her skirt, ran her fingers through her hair.

"That's my girl, high-five."

Kaye told herself she'd have to lighten up. That other people did this all the time.

"Irish girl, you got tables," George roared above the crash of cutlery, dishes, chatter.

"Just remember." Melissa whispered. "When you get the chance to fuck, take it."

"I did!"

CHAPTER FIFTEEN

New Jersey Transit trundled through Trenton, Elizabeth, and Newark, speeding past billboards, factories, chimneys, railway tracks, motels, and high-rise apartment blocks.

At Lou and Matt's wedding, Kaye had been given the role of trainbearer. Her three-year old mind had envisaged holding onto an actual train until her mother explained it might be the veil she'd be holding, or the end of a long dress. But Kaye had been disappointed in the end when Lou arrived at the church in knee-length lace, a veil tipping her shoulders, not a train in sight. For the rest of the day, she had been unsure of her role.

The train stopped in Princeton – where F. Scott Fitzgerald had been a student. Kaye had done her thesis on *The Great Gatsby – An American Dream Beneath the Glittering Surface*. Little did she know. Next stop, New Brunswick, where this fella Olivia had met in Dun Laoghaire baths was from. She went out with him for a whole summer, while Kaye read all the books in her mother's bookcase.

When the train stopped at 30th Street station, it didn't take long to spot Lou and Matt on the platform. Matt, tanned and handsome with distinguished grey streaks in his black hair, was a psychoanalyst with his own practice. Lou, still sparkly and diminutive, was wearing kohl eyeliner now, her curls carroty red, not black how Kaye had remembered them.

"You look wonderful." She gathered Kaye into her arms. "We're thrilled to have you."

"Nice to see you, Katherine." Matt kissed her on the forehead. "You look swell."

They whisked her out of the station into a waiting cab.

"I don't drive." Matt explained. "Don't need to, as I work and live in this great city."

"Did you lose weight?" Lou eyed her up and down.

"No," said Kaye, "put it on, more like, the same five pounds I keep losing and gaining."

"How's New York?" asked Matt.

"Grand."

"We were there years ago to see a show." Lou sighed. "I'd love to go back."

"It's only up the road?" Kaye looked at her aunt, but she didn't reply.

Matt asked the taxi driver to take them into the city to show Kaye the Clothespin.

"You're the image of your mother," Lou said. "She was wearing a green-and-white striped dress the first time I met her, and your dad joked about what horse she was riding."

"Is that the time you pinned the doily inside your jumper?"

"It was a top really, with a low neck. We were at a dress dance. Your father's friend called to the door and invited me when I was down on my knees scrubbing the floor."

"There's the Liberty Bell; we'll take you tomorrow," said Matt.

"*Bell, bell, my Liberty Bell,*" Lou started to sing, "*I'm so in love with you.*"

"And that's where Betsy Ross made the flag."

"Your mother gave me a lovely yellow swing jacket when she was pregnant on you."

"She made it herself, like?"

"Yes, hand sewn."

"No, her aunt had sent it to her from England."

"The flag?"

"No, the jacket."

"Honey, for Chrissake." Matt cried. "I'm trying to show your niece some history."

"Oh, who cares about that?" Lou waved him away. "I want to talk about Ireland."

"That's City Hall," Matt continued, "and down that side street is my office."

The buildings weren't as high as in New York and the neon lights not as bright. There was less shouting and less beeping.

"Did Granddad really throw your mattress out in the shed?" Kaye asked Lou.

"Only the once; don't believe all you hear."

"This is the campus of Temple University where Anna and Matthew are students."

"Sure, we were so innocent back then. All we did was kiss."

"And this is Pine Street," said Matt, as the cab pulled up in front of a reddish-brown house with a porch in front. "Home at last."

"Our lips used to be sore from the kissing." Lou eased herself into a chair on the porch and Kaye sat on a swing.

"Would you like a drink?" Matt asked her. "A beer, soda, glass of wine?"

"A cup of tea would be grand." She was going to take a break from beer this weekend.

"How about a sandwich?"

"That'd be lovely." She rubbed her bloated tummy, what the heck, she was hungry.

"There's Doyle's Tavern where Matt used to work when we came over first." Lou pointed up the street. "And there, on the corner of Spruce was our first apartment."

Matt brought out a giant bag of crisps and ham sandwiches, Irish style. One square of ham between two slices of buttered bread, cut into triangles. The porch was warm, but not humid. Her cousins were out partying, and she'd meet them in the morning. The Butlers would've been made stay in for visitors. Whatever Kaye was drinking did not taste like tea.

The house was colonial style, Lou showed her around. The front door led into a living room, its furniture heavy and dark. From there, they went into the dining room and through to the kitchen, like in 4D. Upstairs, were two more floors with two bedrooms, a bathroom, and a box room on each. One box room was a bureau for Matt and the other a TV room. The walls were covered with family photographs and paintings of Ireland.

When Kaye awoke the next morning, it took her a few minutes to realise where she was. The night before, she had slipped between pink sheets, under a canopy of broderie anglaise, and fallen into a deep sleep. She was about to panic when the familiar photographs caught her eye. And then, came the smell of bacon.

In the kitchen, Matt was whisking eggs.

"Sleep ok, hun?" He placed a plate in front of her, buttered toast on the side.

"Grand," she said.

Anna arrived in soon after and kissed her. "It's so good to see you again."

After breakfast, the girls went to the Gallery Mall, where Kaye bought Eagles T-shirts for Chrissie and Mo and magnets for their fridge.

"It's great to have someone to show around." Anna gushed. "Can you imagine never having a grandmother, grandfather, aunt, uncle, or cousin to spend the holidays with? To never have family to celebrate Christmas, Easter, your birthday, or graduation with?"

"I can. It was the same for us. Kilcoughlan is way down the country, and as you know, the Butlers are on the other side of Dublin city."

On her First Holy Communion Day, Kaye had had no relatives to call on, had made no actual money, only postal orders. Olivia, of course, made loads.

"Do you like turkey and ham?" Lou asked her. "We'll have it for dinner."

"Lovely," Kaye said and was surprised when Lou suggested stopping at a Food Court for a late lunch. Shouldn't she be going home to put on the turkey?

"I'm having McDonald's," said Anna. "How about you Mom?"

"I'll have Chinese. How about you, Kaye?"

"Just a drink, please, a soda."

"Are you sure? How about a slice of pizza? Oh! I know, a Philly steak sandwich."

"No, no, I'm grand." Kaye pulled out a chair. "I'm saving myself for dinner."

"Dinner?" Anna grabbed a tray for McDonald's.

Lou trotted towards Chopsticks in shorts and a tank top. Kaye's mother would never wear trousers, much less shorts.

As they ate, no one mentioned the turkey. Maybe Matt would turn on the oven?

"Why don't you stay?" Lou spoke with her mouth full of chow mein. "You'd get a teaching job here no prob, and you could live with us."

Kaye shook her head. "Not a chance," she said.

She tried to imagine it though. Just for the fun of it. What would it be like? To live in Philadelphia, up to New York for weekends. Visit the places she'd seen listed on the Amtrak board in Penn Station. Home on holidays, telling everyone about her new life. Have people over to visit, showing them around. Getting up every morning to teach in an American high school.

"It would be so much fun," said Anna. "You'd be here for Thanksgiving, for the Army–Navy football game, for Christmas, for Paddy's Day – the best day of the year in Doyle's – and you might make it for my graduation next spring, if I make it myself."

"Sounds great," Kaye said. "But it won't be happening, I'm afraid."

Matt and Matthew were sitting on the porch when they got home. Her cousin, so like his father, reminded her of JFK Junior who'd been in Burger Heaven one day.

"He had apple pie and cream and left Melissa a two-dollar tip," she told Lou.

"Did ya meet anyone else famous?" Her aunt sat into a hammock and reached for an iced tea, apparently with no notion of getting dinner ready.

"Em. Kathleen Turner, and some comedian?"

"Would you like to eat now, hon?" Matt asked her. "Or later?"

"I wouldn't mind now." She followed him into the kitchen where there was no smell of cooking; no sign of steam; no pots and pans on the cooker. "Whenever it's ready?"

"It's ready when you are." Matt opened the fridge and took out a ball of white turkey meat and plastic-wrapped slices of ham. "Would you like coleslaw or macaroni cheese?"

Kaye held onto a chair laughing. "Matt." She spluttered and had to sit down.

"What's the matter, honey?" He ran to her.

"I was expecting …" Kaye held her tummy.

"You're expecting?" echoed Lou, who had just arrived in.

"No, no." The tears rolled down Kaye's cheeks. "I was expecting roast turkey with stuffin' and gravy and mashed potato, baked ham. I've been savin' meself all day for it."

"Oh, dear." Matt forced a smile, but Kaye could see he didn't get it.

"Are you kiddin' me?" Lou cried. "Roasting a turkey in this weather?"

"Cooking is not one of my wife's strong points," said Matt.

"What's so funny cuz?" Now Matthew had arrived in.

"She thought we were having a roast turkey dinner, with all the trimmings, and a ham baked in the oven. Is she crazy?" Lou set the table with paper plates.

"You won't get anything like that around here until Thanksgiving." Matthew laughed. "Even then, we have bets as to how many cans Mom will use. I guess cooking ain't a strong point with the Irish, not with all that drinking."

"That's not true." Kaye was on the defensive, like when customers asked silly questions about Ireland. "Dad doesn't drink, and Mam's a great cook. Auntie May too."

"They must have had lessons since I was there," said Matthew. "I loved the desserts and candies, but the dinners were pretty bland."

"Oh, I miss the sausage." Lou sighed. "And the bacon and cabbage. And, by the way, don't put her off my cooking, she might be here for Thanksgiving."

Kaye placed a slice of turkey on a square of white Wonder bread.

"That'd be great, honey." Matt spread mayonnaise on his and covered it with ham. "It's my favourite holiday of the year."

"Ah, a pity I won't be here."

"Yeah," said Matthew. "It's Christmas without all the fuss."

Kaye munched her sandwich. "I have to go home. Dad lost his job."

"We heard." Lou looked forlorn. "But, years ago, people went away and sent the money home. You'd be a much better help to them from here, surely?"

"Not working as a waitress, I wouldn't. It's so uncertain. And I am illegal."

"Oh, that's too bad." Matt opened a can of beer. "Because you seem much happier than you were when we were last home."

"When was that?" Kaye asked him.

"Four years ago."

After the dinner dance in the Glenview, Kaye didn't see Liam for weeks, although she had her eyes peeled for him at her Wednesday-night typing class and dreamed of bumping into him in the corridor. She watched every day for the red Fiesta gliding down Herbert Road, and every Friday in the Harbour Bar, thought this could be it, this could be the night.

When Lou and Matt arrived on a holiday that summer, Kaye was still berating herself over what could've caused Liam's disinterest. Had she spent too much time chatting to his friends? Drank too much? Because she fell asleep in the car? Was she too fat in the dress?

Dad drove the visitors up Bray Head and pointed out Killiney Hill and Dalkey Island, telling them proudly that the view was often compared to the Bay of Naples. Kaye spent the whole time wondering where Liam was.

After dinner, Lou, Matt, and Kaye went over to Doyle's. Matthew was out clubbing with his buddies, and Anna had a date with her boyfriend, Mario O'Brien.

The three of them sat at the bar with another ten or twelve, who, in the course of the evening, all shuffled over, to be introduced to Kaye.

"Next time I'll wear a T-shirt with, I'M HIS WIFE'S NIECE FROM IRELAND written on the back." Kaye giggled. "Save him the time."

"Oh, don't worry," Lou said. "He loves it."

Photographs of the bar during Prohibition, covered the walls. Matt explained how liquor had been made illegal and how gangs back then had smuggled it in. How bar owners were forced to find ways to sell the "hooch" without attracting the cops.

"I used to sit there on a Saturday night. In my black cocktail dress." Lou tilted her bright red curls at the tables and chairs behind them. "With Matt's two aunts who'd come over years before us, and we'd watch him work. Otherwise, I'd hardly have seen him at all."

"There's Old Man Doyle." Matt pointed at a photograph of a crinkled face under a soft cap: an Irish version of Al Capone. "He gave me my first job in America," Matt said proudly. "And see those teacups on the tables? Whiskey."

"Whiskey?"

"During Prohibition this place was a tearoom, serving bootleg whiskey."

"I waited and waited for word from Dad. In those days, the mail from Ireland used to take two weeks." Lou's cigarette was red from her lipstick. "I waited to get pregnant, which I did after six months. Matt worked and went to school. Then I had the kids."

Where, wondered Kaye, was the vivacious girl in the photographs? Doris Day beside a swimming pool? The devil-may-care heroine of Kaye's childhood?

"I would love to have lived in the suburbs." Lou blabbered on. "The kids could've learnt Irish dancing, joined the GAA, played hurling and football, camogie. But Matt's job kept him here, in the city." She stubbed her cigarette and lit another one.

The barman, a sinewy little man, banged an ashtray on the counter and called, "*Ciúnas*" in that bizarre mix of an Irish American accent that she'd noticed in people who'd been here a long time. Lou sang '*When Irish Eyes Are Smiling*', and then volunteered Kaye, who didn't think Mary Black would suit this crowd, so she tried '*Spancil Hill*' and it was a hit. When Matt sang '*Danny Boy*', they dabbed their eyes with hankies, tissues, sleeves.

No way was she staying in this country.

On the way home, they passed the Chinese laundry where Matt had his shirts pressed, the diner where he ate his pancakes every morning, the stand where he had his shoes shone, and Thriftway, the supermarket Lou had been afraid to go into when she arrived over.

Lou went straight to bed. Matt opened a cooler and retrieved two cans of *Coors*. "Don't you have a love?" He handed one to Kaye. "You're too interesting to be alone."

Kaye swung back and forth on the swing, the sky full of stars, and told him her story.

They had a cookout on the Sunday. Burgers were grilled on the barbeque, and Matthew had been telling the truth: mashed potatoes, onion rings and pickles out of a tin. The old dears from Doyle's were there and the next-door neighbours. Someone asked Kaye how she was enjoying her weekend.

"Great," she said. "Except for the heat. I was baking all day."

"How nice, were you making desserts?"

Kaye fell into the kitchen laughing.

"Are they gonna get a shock," Lou laughed with her. "The only baked goods we're having are *Entenmann's*." She pointed to a stack of cardboard boxes.

"We'll hide the boxes and pretend I made them," said Kaye.

The next morning, Kaye's throat felt tight, saying goodbye. She hadn't expected to feel so sad.

"Think about staying." Lou hugged her.

Kaye hadn't the heart to say she had no intention. "Maybe." She walked to the cab.

"And send that young man back home a card. Matt told me all

about him."

"You should." Matt paid her fare to the driver. "Maybe he needs to hear from you?"

Send him a card?

Exactly what she had wanted to hear.

CHAPTER SIXTEEN

She scurried down 34th Street from Penn Station, along Lexington Avenue up to 56th and spun through the door of Burger Heaven, just as the small hand on the bronze clock hit two.

"It's ten after ten." Tina didn't lift her eyes from counting bills. "How was your trip?"

"Great."

Melissa passed by with four plates propped along her left arm and a Coke in her right hand. "Hey girl. Have a good trip?"

"Yep."

"You're late," George hissed. "Hurry up and get your side work done."

"Hey Mama." Fernando was scrambling eggs. "How was your trip?"

You'd think she'd been in the Antarctic.

"I was only down the road."

She bolted down the stairs, pulled her shirt over her head and tightened her tie. Well, not a tie, but the leatherette string with a silver acropolis at the throat that George had brought them all back from Crete.

Perfecto had been lifting a tray of corn muffins out of the oven, and the smell of them, along with ground Columbian coffee beans, carried her back upstairs.

"You marry me, Mama?"

"If you make me buns like that, I might." She tied her apron.

He looked at her wide-eyed.

"Confusing the help again, Kathy?" Melissa approached the wait station.

"Is your man on the warpath today?" Kaye jerked her head at George.

"Excuse me?" Melissa said. "I don't have a man?"

"I mean George." Kaye grabbed a bunch of knives for shining.

"He's not my man." Melissa rolled her eyes. "And by the way you have tables. I already gave Seven his soda and I'm leaving Two to you."

"Gee, thanks." Kaye gave Table Seven the thumbs up to let him know she was on her way and then spotted the forlorn figure at Table Two. "I see Decaf's here already."

"Yep. Wouldn't have anyone but you; said you're the only one who listens to her."

"Pity she wouldn't drink a decent cup of coffee." Kaye picked up a mug and poured from the pot. "Maybe she wouldn't be so depressed." She dropped the coffee on Two with a "how ya doin'?" and listened to its occupant describe exactly how she was doing.

"You Irish not into decaffeinated?" Melissa met her again at the coffee machine.

"Wouldn't dream of it. We were weaned on tea in our baby bottles."

"Get ouda here. So, how's the cab driver?"

"Who?"

Kaye picked up two specials and a cheese deluxe from the hatch. She had decided that the only way to deal with what had happened with Andy was to act as though it hadn't happened at all. At least here, in the restaurant, she was too busy to think about it.

She dropped the food and went on to her next table. The rush had begun, and she was in the weeds already, Tina slamming her with tables.

"Hi there!" Bernard dashed by, balancing a tray on his shoulder.

"I thought he was fired?" Kaye hissed at Melissa.

"Walked out, remember" said Melissa. "Now, he's with an agency and they sent him over to cover lunch today."

"I don't believe it. In Ireland you'd never walk out of a job, and if you did, you'd never come back."

"You're not in Ireland now."

"You can say that again." Kaye dashed to the hatch where Fernando was bouncing on the bell.

"You're not in . . . oh forget it." Melissa was hot on her heels. "Need some help?"

"Oh, you're a star. Can you imagine, my aunt wants me to stay?"

"In Philadelphia?" Melissa picked up some plates. "Would you like it?"

"No!"

"How about New York?"

"No!"

"Alright, alright."

But apparently Melissa wasn't happy to let it go because when they were finally upstairs with their French fries, onion rings, and tuna melts – one with Swiss on rye and the other with cheddar on whole-wheat, she brought it up again.

"So, what did your aunt say?" Melissa chewed on a pickle. "About stayin'?"

"Ah, don't mind her, she only wants the company."

"Nothin' wrong with that."

"No, I'm not staying. I don't know what makes people think I might, all of a sudden. I only came for the summer."

Melissa put up her hand in mock defence.

"Anyhow, I couldn't stay illegally, not being able to go home whenever I wanted."

"What's so great about home?"

"Well, my family. Obviously."

"What else?"

Kaye didn't answer.

"You've a man over there?"

"Yes. No. Sort of. I don't know."

"What's his name?"

"Liam. But he's. Then there's my friend Olivia."

Melissa looked at her. "You think there's something between them?"

"No! I didn't say that."

"Well …"

"Anyhow, I'm not staying. I don't want to end up like Mo. And Nick. And Pete. Andy even. And all the old dears in Doyle's Tavern, crying every time I hear *Danny Boy!*"

"Whoa." Melissa held up her hand again. "Are you in a soap opera?"

"Something like that." Kaye sighed.

"What does Kathy want? Forget about everyone else. What do you want."

"Wow. No one has ever asked me that before."

Melissa shrugged.

"I want Liam." She hated how her little voice came out in a whine.

"He must be somethin' else."

"He is."

"You got a teaching degree, right?"

"Yeah, well I got an arts degree, and a diploma in education. Why?"

"Because I heard that the Archdiocese is hiring. They don't pay as much as the public school system, but George would probably let you work Saturdays. We could go see the Christmas tree at Rockefeller. Ice skate in Central Park. You could come to my house for Thanksgiving. You'd love it."

Kaye swabbed her plate with a crust of rye bread. "Get a grip."

"You could do your Masters." Melissa swished her hand at the window. "There's CUNY colleges in the city, or SUNY, elsewhere in the State, but they're more expensive. You could apply for financial aid. There's TAP, PELL – that's the one I got – or a William Stafford loan. You could come to Queensboro Community College with me."

"You're losin' the run of yourself, as me mother would say." Kaye emptied her pockets onto the table. "I came for the summer, I'm staying for the summer, and then I'm going home. That was always the plan."

"The plan?"

"The plan was to come for the summer and go home a new woman who Liam will fall instantly in love with."

"Oh, Kathy." Melissa shook her head in dismay.

"Anyhow, my father lost his job, so I have to go back and help out." Kaye started counting her tips, trying to forget that look of pity she saw on Melissa's face.

"You could help out better from here. Think of all the money you could send?"

"You've an answer for everything, don't you?"

For a Monday night, there was a good crowd in the Terminal. Sil and Seanie perched in their usual positions inside the door, like the pair in the Muppet Show. Kaye took a stool and tried to pat some warmth into her arms. She kept forgetting to bring a cardigan. There was no sign of Chrissie, even though she had called before Kaye left work, to arrange them meeting here. She took out the card she had bought for Liam. On the front were two teddy bears sitting at a table, drinking from two cups. On the outside: WHY DON'T YOU CALL? On the inside: AND WE'LL HAVE SOME TEA?

'Having a ball,' she'd written.

She would post it in the morning.

"Hi." Mo was next in. "Did ya have a good time?"

"Yeah, yeah." Kaye sat up straight, stuffed the card in her handbag. "Did Chrissie tell you about her and Tim?"

"No? She just told me ye were meeting here, and that was it."

"She was with him Saturday night."

"What?"

"Brought him back to our place."

Tim was sitting half-way down the bar, conked out as usual. There was no sign of Izzy. Nick sidled towards them waving two bottles of *Amstel*.

"Awesome." Mo grabbed hers as soon as he'd knocked off the cap. "What's new?"

"Nothing, since Sunday." He bowed towards Tim, then at Chrissie, who had just arrived in, cheeks burning.

"What are yis talkin' about?" She plonked her bag on the counter, as Nick moved away. "Ya told her about me and Tim, didn't ya?" She said to Mo.

"Em, no."

"Ya did so. Anyhow nothin' happened. So what?"

"Where was Izzy Tops at the time?" asked Kaye.

"You mean Iggy Pop," said Mo.

"Izzy's in the Hamptons with the Fingers." Chrissie's eyes never once met Kaye's.

"What's gonna happen now?" Kaye wanted to know.

"Nothin'! Nothin' has happened. And nothin's gonna happen."

"Shush." Kaye tilted her head at Tim. "He'll hear you. So, what about the weddin'?"

"What about the weddin'? We were only chattin', that's all."

"You can say that again." Mo laughed. "I could hear ye through the wall. I thought ye'd never stop. Chatting, that is. What on earth could you have to say to Tim?"

Kaye was sorry she'd come. She'd love to be at home now, curled up in bed, with a nice big mug of tea. And she meant home. Dublin, as far away from here, as she could get.

"Chrissie, are you ok?" she asked her cousin after Mo went off to join Seanie.

"Yeah, why?" Chrissie turned her head away.

"I dunno, you just seem different, that's all."

"I am different; I'm in America, aren't I?"

"It's only been seven months?"

"Well, it seems like a lifetime." Chrissie sighed.

"I know what you mean. How long are you planning on staying?"

"Ah, I'll stick it out the year anyhow. D'ya want another drink?"

"I'll try a *Coors Lite* this time."

"Hey, look who just walked in." Mo was back, nudging her. "Andy, Andy, over here. I have to go to work now, so I'll leave ya to it."

"Well, look who it is." Chrissie unhooked herself from Sil who was now on her other side. "Come sit with us."

"Jesus!" Kaye hissed. "You'd think he was the Pope."

"Hey, guys," said Andy. "Let me buy you a drink."

"No, let us buy you one." Chrissie pushed Kaye. "So, what'll ya have?" She asked him.

"Tia Maria on ice, remember?" He held up a clump of money at Nick.

Kaye couldn't take her eyes off Andy's lips. She'd love a kiss, that's all, just a kiss.

"We're leaving now." Chrissie poked her in the back.

"You wanna come back to my place for coffee?" Andy didn't waste a second.

Nick was stacking glasses; Tim still staring into space. He and Chrissie hadn't exchanged a glance. Maybe all was fair in love. It was nice to be desired. But she wasn't attracted to Andy.

Don't stray too far from your nature, Liam told her, when she'd begged him to take her home to his new house overlooking Greystones harbour. When, after much drinking and kissing, Kaye had decided she was going to stay the night. When he'd knelt down and banged his head on his sitting-room floor, moaning, 'I'm going mad. Mad,' and then led her to a spare room, her heart in pieces, her mind going over what might have been, might have been. He was going to get help he said the next morning; make an appointment with a therapist. They never discussed the subject again.

"Nah, I don't like coffee, that much." She told Andy, swivelled off the swivel stool, waved at Nick and left.

CHAPTER SEVENTEEN

K aye sat on the windowsill and stuck her head out the window, gasping for air. Bed was a lost cause because of the heat. It was dark now, only a few lights from the pastel houses opposite, but the sign on the corner *Bodega* still flickered OPEN in neon, and the neighbours on their sidewalk chairs, laughed and talked and clicked their beads to a salsa beat.

It wasn't only the heat and the music that made it impossible to rest. She was in a state, had been ever since Trish had called collect from a public phone somewhere on Long Island, where she was visiting college friends. Every time Kaye had tried to ring back, Trish couldn't hear her. Then she'd tried the operator and had banged down the phone with frustration when she couldn't get her through.

What would Liam think of her, if he saw her behave like that? It wasn't exactly the transformation she was going for.

Liam, who could have had his choice of girls. Yet, she had to face it, the only one he'd ever seemed interested in was herself and if she was being perfectly honest, he hadn't even been that interested in her.

She and Olivia had mulled over it for hours, the way he was so slow to make a move.

Then, out of the blue, "I know what his problem is."

It was Olivia, on the phone.

"What?" Kaye had called her from a kiosk in Loughlinstown, Lucky at her feet.

"He had mumps as a child."

"So?" Kaye quivered with the cold, the dog's eyes pleading with her to go home.

"So, he might be sterile."

"Sterile?"

"Yeah, it's one of the side effects, for boys. So that must be it."

Olivia sounded pleased with herself.

"That's why he won't commit."

"How do you know, anyhow?" Kaye lit a cigarette. Lucky lay out on the floor.

"He left his personal file here, after a meeting."

"And you read it?"

"Yeah, just scanned through it. Thought it might help you get over him."

She wandered into the kitchen for water, soda, iced tea, anything. The idea of drinking cold tea would have sickened her before, but the tangy lemon and crushed ice was great for quenching thirst. She sat in the dark kitchen, cradling her glass, relishing the silence, no longer aware of the sounds on the street, thinking about Nick instead.

Be careful.

He's living a lie.

A bit of a lad.

What did that really mean? Kaye had no evidence of Nick being a womaniser. In fact, she'd never once seen him leave the Terminal with anyone, except for his trips out the back door to Chrissie, but Chrissie insists she's never been with him.

Melissa and Kaye were counting their tips in the back station when the doorbell rang, Kaye stacking the quarters and Melissa separating the one-dollar bills from the fives. They hardly ever got a ten or a twenty, and when they did, they cried "Yoo-hoo" to let the other one know.

"Feck it," said Kaye, the doorbell making her lose count.

"Feck it," Melissa mimicked her in a stage-Irish accent. "Why don't you just say, 'fuck it' like everyone else, Kathy. Why don't you just lash out?"

Kaye swept the coins off the table and back into her pocket.

"We're closed." Tina didn't take her eyes off the cash she was counting.

"I'm looking for me sister."

It was Trish, standing in the doorway.

"Agh!" Kaye bolted out of her chair scattering their tips all over the floor. "What took so long. Ya should've been here hours ago."

"Thanks Kathy," Melissa said. "Now I have to start all over again."

Trish gave her a "who's-yer-one?" look, as Kaye showed her to a seat at the counter.

"I missed the train." Trish whined. "And had to wait for the next one." She plonked herself on the stool. "I'm wrecked," she said. "And starving."

"Oh! The kitchen's closed."

Fernando was scrubbing the grill with a wire brush.

"And I don't know if 'Hear the Drums' will want to turn on the fire again." She waved to Melissa. "Come meet my sister; you too, Fernando."

"I was already told that you were closed," said Trish. "Yer one nearly took the nose off me when I walked in the door. And what drums are ya talkin' about?"

"His name is Fernando. I call him 'Hear the Drums'. This is winding down time," Kaye explained. "We're all dyin' to get outa here after the long shift."

"Is that the takin's for the day?" Trish gaped at the pile of money on the table.

"That's our tips," said Kaye, handing her a coke. "Fernando, any chance of a burger? *Por favor*, like?"

"Pour fa-vore?" Trish eyed Kaye.

"Anything for you, Mama." Fernando smiled. "And your seester, she nice too."

"And a few fries?" Kaye joined her hands in prayer. "*Mucho, mucho gracias*, Nando. My seester, she very hungry. *Tiene hombre.*"

"*Tiene hombre?*" Fernando raised his eyebrows. "She like me, maybe?"

"I mean *hambre*. I always get that mixed up." She turned to Trish. "I said 'she wants a man' instead of 'she's hungry'!"

Trish was looking at her spellbound. "I thought, maybe you'd have an American accent, but ..."

Then, she looked Kaye up and down. What on earth are ya like? The get-up on ya."

Kaye patted her uniform. "What's wrong?"

"Just look at yourself." She turned Kaye around to a mirror-lined wall.

"I suppose I do look a sight." She did a twirl and then exploded into laughter. "No wonder the customers are always askin' if this is my national costume. Mam would kill me."

"You look cool." Melissa lit a cigarette for Kaye and one for herself.

"Does the sista smoke?" she asked.

"No, thank you very much."

"Does she have an Irish attitude too?"

"I beg your pardon?" Trish frowned at Melissa, then at Kaye.

"I'll go and change." Kaye flicked some ash into a saucer. "And ya know what?" She paused before descending the stairs. "I like the way I dress over here. Nobody knows me and nobody cares. I love that about New York. I love being anonymous."

"Oh, I thought you didn't like it at all." Trish was still shrugging her shoulders.

In the cupboard they called a bathroom, Kaye wriggled out of her uniform, careful not to shove her elbow through the cardboard wall. She squeezed into the black canvas skirt she'd bought in Philadelphia and had been hoping to slim into, a black top and sandals. Their mother was always praising Trish's skinny legs, her straight hair.

'Ya'd better be off the road before she starts out.' Her father would mutter from behind his newspaper,' or she'll steal all yer boyfriends.'

She blotted her nose and forehead with toilet paper and smeared foundation across her cheeks, dampened her hair with tap water, puckered her lips for pink gloss and was done. Her only accessory was silver loop earrings. She studied her reflection. She'd do.

On their way to the subway, Trish photographed hot-dog vendors; a policeman on a horse; the queue for Carnegie Hall in case there was anyone famous in it; the bouncer outside Hard Rock Café in case he was famous, and the giant rolls of salami in the window of the New York Deli, which were famous. Then, the two of them posed, their legs entangled, outside Bloomingdale's, their fingers in a V behind each other's heads in front of Tommy Makem's Pavilion on 57th Street; reading the menu in the Russian Tea Room and hoisting their skirts up beside the statue of Columbus at the station. More snaps were taken on the escalator, buying their tokens, and wrapped around a pole on the platform.

"Sit beside two fine things when we get on the train." Trish told her. "And we'll pretend to people at home that they're our boyfriends."

Olivia did that in Athens. She'd sit beside a hunk, and have Kaye take her photograph, then pretend to everyone in the Tech that she'd got off with him.

"Yer not on a Greek island now, you know."

"A Greek island?" Trish looked confused. "What would I be doin' there?"

"Oh, nothin'." Kaye fell into fits of laughter. Sometimes, she got her daydreams confused with real life.

"The heat is gone to yer head." Trish flapped her shirt for air, if there was any, to circulate. "If anyone asked me to dance right now, I could actually say, 'I'm sweatin', ask me sister' and mean it. What's that smell? It's like petrol? Mechanic's aftershave?"

Trish continued her snapping spree on the train. One of the two of them with their knees crossed over one another, another of the two of them sitting on each other's laps, embracing, and one of them waltzing to a barbershop quartet singing '*Danny Boy*,' after which there was a burst of applause.

"Shoot me if ya ever catch me cryin' at that song," said Kaye, as she took the camera off Trish just in time to stop her from snapping the man wheeling by on a skateboard.

"He's got no legs." She whispered. "Respect."

Trish clasped her mouth. "I'm sorry. I thought he'd fallen in between the carriages."

"I thought that my first night too and felt awful."

"I like the way you said 'respect', it's so American."

Kaye sank back into her seat. She was showing off New York like it was her hometown. Next, the Terminal.

At the bar, Trish raised her bottle. "The highlight of the trip so far. We might never again be in the same place with the same people. Right?"

"Wrong." Chrissie tipped her bottle. "We'll probably be here again tomorrow night."

"That suits me fine." Trish spun around on her stool.

"Hang on a second," said Mo. "You're saying you've been to California, Chicago, and the Hamptons. And this." Her hand swept the bar, a look of disbelief on her face. "Is the highlight?"

"Well, at first I was working all hours in a snotty summer camp in San Diego. In Chicago, I spent all my time sightseeing. Southampton's too posh. Now, all I want to do is have the craic, and get off with an American."

"If ya can find one!" Kaye laughed.

"Are there none here?" Trish spun around again.

"Not too many in the Bronx," said Chrissie. "We haven't found one, yet."

Trish slowed down, tilted her head. "Who's the fine thing of a bartender?"

"Ya mean, Pete?" Kaye said.

"No. Over on the other side." Trish was craning her neck.

"That's Tricky Nick," said Chrissie. "He's a friend of ours. Wouldn't mind getting into his pants either if the opportunity arose. Literally." She clicked all their bottles.

"Would ya go the whole way?" Trish asked her.

"Oh! All the way, baby." Chrissie licked her lips. "All the way."

Trish looked at her in awe. "Ya always have loads of men."

"I do not. Hey, Pete," Chrissie roared. "Another drink over here, we're gaspin'."

"Don't get yer knickers in a knot." Pete appeared, shaking his head, as usual. "Now, girl." He looked at Trish. "D'ya know what yer getting into? Partying with these ones?"

"I know. Kaye's me sister." Trish was trying to light her cigarette at the wrong end.

"Trish, is it?" Pete turned the cigarette right side up. "The Dish," he said, holding out his hand and Kaye groaned. "Kaye's sister? Well, if yer quarter as nice, yer welcome."

"Ah now, Peter." Kaye couldn't help beaming. "Will ya go 'way out a dat."

He fanned four beer mats in front of them. "A drink comin' whenever yis are ready. Meself and Nick were just remarkin' on how yis are always in good humour, always good for a laugh, never gettin' into fights or anythin'. The cool chicks, right, Nick?"

"What's that?" Nick slithered over.

"Meet my sister," Kaye said. "Trish, this is Nick."

"Enchanted." He took both of her hands in his and covered them with butterfly kisses. "So, this is Trish the Dish?"

"And you're Nick the Trick." Trish fluttered her eyelashes.

"Em, right." He looked at Kaye and then back at Trish. "You don't look alike."

Yeah, right.

"You don't have Katie's nice wavy hair." He flashed Kaye a smile.

Kaye sprung her finger away from a curl she'd been twisting.

"We'll have one for the road," she said, beaming at him.

They linked Trish out to the cab later.

"Is that the fella you got off with?" She prodded the back of Andy's seat.

Kaye nodded. Yes.

Trish opened her mouth in an O.

"So, what are your intentions now regarding my sister?" she said to Andy. "Me fader will be wantin' full particulars, you see."

"What is she talking about?" Mo said, irritated.

"Don't listen to her." Kaye snarled.

"Yeah," said Chrissie. "When are ya gonna make an honest woman ouda her?"

"Leave Katee alone." Andy's eyes caught hers in the rear-view mirror. "Eh, Katerina?"

"Yes," Kaye said. "Leave me alone."

"You better." Trish lay back on the seat. "Before me fader comes over with a shotgun."

"This is ridiculous." Mo was getting more aggravated.

Kaye could see Andy's face in the mirror, contorted into creases.

"She's only jokin," she said, meeting his gaze. "Dad hasn't a notion of getting on a plane at his age."

How was he to know that her parents were off to Lanzarote for two weeks, as soon as he'd finished work. Or that she had no intention of going out with anyone over here?

"Would ya not prefer that Nick the Trick fella?" Trish whispered.

Andy glared.

"I don't prefer anyone," said Kaye, as the car pulled up.

Except Liam.

Before she got out, Andy turned and looked at her.

"What's up?"

"Be careful of the Nick."

"For God's sake, I've no interest in Nick." Kaye pushed Trish out the door.

"Did ya see his poor face?" Trish crawled up the three steps. "He was like the Cabbage Patch Kid."

Inside the door, she turned to Kaye. "Are ye annoyed with me?"

"Yes."

Mo steadied her upright.

"Don't worry." Kaye linked her along the marbled foyer to the stairs. "I've been like this too, several times. The drink is lethal over here."

"I mean about Andy?"

"Nah." Kaye laughed. "I don't know why he felt he had to warn me about Nick though."

"Ah, like I told you." Mo sighed behind them. "Nick's a bit of a stud, is all."

"Not that Andy can talk." Chrissie opened the apartment door.

Kaye lugged Trish down to the bedroom and somehow got her onto the bed.

"Kaye?" Trish's face was muffled in the pillow.

"Yeah?" Kaye slipped in beside her.

"I'm glad you're here."

"Why is that?"

"Because I haven't had this much craic with you in ages."

CHAPTER EIGHTEEN

She couldn't sleep thinking about what Trish had said. She'd always been known for her sense of humour, in school, at home, down in Kilcoughlan. Olivia maintained it was her way of seeking attention; that Kaye loved attention. Kaye had sent her a Peanuts birthday card once with Lucy on the front shouting: ATTENTION! ATTENTION! CAN I HAVE YOUR ATTENTION PLEASE? Inside it said: BECAUSE I JUST LOVE ATTENTION. It's not that she loved attention but being funny had been her way to get it. She'd tried to win Liam at first by being outgoing and gregarious, the life and soul of all the sessions.

Chrissie had introduced her as the funniest girl to hit the Bronx, but Trish was right, she hadn't been much craic lately. Maybe that's why Chrissie wasn't the same, because Kaye wasn't the same either? She'd have to make up it up to her.

"I don't understand why you just don't stay," Trish said. It was her second night in New York and Chrissie had cooked Bolognese to celebrate. She'd also insisted that the girls dress up and make it a right, proper dinner party. Kaye and Trish were in the bedroom doing just that. "It's not like there's anything to go home to." Trish told Kaye. "And you could always send money back, if that's what you're worried about."

"Gosh, it didn't take you long," Kaye said.

"What didn't?" Trish looked at her bewildered.

"To join the chorus of why I should stay here." Kaye vigorously applied foundation. "It's like the whole world wants me to stay, except the two most important people."

"Who?" Trish nudged her away from the mirror.

"Chrissie and Mo," Kaye said. "I'm not absolutely certain they'd be thrilled with the idea, and neither would I!" She hurrahed down to the sitting-room.

The table was all set with a white tablecloth, sparkly wine glasses and cutlery polished until it shone.

"It's him, isn't it?" Trish was hot on her heels. "You still think you have a chance with Liam." She plopped herself down beside Kaye.

"Not this again." Chrissie arrived in with a bowl of pasta, rolling her eyes at Mo who carried a dish of Bolognese.

"She's a different person here, Kaye." Trish looked at the others. "You should have seen her this time last year."

Over dinner, Kaye recalled how she and Olivia had spent every weekend of the previous summer in Peekers, a local nightclub; Olivia whining about Morgan, who was by then on baby number three. And Kaye hoping to catch sight of Liam. The two of them drinking oodles of ninety-nine pence beers and lining their stomachs with seagull stew.

"With *what*?" Mo looked like she was going to get sick.

"Bren's name for their chicken curry."

"I got off with a few fellas alright." Kaye told them.

"Only because you hoped Liam would find out and be jealous." Chrissie scoffed. "How did that work out for ya?"

"Well, I did bring one lad to the pitch 'n putt day in Begnet's, and he did seem a bit put out." Kaye insisted, even though he wasn't really.

Trish was struggling with curling the spaghetti around her fork. "Not enough to ask you out properly though."

"How did you stick it?" Mo grated some cheese over hers.

"I dunno." Kaye shrugged.

She didn't really stick it, there were days when she cried with frustration, and disappointment.

"This is perfect hangover food." Trish licked tomato sauce off a spoon. "Just what the doctor ordered. Ya'd have to feel sorry for Olivia, all the same," she said. "She had a hard life."

"Hard life my ass," said Mo. "We've all had a hard life."

"I remember when she used to come out from the Home on a Sunday," Trish continued. "And you and her ..." she pointed the spoon at Kaye "... would spend the day laughing. She'd be real sad going back that evening and Mam would say, 'Ah, God love her.'"

"Gimme a break," said Chrissie. "My parents spent their day on the farm. I often had to get the dinner for the workmen, and at weekends we were left to our own devices."

Kaye's memory of Auntie May was that she was always in the kitchen.

"My mother used go back to her homeplace for days," Mo said.

"And we'd be let run wild on the streets. It's a wonder the neighbours didn't report us to social services."

Jaysus!

It was all coming out.

"I suppose I never got on with my father either," Kaye admitted for the first time ever, to anyone. "They say that's a girl's first romantic relationship. If you screw up with that one, there's no hope."

"That was your own fault." Trish piped up. "You always find fault with him."

"I do? Well, you would say that; you're his favourite."

"Will yis stop it!" Chrissie snapped off a crust of garlic bread. "You should have rode the arse off Limo and left it at that," she told Kaye.

Kaye tried to hide her surprise. "A ride home would've done. Even a kiss."

"It was romantic, in a way." Trish went all dreamy. "That it wasn't about sex."

"I still don't know why you didn't give up, sooner," said Mo.

"To be fair," said Trish. "He was always asking her to some 'do', and she'd get all dressed up and look fabulous and they'd have a great time and meet all his friends. Then he'd drop her home and mumble about seein' her again, keepin' her hopes up."

"He never had anyone else," said Kaye. "It was me he took for a walk on the prom after work and for an ice cream or into Martello's for a drink. He had studied English with PE, so we'd discuss books and poetry, and we both liked Christy Moore and Planxty, the GAA. And there was never anyone else. That's what kept me hopin'."

At one of the Christmas parties in the Royal, he pranced across the dancefloor, limbs flaying, stopped right in front of her and curtsied. "Can I have this dance, Mademoiselle?"

"Sure." She was afraid to curtsy back in case she fell on her bum.

She was wearing a blue and yellow dress with blue shoes. Everyone had told her she looked gorgeous, yet Liam had spent most of the evening rubbing Olivia's back. Olivia who was supposed to be heartbroken for Morgan but seemed blind to Kaye's 'get out of here' glares.

"I hope you don't think I'm being presuming." Kaye followed him out to the carpark later, a lift home her intention all along. She had even been considering suggesting a drink some night.

"It's not presumptuous at all." He smiled.

Presumptuous. That's the word. Damn him.

"Great party." She stretched out her legs in the car, pulling her dress up above her knees, planning how she'd tempt him in for tea.

"Jesus Christ!" He jammed on the breaks at the hotel gates.

"What's that?" She saw a bundle slumped on the driveway. "Is it a tramp?"

"It's Olivia." He leapt out and ran to the body, lifted it up in his arms like Rhett Butler in *Gone with the Wind* and carried it to the car. "I'll drop you first," he said. "Then take her."

"Ok." Kaye sucked in slowly, her heart deflating. "No prob."

Like Tess d'Urberville, of all the stars in the sky, Kaye wondered why was she born under a blighted one? Of all the boys in the world, why had she fallen for this one?

"Oh, that's lovely!" Chrissie's mouth was full of spaghetti and red sauce. "Tess who?"

"You and that Olivia one spent an awful lot of time on one man," said Mo. "Her and that Morgan guy, you and Liam?"

That had never dawned on Kaye before, but right now, she didn't care, because she had them all talking about Liam, and she hadn't even started the conversation.

Mo turned to Chrissie. "What did you make of it all this time?"

"Well, I'd hear bits and pieces over the phone, and I'd always be encouraging her. Why not? Then I came up to work in Dublin and met him out in their GAA club."

Kaye held her breath. She'd never known what Chrissie really thought.

"He was nice," she said, not all that enthusiastic. "A bit of a smart Alec, like a lot of Dublin fellas. Good-looking, I suppose, but not worth all the time Kaye gave him, and the patience, and the waiting. He did seem to fancy her, at first, but then he didn't. Seem to, that is. That was the worst part, I always thought, his blowing hot and cold."

"So much time wasted." Mo shook her head. "And I thought he was from Bray, isn't that Wicklow?"

"Well, it might as well be Dublin. And, I'm going to get wasted too," Chrissie poured more wine. "Anyone else?"

"They're right." Trish held out her glass and looked at Kaye. "No more time-wasting, stay here and forget about him. Find someone else."

"She has a point." Chrissie looked at Kaye. "Aren't the Catholic schools here crying out for teachers?"

"They are?" Trish looked at her too.

"So I heard." Kaye jumped up and pushed back her chair. "But I haven't a clue how to go about applying, and I have no intention of finding out either. I'm going home, that's it. I'll get more part-time hours teaching typing and I'll be right there if an English position comes up. What does that auld Dean know anyhow." She marched out of the room, her footsteps heard the whole way down to the bathroom, the three girls shaking their heads at one another, not saying a word.

The night before Trish left, Kaye took her to Doubledays, a restaurant she passed every day on the bus but had never been inside. The circular counter was mahogany, the seats intact. There was a popcorn machine and a pinball alley, aromas of butter and salt, tables with green check tablecloths and stained-glass lanterns.

"It's so American." Trish glided onto a stool and checked its swivel capacity.

"The customers are too." Kaye nodded towards a gang of tanned lads in cut-off shorts and sleeveless T-shirts, baseball caps back to front. They were knocking back shots and screaming at a game on television. Kaye liked that there was a bar in a restaurant. She'd bring Chrissie and Mo here for a meal before she went home.

"Now, what are ya havin'?" Trish took out her purse. "And do I have to leave me money on the counter? Say if someone swipes it?"

"They won't." Kaye assured her. "Em, I think I'll have a vodka and cranberry."

"What's that like?"

"Nice, you'll like it. Refreshing, good for your urinary tract. I can't take anymore beer."

"Ah, gimme a bucket! You're gettin' very American with your 'urinary tract'. Next ya'll be havin' allergies. Hey barman." She gave their order.

"This would be a nice place to work." Trish looked around. "Closer to home too." Trish clinked her glass, "I know you don't want to be a waitress for the rest of your life, after killing yourself in college. It would be such a waste, but alright while you're waiting for something else. It's surely not that hard to become legal?"

"Will you just give it up." Kaye sipped her cranberry cocktail. "I'm not staying here, and college was never a waste."

"Oh you know what I mean!" Trish gulped down her drink. "It would be nice to use your qualifications after working so hard for them, that's all I meant.

"And then, there's Liam. I don't think I can give up on him, just yet. In fact," she took a breath. "I can't imagine my life without him in it."

"Really?" Trish tapped her glass on the counter. "I've never loved anyone like that," she said wistfully. "But it's just."

"Just what?"

It was a relief for Kaye to be able to mention his name without a barrage of protests. She appreciated her sister for that.

"It's just you've got so much going for you, and they say America is the land of opportunity, and I can imagine you here, even if you can't, and …. Oh I don't know, I give up!" Trish flapped her hands in exasperation.

"I'll be grand, I can find everything I want at home too." Kaye squeezed her sister's arm. "It can be hard for people here too, you know, it ain't all sunshine, as they say."

"On the other hand, you keep changing your mind." Trish was on a roll again. "You couldn't wait to get into the bank, then you hated it. You could've gone to university after you left school, but oh no, you didn't want any more studying. After a few years, then you decided to go. You'll probably get fed up with the Tech too, then what? There are not too many choices at home right now."

Kaye hadn't considered that. Trish obviously had. Mam and Dad too, probably.

"I know." Trish tapped on the counter. "Anyhow let's have another drink. Barman? Two shots, please. Pardon? Oh! Surprise us. Cheers. Here's to two sisters celebratin' our last night together until September."

"Alright!" The barman high-fived them. "Call me Chuck."

"Alright Chuck!" Trish slapped his hand.

"Anyhow," she said to Kaye. "Let's forget it for a while and enjoy the night." She jumped off her stool. "I'm going to have some popcorn. The smell is drivin' me mad."

"Will I order mozzarella sticks?"

"Wha'?"

"Sticks of cheese dipped in breadcrumbs, deep fat fried, served with barbeque sauce."

"Game ball," said Trish. "I'll get the popcorn."

The waitresses were dressed in green-and-white, very sophisticated. The American guys slammed their shot glasses on the counter, called for more beers, taking a swig out of a bottle of port every time their team scored. The Irish might have a name for drinking, but every nationality was good at it.

"Well, look who's here," said a voice behind her.

She twirled around and found herself face-to-face with Nick.

"Oh."

"We're not that busy tonight, so I clocked off early."

"Oh."

Chuck arrived with the mozzarella sticks, shook hands with Nick, handed him a beer, put two more vodkas beside the girls' half-filled glasses, found a stool for Trish who had returned with the popcorn, then knocked on the counter shouting, "On me."

"I'll be on ya, if ya like." Trish shuffled onto the stool without spilling the popcorn.

Nick took her hand when it was free and kissed it. "Hi, the lovely sister, again."

"Heh, heh." Kaye giggled. "Flattery will get ya everywhere."

"It always does." He clinked her quivering glass. "Always does."

"I wish it worked for me."

"It worked for you one night." Nick narrowed the tea-leaf eyes, sucked on a cigarette. "When you left with the cab driver." He puffed out a ring of smoke.

"Andy?"

"Yeah." He tapped ash into a nearby ashtray.

"The one I frightened the life out of?" Trish asked. "Tellin' him Dad was comin' over with a shotgun."

"Excuse me?"

"Trish!" Kaye pleaded with her.

"Dad's not comin' over," she assured Nick. "It was just a joke."

"Be careful of those cab drivers," Nick said. "That right?" He said to Chuck who'd just appeared with some shot glasses.

"Yeah, sure!" Chuck nodded in agreement.

"I was told to be careful of you too," Kaye said to Nick.

"You're kiddin' me. Who told you that?" He grinned, resting his elbow on the counter.

"No one," she gulped. "Everyone."

"Stick to your own would be my advice." Chuck poured shots of Tequila and sliced a lemon, sprinkled salt on their fists. Demonstrated how to lick the salt, bite the lemon, and knock back the liquor.

Trish managed without any bother.

Kaye inhaled the salt, choked on the lemon, spilt the tequila down her front.

"You seem to have a problem with foreign objects in your mouth." Nick smiled, referring to her escapade with the BJ shots in Celtic House.

Kaye spat the lemon into a napkin and wiped down her crochet top. Tried it three more times until she got it right. Trish stood up and called for a round of applause from the other bartenders and the waitresses cleaning up in the restaurant. Kaye felt light-headed.

"Let's go for breakfast." Chuck suggested after a few more rounds. Doubledays closed earlier, it seemed, than most other joints.

"Sounds like a plan," said Nick. "Ladies?"

"Game ball," said Trish. "I'm all on for it. Breakfast in the middle of the night? What could be better?"

Waves of tequila were rising from Kaye's stomach. She clamped a hand over her mouth and signalled at Trish to follow her into the bathroom.

"Are ya doin' a Huey in the toilet?" Trish admired herself in the full-length mirror.

"No, I'm not." Kaye burped from the cubicle. "What are we goin' to do?"

"Well, I'll have yer man, Chuck," said Trish. "Because the other one wants you."

"Ya must be jokin'. I wouldn't be able for him." Kaye came out to the sound of a toilet flushing.

Trish shrugged at her through the mirror. "I just want to kiss an American."

"They'll be lookin' for more than that."

"Let 'em look - every time you have sex with a stranger, you give part of yourself away. I read that in a book once."

Jaysus! She was surrounded by philosophers.

"Chrissie's havin' a ball at it."

"I bet she's not, and I bet she still likes Billy."

There was a banging on the door. "You girls done in there?" Chuck roared at them. "Because we're outa here."

"Yeah, comin'," said Trish.

"Already?" Chuck guffawed. "And I haven't even started."

"Said to bishop to the actress. C'mon." Trish caught Kaye's arm. "Bacon 'n' eggs 'n' greasy kisses. What more could a girl want?"

Chuck sped along the expressway, screeching to a halt outside Yonkers Diner.

Nick smelt of cigarette smoke and cologne, as he took her hand and helped her out of the back seat. She brushed against him, felt a spark. They sat opposite one another in a booth in the diner and ordered. Her knees skimmed his. There was no sign of Trish and Chuck.

Nick looked into her eyes. "Talk to me, Katie. Tell me all about yourself."

She swept back her hair. "Well, I was born in the Midlands, but grew up in Dublin. I've just finished college, so now I can teach, but there's no real teaching jobs at home."

"You're a teacher? I didn't know that."

"Well, I've just qualified." The waitress put down two lumberjack specials – pancakes, eggs, sausages, bacon, and toast. She should've ordered the fruit salad.

"What did you get your Bachelors in?" He chopped his food, left the knife aside and ate with just the fork. Like the customers in Burger Heaven.

"English and economics." Kaye savoured the salty bacon, the sweet syrupy pancake.

"A nice combination. What were you doing before that?"

"I was in the bank."

"And you left it? My father would turn in his grave. A job for life." Just what Liam had said.

"Yeah."

"So what made you go to college?"

Liam?

"Em, I dunno. I was good at English at school." A lie. "I wanted to travel." True. "I had hoped I would be transferred down the country, just to get away for a while." True. "But I was sent to Bray, five miles away." A disappointment. "I always loved literature and wanted to learn more." Sorta true. "So, I went to college at night, and resigned from the bank in order to do the H. Dip by day." She didn't mention getting an honours degree. "That's the Higher Diploma in Education."

"I know what it is. Gosh you were really serious about this. I majored in English too," he said.

"Really?" She coughed. "Oh, I didn't know. Have you tried teaching?"

"Nah, there's more money in bartending."

"Really? I believe the archdiocese are hiring, but I don't know where to call."

He took a biro out of his shirt pocket and scribbled a phone number on a napkin. "My high school principal, Brother Vincent, is head honcho over there. Give him a call." He handed her the napkin.

Feck, what was she going to do now?

And then Nick began to talk.

He was born in the Bronx, he said but his parents had returned to Crusheen in County Clare when he was ten. He'd come back to New York for college. Chrissie was wrong, he hadn't been here since he was six. He had always considered himself Irish until he lived there and found himself being called the Yank, teased for his accent. In the Bronx, he'd spent every Sunday in Gaelic Park, learnt Irish dancing, marched in the parade. In Clare, boys his age were obsessed with hurling; they couldn't have cared less about step-dancing. Paddy's Day was just a Sunday in the middle of the week.

He lit her a cigarette and one for himself.

So, she thought, Nick didn't know where he was from either.

"If the others are not gonna join us," he said, "I'll get the check."

"Nick?" she asked, after the bill had arrived.

"Yeah?" He flicked thirty dollars on the table, plus a twenty-dollar tip.

She wanted to ask him about the rumours, but then those eyes were on her, and she lost her nerve.

"Never mind."

As Kaye clicked open the back door of the car, she caught a glimpse of Trish and Chuck untangling themselves.

"How was breakfast?" Chuck turned the key in the ignition.

"De–lish," said Kaye. "Ya missed it."

The Bangles were singing '*Eternal Flame*' on the radio when Kaye's hand found itself in Nick's. Without thinking, she turned to face him, to find him looking back at her. Before she knew it, his lips were on hers. The Bangles were asking did someone feel the same, as his tongue gently sought hers. The Bangles were wondering if they were only dreaming, as their tongues probed deeper and deeper. His face bristled hers, his eyelashes brushed her temple, a thigh pressed against her, his arm snuck around her shoulders, scrunched her hair. Is this burning some sort of flame? The Bangles wanted to know, reaching a crescendo, as Kaye and Nick pulled away from each other.

The candy-coloured houses came into view.

Chuck jammed on the brakes outside the apartment block.

Nick kissed her cheek. "Goodbye." His lips were soft, like before.

"So," she said to Trish, as they clobbered up the stairs. "Chuck the Fuck, how was he?"

"Unbelievable kisser."

They burst into 4D, scurried down to the bedroom and belly-flopped onto the bed.

"Kaye?"

"Yeah?"

"We kissed Americans!"

CHAPTER NINETEEN

August draped a blanket over the Bronx. At night, the girls gathered around the fan, desperate for cool air.

"Oh, I'll never sit in the sun again." Chrissie lay on the floor, flapping her legs.

"D'ya hear her?" Mo scraped her brownish wisps into a ponytail, not a bead of perspiration on her pink face. "And she covered from head to toe in tin foil on Orchard Beach back in May."

"Jesus!" Kaye took off her tee shirt. "You could've been burnt alive."

"That was the idea, ya thick." Chrissie extended her legs so that her toes touched the wall and the hem of her nightie inched up her thighs, waiting for the fan to whisk by.

"Her skin broke out in blisters." Mo continued. "And one of the kitchen guys insisted on rubbing yoghurt on her boobs. Said it was a cure for sunburn."

"And it was too." Chrissie mopped her face with a towel.

"I'm sweatin'." Kaye stuck hers in the fan, as it swished by.

"Women don't sweat," Mo said. "We glow."

"Well, I'm sweatin'." Chrissie sat up on her hunkers. "And gaspin' for a drink. Will we go down to the Terminal, at least we'll have AC there?" She stood up. "Jaysus, I'm stiff."

"You're getting old." Mo loosened the rubber band and shook out her hair. "Ticking the 'over 25' box now."

"And you're not far behind me." Chrissie crashed onto the floor again, her back against the couch. "So, are we going out or wha'?"

"Don't have the energy to lift a glass right now." Kaye pinched the roll of fat around her middle. "I feel so bloated, it's disgustin'."

And she wasn't ready to see Nick.

"Think of all that lovely cold air whirling around the air-conditioned bar," Chrissie padded down to the bathroom. "Bags the shower first."

Kaye hadn't told her about Nick, yet.

"Well, it looks like we are going out." Mo wriggled upright. "Are ya comin'?"

"I don't know what to do." Kaye pinched her abdomen. "I'm hot, and I'm fat," she said. "And I have an interview with this Brother Vincent, only because Nick gave me the number, and only to get Trish off my back." She couldn't believe she was spilling all this out to Mo.

"You're not fat," Mo said. "You're just curvy, that's all. As for the interview, there's no harm in going in to find out what they have to offer. Nothing is written in stone."

Kaye had an image of the Ten Commandments written on a big slab of stone.

"I just want people to leave me alone, to let me do my own thing."

"Well, no one is forcing you to go for the interview, or take a teaching job."

"I know, I know." She hadn't meant to sound so grouchy.

There was still no reply to the card she'd sent Liam. Unless she counted the breezy letter that had arrived from Olivia, all about what her and Liam were up to. And then, as an afterthought: *That card you sent him was so cute.* Why had he even shown it to Olivia? Were they laughing at her behind her back?

"Are you thinking about Nick?" Mo tilted her head.

"No." Kaye's tone was sharp. "Why would I be thinking about him?"

"A little bird told me there'd been a kiss?"

"Who told you? Oh, Trish, I'll kill her! Does Chrissie know?"

"No, but I wouldn't worry about Chrissie."

From the bedroom came the sound of a hairdryer. "She has her own issues, and she has Sil, after all."

What issues?

"As for Nick." Mo sauntered across the room. "Aren't you going after the same sort of man again?"

"The same as who?"

"Liam and Nick have commitment phobias, it seems? Anyhow, let them decide, men prefer the chase."

"That's what Mam used to say. And Olivia said there was no harm in letting them know. And then Auntie Lou said to imagine a man loving me as much as I love him." Kaye shook her head. "I'm addled from them all."

"And I say, marry a man who loves you more than you love him."

"Hmmm."

"Look, go for Nick, if you want a fling, but don't expect anything more."

"I don't want him, and I don't want anything more."

"Yeah, yeah. I know, I know. You're saving your heart for whatshisname."

Mo was clicking her fingers.

"Probably just as well, because there's something holding Nick back too, I just haven't figured out what it is, yet. There are rumours, of course, but ..."

"What rumours?" Kaye stuck out her head out the window, stealing herself for what Mo was going to say, the heat like a blast from a gigantic oven.

"My lips are sealed." Mo put a finger on them. "Don't want to be quoted."

Never carry a story, Mam had always taught them.

"Having a man isn't the greatest thing in the world, you know."

And her with two of them.

"We're always afraid they'll leave us."

Chrissie appeared in the doorway. "Don't mind that one. It's nice to have someone to go out with, for a chat, a laugh."

Kaye wondered how much she'd heard. "Like we're havin' now?"

"You know what I mean."

"If being single is not making you happy," Mo said, "change. If you don't, everything stays the same. Unless you're afraid to hook up?"

Was she? Afraid?

Mo took Chrissie's hand, and they pirouetted in front of the fan, their only fan, out into the hallway. "I'm going to have a shower," she said to Kaye. "Are ya comin' out or not?"

"I think I'll stay put."

Brother Vincent was wedged behind a wide mahogany desk, his shiny red face lit up like a Christmas tree. Kaye's second New York interview went as well as the first, despite her new, black-and-white silk dress from the Chinese shop clinging to her. Over the lens of his spectacles, Big Brother, offered her a five-year H1 visa and a tax-free salary for three.

"The nuns will love you," he said in a voice like President Kennedy's, wiping his face with a rumpled white handkerchief. "It is a little late to be applying," he continued, "but you might get substitution for this term. As soon as you find a position, let me know and I'll start the paperwork." He handed her a list of schools requiring teachers. "In the meantime, I'll pass your particulars around to places that I know need someone. Any questions?"

"No."

"The kids are the same as the kids in Ireland, I'm sure." He leaned forward and shook her sweaty paw. "Deep down, a kid's a kid, right?"

"Right."

"And say hi to Nicholas for me, he was one of my best students."

"I will."

A pity she couldn't give it a try, she thought, as she walked in the sunshine back down Lexington Avenue. It's what she'd studied for, after all. Well, not really. She went to college because of Liam saying she could be doing better.

She'd spent First Year on the bus to Belfield four nights a week, her lunch hours and weekends writing essays, only to be told, after she got honours in her exams, that she could only complete an honours degree by day. The bank manager suggested a Career Break.

"You'd be mad not to," Liam said.

She had loved the grassy campus with its man-made lake, the soothing silence of the library, the greasy chips in the canteen, being able to wear jeans and desert boots – no more tweed suits and tights, no longer concerned about whether her earrings matched her lipstick. She had loved discussing literature in the Belfield bar - Donne and Shakespeare, Restoration, Renaissance, Romanticism. Being a full-time student had given her more satisfaction than anything ever had before. Except, of course, loving Liam.

"Awesome." Melissa gave her a high five when she told her about the interview. "We are definitely going to hang out."

"No, we're not." Kaye tied her apron around her extended waistline. "I just did it to keep everyone quiet."

"C'mon." Melissa held out her hands. "How about that visa, you must be tempted, eh?"

"Well," Kaye hesitated.

"You are, you are, you are tempted. Go girl!"

"I am not. I'll be on that plane on the 18th and you'll never see me again."

"That's too bad." Melissa walked away shaking her head. "Too bad."

"Oh, I didn't mean it like that," she said to Melissa's retreating back.

Why couldn't she just keep her big mouth shut.

"Sorry I'm late." She ducked a swipe of Perfecto's cloth. "Did ye get on alright without me?"

"Yes, Kataleena, we get on. Your friend Meleesa, cover for you and I bus your tables."

Fernando banged on the bell.

"Don't get your knickers in a knot. Where's this food going?"

"Twenty-five. How's my Irish princess today?" His yellow teeth flashed. "Where were you till now, at a par–ty, or out for a glass of wat–ter? Say 'butter' for me, Kataline, just once before you go, butt–ter, and remember, smile."

"You want me to butt her?" She balanced two plates on her wrist and headed for Twenty-Five. Kataleena? Kataline? Katherine? What would she be called next?

"Hey Kathy Lee, wanna come to my sister's birthday party on Saturday?" Melissa hollered.

"OK." Kaye hunkered down to grab crackers for a cup of soup, relieved that Melissa didn't seem that mad with her.

Melissa had been waitressing since she was sixteen, after all, she was probably used to this shit. Had worked her way through high school and college. Her father having walked out when she was three, leaving her mother with five screaming children, trying to wrench his suitcase from him. It would be interesting to meet this family, to see another side of New York, other than the Bronx, and Manhattan.

But, when Kaye rang her on Saturday morning to tell her what time she was arriving, Melissa sounded vague. Not at all as chirpy as she was at work.

"It's like she'd forgotten I was coming." Kaye joined the girls on the roof, sunbathing on the blistering tar. "It was like she didn't know who I was."

"Stay with us so." Chrissie lathered on the baby oil. "Ya'll have more craic, right, girls?"

Izzy and Mo mumbled.

Chrissie was right, but Kaye wanted to try something new, for a change.

"Are ya goin' to be friends with her now and not with us?" Chrissie wanted to know.

"Don't be silly." Kaye closed her eyes, secretly delighted that Chrissie wanted her to stay. She would have liked to. Sizzling on the concrete with the girls was more preferable to spending the best part of a Saturday morning on a subway.

But she'd promised.

Melissa's maroon *Buick Skylark* screeched up to the Flushing Meadows sidewalk where Kaye was waiting, in a new yellow-and-white striped shirt she'd bought in Mandee's, tucked into yellow shorts. It was ninety degrees and soaring.

"Your car's lovely," she said, placing her new GAP denim backpack on her lap, careful not to scuff her new white Reeboks. Chrissie had been right; everyone wore them over here.

"Everything's lovely with you." Melissa chuckled. "This is an old lady's car, for God's sake; it belongs to my mom."

They sped along Bayshore Boulevard, past boats and yachts and people jogging along a track. Like Bray and Dun Laoghaire, except for the sun, sapphire water, and cloudless sky.

Kaye stuck her elbow out the window.

"Close it! We have AC, ya shmuck."

"I will in a minute, I want fresh air first."

Kaye was afraid she'd get facial paralysis again. It had taken eight months of electric shock treatment to get her face right the last time. At only thirteen, she had been so self-conscious of her crooked mouth and weeping eye but had loved getting off school three times a week, with an ice-cream from Woolworths afterwards.

Melissa was quieter and more subdued that morning and not as pretty in a check shirt and jeans cut to her knees. Kaye had asked her what she was going to wear, and Melissa said a jumper. It took them a while to figure out that in America, jumper meant what the Irish called a jumpsuit. Whereas in Ireland jumper was a sweater. Kaye had had visions of Melissa turning up in nothing but a sweater. Looked like she hadn't even bothered with the jumpsuit. Looked like she hadn't slept; her hair straggling down her back; feet bare; the car reeking of cigarettes and perfume.

"I'm glad to see you." She patted Kaye's knee, as they swerved onto a highway.

"Really?" Kaye said. "My father's cousin lives near here." She'd been checking the exit signs. "He takes the Long Island Expressway to work every day, said it was like a carpark."

"The LIE is seventy-one miles long," Melissa chuckled again. "He could be anywhere."

"There it is. That's it." Kaye bopped up and down. "Great Neck. What a name."

"D'ya wanna go visit him?"

"No way, sure he'd never remember me."

Kaye recalled the lovely American telling the story and now here she was, on the LIE.

"Oh, I'm sure he would, Kathy, I'm sure he would." Melissa changed lanes and exited at the sign for Long Beach. "I'm excited for my sister's surprise." She stopped outside a two-storey house with a balcony upstairs.

"Well, she'll get a surprise seein' me anyhow."

Kaye followed her into a living-room full of people, the walls, carpets, curtains, and couches all white, the cushions covered in plastic. Pictures in frames and party balloons provided the only splashes of colour. On the ceiling, a fan whirred.

"Hey, how ya doin'?" Melissa brushed hands with everyone.

"Here, Missy, take these." A big guy handed her a bunch of balloons.

"Missy?" Kaye whispered.

"Hey, you're called after a letter in the alphabet and you gotta cousin called Crispy."

"True." So far, nobody had batted an eyelid at Kaye.

Melissa stopped in front of two thinnish girls with hair blacker than hers and after exchanging a few words, screamed, "He hasn't sent me a birthday or a Christmas card since the day he left. Not since I was three years of age. I sure ain't gonna speak to him now!" Then she glared at a long, thin man, with black circles around his eyes, and cheeks sunken in a rectangular face, sitting on one of the plastic-clad couches.

Kaye blew up the balloons, for something to do, wishing she was on the roof with the girls, with nothing to worry her except what to wear to the Terminal, what she was going to say to Nick, hoping he'd talk to her, how to avoid Andy. Nobody here offered her a drink, something to eat, nothing. Thank God she had cigarettes, and balloons.

When the birthday sister arrived, she showed no reaction to the surprise, didn't seem happy about the party, and couldn't have cared less about Kaye.

After some burgers, they played a game which involved things they'd take to a picnic that started with the initial of their name. Kaye shouted knickers. 'Something to eat' they screamed back, so she had to take a swig of beer. Next turn, she roared Kellogg's, which they reluctantly accepted, and after that, Krispies. She was getting attention, which was better than being ignored.

At ten o'clock, the party ended; the time an Irish one would be starting. Melissa's brother offered her a ride home, if she paid for gas, but nobody knew the way to the Bronx.

She had to phone the girls.

"Mo says there's a Triborough Bridge, but she hasn't a clue after that." Chrissie told her. "Are ya havin' a good time?"

"Yeah, brilliant. Her family are gas."

"So, will ya not be botherin' with us anymore, then?"

"Of course, I will; don't be so silly." It was great to be missed.

"Why don't you ring Nick?" Chrissie yawned into the receiver.

"Wha'?"

"Call the Terminal and ask him how you'd get home?"

"Oh, em I dunno. Sure, give us the number, anyhow."

But Kaye couldn't bring herself to dial it.

"Maybe I won't bother. He'll think I fancy him," she told Melissa.

"And do you?"

"No!"

"You Irish!" Melissa handed her the phone. "It's only a freakin' call. No big deal!"

Only a freaking phone call that he hadn't bothered making himself. Not a word out of him since their intimate breakfast. But maybe Melissa was right, it was no big deal.

"Terminal!" The voice was husky, *Papa don't Preach* belting out in the background.

"Oh, hi, this is Kaye Butler." She tried to sound offhand. "Who's this?

"Hi, K for Kaye Butler, what's up?"

"Oh, em, Nick, is it?"

"That's me. What can I do you for, pet?"

"Em, well, I'm over here in Queen's and I was wonderin' how I'd get home?"

"Wondering how you'd get home? From Queens, let me see. By car, cab, bus? And what has you so far away?"

"Well, I'm at a party and this guy will drive me home, but I don't know the way."

"So, you picked up a guy and he's driving you home and you're asking me the way?"

"Oh no, it's not like that, he's my friend's brother, just giving me a lift."

"Aim for the Triborough Bridge, take the Deegan North to Exit 11, and we're right around the corner. You'll see the elevated train tracks. What can I get ya, darlin'?"

"Pardon? Oh, sorry, OK, Triborough, Deegan, Exit 11."

Kaye scribbled across the front page of the *New York Post*, as Melissa relayed the information to her brother. She could hear the clink of glasses, Madonna on the jukebox, Irish accents, Pete's laugh, Nick's voice close to her ear, the cash register ringing.

"Bring your date in for a cocktail," Nick said. "Gotta go now, Katie. Talk to ya."

"He's not a . . ."

He was gone.

"He thinks I'm on a date."

She lit a cigarette.

"Good, that'll keep him interested."

"No," Kaye took a pull. "He's just ..."

"Anyhow, there's been a change of plan." Melissa interrupted her. "Little bro' says he ain't going to no Bronx, it's too dangerous over there, so looks like you're stuck with me." She jangled her keys. "And we're goin' clubbin'."

Dangerous? They tiptoed through the yard, sidestepped around a bench, and a barbeque, and hopped over a variety of garden gnomes.

"My family loved you." Melissa accelerated away from the house.

"They did?" Kaye said, thinking she'd never have guessed.

After a short drive, they pulled up under a neon sign that flickered: SAL–I–VATING; girls in jumpsuits lined up under it.

"Nice body." Melissa beamed her headlights at a Barbie blond in a white canvas jumpsuit. "I mean, I'd like a body like that."

"Cute cop." She smiled at a policewoman in the parking lot, smacked hands and back-patted more girls on their way in.

As soon as Kaye bought the drinks, Melissa left. Salivating! And Nick thought she was on a date?

The club was full of women. Not a hunk in sight. Gloria Gaynor and Donna Summers blaring. When the barmaid leaned in to light her cigarette, a switch went on in Kaye's head. She looked around. People were dancing, singing, chatting, laughing, drinking. Just like any other bar. Except there were no men.

"We come here for the music." Melissa seemed jittery when she returned. "And because the beer's less expensive than other places around here."

"I see."

Kaye remained seated, her gaze straight ahead, and not on any of the erotic postcards on the wall behind the bar.

To celebrate her exam results, Liam had taken Kaye for a meal in the Katmandu in Dalkey. All he could talk about was his future, and where he saw himself in five years' time. Life wasn't a dress rehearsal, he kept insisting, it was the real deal.

Eventually he turned his attention to her. "Miss Kane was right," he said, raising his glass and quoting Kaye's former colleague. "You have far more brains than I have."

Kaye smoked and babbled on about whether to do a master's or the Dip.

"Do the Dip," he said. "The world is your oyster then. It'll take you anywhere you want."

"But I want to stay right here with you." She heard herself say.

"Oh, Kaye." He sighed. "Don't." He kept rubbing her back, like a child's.

And though that was not the reply she'd been hoping for, she felt like a bird freed from its cage.

In the carpark, Melissa was reclining against the *Skylark*.

"Hey, what you doin' here?"

"Looking for you."

Kaye eyed the broken mirror in Melissa's hand, the white powder.

"I'm sorry." Melissa looked sheepish. "I didn't want you to know."

Kaye kept staring at her.

"Are you mad at me?" Melissa was kicking stones, bits of black hair in her eyes.

Kaye was more shocked, afraid, as well as annoyed.

"What if the policewoman sees you?"

"That's not a real cop," Melissa chuckled. "Just a girl wearing the outfit."

Jaysus!

"Let's go home." Kaye gestured at the Buick.

Melissa chattered nonstop the whole way home. Kaye couldn't even believe she was driving but was beyond caring. She just wanted a bed. When they got to the apartment, Melissa rolled a joint, to wind down, she said, otherwise she wouldn't be able to sleep.

"You shoulda stuck to beer." Kaye yawned and stretched out on the couch. "If you'd stayed with me and drank *Bud* all night, you'd be well able to sleep."

"I'm sorry."

Melissa threw a sheet over her and lowered her head close to Kaye's. "How about you forget about all those loser men in your life and try a woman?"

"Get lost!"

"Only kiddin'" Melissa moved closer to rub noses. "I do have something to tell you though." Her lips softly brushed Kaye's.

"I think I know." Kaye turned on her side and pretended to fall sleep.

CHAPTER TWENTY

The telephone shrilled. Kaye leapt from her bed. It was four o'clock according to her bedside clock. Home, she thought, as she ran down the hall. Something's happened at home. She yanked the receiver off the wall.

"Help, help!"

"Who is it?"

"I lost my case." It was Mo, howling, "Please help me."

"Your what?"

"Oh, God, please help me. What will I do if she's been kidnapped? Killed?"

"What are ya talkin' about?"

"What's wrong?" Chrissie appeared beside her, knotting the ends of her T-shirt.

"I don't know. Mo's on about her case being lost?"

"Mrs. Polansky is lost?" Chrissie shrieked. "How on earth did that happen?"

"Jesus, I don't know. Mo, Mo, are you alright?"

"No, I'm not all right. You've gotta help me find her before the day nurse comes on."

"OK, OK, give me the address and we'll be there in a jiffy."

Kaye dialled Andy's number. "Come quick," she said, then rushed into her bedroom to change into shorts, the perspiration pumping out of her.

On her way back, she met Chrissie in the hall dragging on a pair of jeans. "How can you wear those yokes in this heat? Turn off the fan and I'll put on a tape."

Izzy's head popped out of 2C. "What's all the racket? Are yis goin' out at this hour?"

"Yeah, sorta."

"Tim's on the graveyard shift. I'm waiting up for him. See yis."

"Yeah. See ya."

The cab raced along the expressway, Andy's curtain of hair brushing against her face every time he swung around a corner. She liked the silky feel of it, the citrusy scent.

"You girls." He kept shaking his head. "What you do now?"

Traffic was light, yet there were people waiting for a bus outside Yonkers Raceway.

Andy stopped the cab at a green gate, where Mo stood, her face white.

"What am I going to do?" she sobbed. "Say if I'm deported?"

"Deported?" Chrissie jumped back into the cab. "I'm ouda here."

"Me too." Andy turned and sped off, Chrissie rocking from side to side in the back seat.

"But you're a citizen?" Kaye looked at Mo. "Weren't you conceived in Boston?"

"I know, I know," Mo cried. "But I could still be arrested, right?"

"I've no idea. What exactly happened?"

"As soon as I had my client settled, I fell asleep in the chair. Only for a few minutes."

"A few minutes?"

"Well, maybe half an hour."

"Half an hour?"

"And when I woke up, she was gone. The front door wide open and the gate too."

"We'll have to call the police."

"Oh, no, I'll lose my job," Mo howled. "Be arrested. Sent home."

"Mo!" Kaye yelled. "We have to find that poor woman, or we'll all end up in jail."

"You're right, you're right." Mo balled her fists. "Let's go inside and think."

Kaye followed her up the steps to a porch. All this talk about going home, seemed like she mightn't be the only one on that return flight. A Sister Virginia from Pope Pius High School had called her. Brother Vincent had sent her Kaye's resume, she called it, and the nun had been particularly interested in Kaye's typewriting teaching skills. She'd offered her a three-month contract to substitute for a Sister Clare, who was ill. A real job in New York if she wanted it. It wasn't English though; she wouldn't be teaching English.

Chrissie had taken offence at her remark that waitressing wasn't a real job. "I make more than that," she'd sneered at Sister Virginia's offer of ninety dollars a day. Kaye didn't remind her that she worked more hours too.

Kaye made Mo sit into a recliner on the porch, while she made tea. What for, she didn't know. While waiting for the kettle to boil, she took a look around the house in case Mrs. Polansky was lurking somewhere in the dark rooms, in the musty gloom under the beds, inside the wardrobes, full of clutter.

So this was where Mo spent her time? Here on her own every night. No one for company, a laugh, a chat. Surely a hospital would be better.

When she got back to the porch, Mo was marching up and down, wringing her hands. When Kaye gave her the tea, the cup rattled on the saucer. This was serious, it occurred to her. It could mean jail if the old lady wasn't found, or worse if she wasn't found alive.

And yet, what could they do? Helplessly, she sat on the recliner watching Mo stomping up and down, waiting for her to decide. Why couldn't they just call the cops and let them deal with it. Then again, it probably would be better to sort it out themselves. She began to daydream about living in a house like this, sitting here in the evenings, reading a book, when a movement in the garden caught her eye. She could just about make out the rosebushes rustling; a flash of pink, followed by a clicking sound.

Kaye ran down the steps, gesturing at Mo to follow. Tiptoed towards the hedge that lined the garden. And there she found an elderly woman crouched among the thicket, her dressing gown trailing on the ground, her feet bare, her white hair a waterfall over her face.

"I'm looking for Minnie." Her eyes skittered about the bushes.

"Minnie?" Kaye took the woman's ice-cold hand.

"My dog." She whimpered. "My lovely, little doggie."

Mo shrugged. "There's no dog."

"I'll have a look for Minnie," Kaye told her. "While Mo takes you inside."

"Mo, Mo," cried the woman. "Who's Mo?"

Mo shrugged at Kaye before guiding Mrs. Polansky into the house, shushing at her to be quiet, as they made their way up the stairs.

Kaye sat there listening to the hum of the two of them mumbling, the old lady shrieking every now and then, a toilet flushing, shower swishing, more inaudible conversation, a few more screams, and eventually silence. How does she do it, how does Mo do this every night?

The next thing Kaye was aware of was the sound of the gate clicking open, and a girl walking up the path, the sun nudging the sky scarlet and a kind of gold. She checked her watch; it was now six o'clock. She must've nodded off.

"Everything alright?" the girl asked.

"Yeah, everything's grand."

"Where's Joanne?"

"Joanne?"

"Oh, there she is." The girl was looking at the door where Mo was shaking her head no. "How's Mrs. Polansky?"

"She's fine," said Mo. "Fast asleep. Nothing unusual to report."

"Great," said the girl. "See you tomorrow then, Jo?"

"Yeah. See ya."

Kaye hurried after Mo, down the path and onto the street. "Isn't Joanne your sister who used to work with Chrissie?"

"Yes." Mo hailed a cab. "She was conceived here, not me. I'm using her social security number because I wouldn't have been able to sign on with the carers' agency otherwise. The Short Stop," she told the cab driver. "I'd murder a plate of eggs right now."

Kaye shook her head in confusion. And how could Mo even think of eating?

They didn't speak for the rest of the journey. The air was thick with heat and exhaust fumes when they arrived at 242nd Street, the sidewalk crammed as usual with taxi drivers, stragglers from the pubs, bartenders on their way home and commuters already heading down to the city, the subway screeching in and out of the station.

Tim staggered out of the Terminal, roaring, "Party animals, don't you ever go home?"

Kaye was about to ask him how the graveyard shift had gone when Mo started puking into a bin. She pulled her hair off her face and held her until she was finished.

"Looks like someone had a good night." Tim bellowed.

"Yeah," said Kaye. "Yeah, she sure did."

They were in the kitchen, drinking tea, the fan whizzing around them,

Chrissie's feet propped on Kaye's lap, hugging cups of tea, and pulling on cigarettes, just like it used to be.

"A Sister Virginia called …" Kaye said. "Brother Vincent gave her my number … She needs a business studies and typewriting teacher until Christmas. They're hard to get here …"

"Are you going to take it?"

"I don't know." Kaye stirred her tea.

Just then, the phone rang. Kaye stretched out her hand and unhooked it. "Trish just told me the news!"

It was Mam.

"What news? Is everything alright?" Kaye pushed Chrissie's feet onto the floor. Her mother had never rung her before, said it was too dear. "What's the matter?"

"The teaching job. Trish was telling me all about it. Congratulations. Dad and I are so proud of you. This is your chance. This is what you worked for."

It is? Well, not really, she'd already had the Typing Teacher Diploma, long before she went back to college. Still, she had needed the degree to even apply to the Archdiocese.

"Em, yeah, I suppose …"

But what about Liam, she wanted to say. She'd love to sit down and have a long chat with her mother about Liam, hear what she thought about the whole thing.

"Now, I must go," her mother said, "this is costing a fortune."

"Ok, Mam. Oh wait, how's Dad?"

The phone clicked. She was gone.

"So?" Chrissie looked at her.

"She said I'm to stay."

Later as she was plucking up the courage to phone Sister Virginia, Mo barged in.

"You stupid bitch, I don't believe what you've done."

"What have I done?" Kaye dropped the phone, leaving it swinging by its chord back and forth against her legs.

"Don't act all innocent with me!" Mo's face was red with rage, spit hissing from her thin lips, her eyes bulging.

Kaye stepped backwards into the wall. Mo's voice was vicious, her face unrecognizable. "Mrs. Polansky had a call from Immigration.' She spat out the words.

"About what?" Kaye managed to squeak.

"About what? Little Miss Innocent; Little Miss goody two-shoes, little Miss teacher's head on ya." Mo's garlicy breath was in Kaye's face, rage in her eyes, venom in her voice.

Jesus Christ. Kaye froze.

"I'll tell you what about," continued Mo. "Me not having a visa. Mrs. Polansky breaking the law for hiring me. Her daughter wiggled their way out of it, blamed her dementia, then reported me to the agency who have let me go. Are ya happy now?"

"Why would I be happy?"

"Because you don't like me, it's obvious. You want Chris all to yourself. The looks you gave me. Every single time I came in the door, your face fell. Ya think I didn't notice. But you don't know what I know! Chris needs me much more than she needs you!"

Mo grabbed a chair and slumped into it, put her head on the kitchen table.

"What am I going to do?"

"Look, I don't know what happened, but I didn't ring Immigration. I wouldn't even know where to get the number, wouldn't know what to say to them if I did. I'll admit I was jealous of you and Chrissie. I'm jealous of everyone. It's a terrible trait. I'm really sorry if I made you feel bad. Look, George never looks for papers. He'll need someone when I go. I'll tell him you'll take my job." That last bit came to her, as the words spilled out of her mouth.

"You will? You would do that for me?"

By the time Chrissie came home, Mo was sound asleep in bed, and Kaye's heart had just about stopped pumping.

"Holy Moley," Chrissie said. "She sure overreacted, it is a big deal, after all."

"Did you know she wasn't legal?"

"No."

"Everything is against me staying." Kaye sighed. "You don't want me here either. You were dyin' for me to come over, and now. Oh, I don't know. I suppose I am jealous. Of Olivia and Liam. Trish and Mam. You and Mo. There, I said it."

"Everyone is jealous." Chrissie flopped down on the couch beside her. "It's natural."

"It is?"

"Of course, and I'll bet Mo suffers from it too. And that was a great idea getting her your job, if you can, she'll definitely be delighted with you then."

"Ya think?" Kaye wasn't so sure. Chrissie hadn't seen Mo in such a state.

"I don't think, I know." Chrissie switched on the television Sil had got them from the hotel. "Now, we'll watch *Dateline* and have some real drama, for a change."

Chrissie hadn't denied or confirmed that she didn't want Kaye to stay.

"There's just one thing," Chrissie said during a commercial break.

"What's that?" Kaye was nearly afraid to ask.

"Who called Immigration?"

Chapter Twenty-One

Anna's twenty-first birthday party was in an Italian restaurant in South Philly. Kaye walked through its doors wearing the fuchsia shimmery dress Trish had squashed into her rucksack the night before she left home; her hair cut short and highlighted. And she had lost weight.

It was Labour Day weekend, which marked the end of the summer.

"You look stunning, hon." Matt told her, and she believed him. They were the only ones at the free bar; him sipping a Beefeater Martini with a green olive floating on top and Kaye risking a gimlet. Vodka and lime had always been her drink at home, but she'd had to give it up in the Bronx because of the generous measures.

"Here's to you." He raised his glass. "You'll be the best teacher to hit New York City."

"D'ya think?"

"Sure." He swallowed the Martini in two gulps and tipped his glass on the counter for another. "The kids will love you and the nuns will eat you up."

Kaye didn't want to hear about being gobbled up by a pack of nuns. "I hope so," she said. She still wasn't sure how she'd walked herself into this whole thing. Still, there was no harm in staying another few months. It didn't mean her plan to win Liam was abandoned.

"And just remember." Matt was still talking. "You are the greatest. Say it to yourself every day, looking in the mirror. Watch my lips and repeat after me – I AM THE GREATEST."

Kaye giggled, imagining one of the girls finding her in the bathroom talking to the mirror, but this strong, handsome man with the silver sideburns made her feel safe.

Labour Day weekend also marked the end of Kaye's short career as a full-time waitress. On Tuesday, Mo would be taking over her position, and, as expected, George had offered Kaye a Saturday shift. Kaye, Mo, and Melissa working together, how would that go?

"Look at my bride." Matt gazed at the dance floor where Lou was swinging around with Matthew Jr. and his buddies. She had made several attempts to lure Kaye out to join them, but Kaye preferred listening to Matt. "She's my best friend." His eyes filled with tears. "The one thing constant in my life."

Liam had once told Kaye she was his best friend. He said they'd always be friends, no matter what. On another night that she'd been hoping he might kiss her.

"Any word from that guy?" asked Matt, as though reading her thoughts.

"No, I sent him a card, like you said, but he hasn't replied."

"There's still time and regardless, there was nothing wrong with reaching out to him."

"I sorta regret that I didn't stay friends with him, it's better than nothing."

"Nah," Matt waved at her dismissively, "it was too raw for you. You did what you had to do at the time."

"I still sorta feel that something is going to happen between us, I haven't given up yet." Kaye regretted the words, as soon as they fell out of her mouth.

"Oh, honey, I didn't realise you were still holding out for him." Matt looked at her with what she thought was pity, making her feel instantly stupid. "That must be really hard for you?" He looked at her again, with compassion, the first one to do so, since her story began.

"It is."

It was also the first time anyone had acknowledged this.

"And why did you want this particular man so bad?"

"He's good looking, popular, a great singer, footballer, hard worker. But he says he's a rake and I deserve better."

"He got that right, and you also deserve to know what's going on. He should have told you since what was on his mind that night. He could've told you in his letter. Whatever, he shouldn't keep you in limbo."

"What do I do now?" Kaye was tired of this path already.

"Be gentle with yourself. Treat yourself like a trusted friend. Don't give in to the critical voice in your head; because that's all it is: a voice, not the truth. Wish Liam well, Olivia too, and remember, it's not your fault. Have you not met anyone else you like, here?"

"Well, there is someone I sorta like, but again I can't tell if he's interested. It's the same old story. And I think Chrissie might like him too. She did, I know, but to be honest, I've never seen any spark between them. Here I go again, chasing someone who's not interested. When am I going to learn?"

"You will learn when the time is right. In the meantime, why don't you ask Christine if she's into him, and if she's not, go for it, ask him out for a drink. Is he shy?"

"Nah, he has loads of girls. Well, that's what I've heard. He's a bartender for God's sake, although I've never actually seen him with anyone, come to think of it."

"The ones that seem to have lots of action are the most insecure; they hide behind that aura. Just come right out and tell him how you feel. Don't play games. Be vulnerable."

We are family. Lou was waving from the dance floor and this time, Kaye joined her, forming a circle with Anna, Matthew Jr., and Mario, dancing her heart out.

Her heart was thumping as she climbed the steps up to the mahogany door of the redbrick High School, on the Grand Concourse.

Sister Virginia took her by the elbow to the faculty room, introducing her to the staff, adding, "God sent her to me." The nuns wore tweed skirts, blouses, and knitted cardigans, but the same brogues, as their Irish counterparts. They smoked cigarettes, jangled car keys, and ate pizza. A robust Mister Al asked Kaye what sort she wanted – potato?

Kaye liked the word 'faculty'. So American. Another one to add to her list.

Next stop was a gymnasium packed with teenage boys and girls chattering, their lips glossy, teeth pearl white. The girls in, flawlessly applied make-up, and perfectly polished nails. Burgundy plaid skirts hiked to expose velvety legs. The boys had chiselled jaws, all had beautifully coiled curls; some of the boys sporting mullets and mohawks, chests bursting through burgundy blazers. "Whassup! What's happenin'? How you doin'?" ricocheted through the hall.

As it was Orientation Day, there were no classes, so she sipped coffee and ate doughnuts at various folding tables in the corridor. Notices listed varsity teams and cheerleading squads and schedules for basketball and baseball practice. Arrows pointed towards homerooms and a cafeteria, and there were announcements about field trips. She was accumulating new words, by the minute.

Homeroom was for checking the register and making announcements and changes to the calendar, she learnt. It was an opportunity for the students to complete their homework and come to Kaye if they had problems with any of their classes, to share personal problems with her too. As soon as she met her group and acquainted herself with the typewriting and business rooms, she assumed she could leave, as classes didn't start until the next day. She'd take a walk in Van Cortlandt Park, curl up on the couch and watch the *Oprah Winfrey Show* that Melissa was always raving about. Have time to herself before the girls got home.

She was about to slip back out the mahogany door when Sister Virginia grabbed her by the arm. "Is your portfolio ready?" Her steel blue eyes had stopped twinkling.

"Pardon?"

"I'll need class plans at the start of every week and extra ones for when you're sick."

"Huh? Em." Kaye fidgeted with the collar of her black-and-white dress. "Ok. I'll put some together for you now."

The keyboarding room was empty, the manual typewriters silent. In the Tech, they'd already advanced onto the golf-ball electric, but not here in the South Bronx. She tried to recall what she'd learnt about aims, objectives, instruction, demonstration, application, revision, and other pedagogical mysteries she'd mulled over for the Teachers' Diploma.

The room was musty, chalky, inky. Outside the cell-like window were the usual traffic and sirens, and machines cranking on a nearby building site. Inside was still. Deserted. Everyone else must have their plans done.

The teachers in the Tech never talked about lesson plans. She'd had a portfolio for teaching practice, in case the Inspector wanted it, but he never did. Kaye racked her brain trying to remember its contents. By four o'clock, she had eight plans to cover the following four days, and two more, for which she had to gauge the level the class would reach on some obscure day in the future when she would be sick.

"And by the way ..." Sister Virginia flicked through the manila folder Kaye had handed her. "... I don't want to see you smile until

December."

That shouldn't be too hard.

The walk in Van Cortlandt was postponed, but she made it home in time for *Oprah* who was discussing women who hadn't had a date in years. Kaye lay on the couch marvelling at forty to fifty-year olds announcing on national television that they couldn't get a man.

Oprah told them if they weren't being asked out, it meant they weren't open to it.

Weren't they a bit old?

Oprah asked if they'd let people know they were available for dating?

Imagine telling the lads in the Terminal that she was available for dating?

The apartment was quieter in the afternoon – the only sound that of children in a distant playground. And she was alone, for a change. At home, Mam and Dad would be watching the nine o'clock news; Olivia playing squash; Trish preparing to return to college; Gary at training. And Liam, what would he be doing? Coaching one of his teams, maybe, or playing his mandolin, or out hiking.

Oprah said people don't want to change. Pain is familiar. We want to hold onto it.

Chrissie charged through the door, flung keys and apron on the floor, tossed mail on the table, and filled the kettle with water. "How did it go? What were the pupils like? Were the nuns alright?" She hurled the questions, without waiting for an answer.

Presently she came into the living-room, carrying two mugs of tea and a packet of Jacob's Cream Crackers.

"There's no budder, we'll eat 'em dry." She sat cross-legged on the floor. "So, tell us."

"A doddle, except for I had to provide lesson plans for when I'm sick. Nothing major." Kaye sipped her tea.

Chrissie crammed a cracker into her mouth, the crumbs spilling down the front of her GIMME A BREAK T-shirt. She slurped some tea, splashing amber spots on her chest.

"Jaysus! Me tits are scalded." She jumped up, pulling the shirt over her head to expose mounds of blue veined breast, and raisin nipples.

"I've never seen your boobs so much in me whole life." Kaye spun her head away.

Later, they watched *Falling in Love*, ogling over Meryl Street and Robert De Niro eying one another up on the Metro North, place names now so familiar flashing by the window.

"I'd love to be able to do that," Chrissie sighed.

"Fall in love?" Kaye curled into a foetal position. The film was making her feel fuzzy.

"No, eejit. I mean lie out on the couch like you. My legs would dangle over the sides." Chrissie squeezed in beside her, moving Kaye's feet onto her lap.

"But would ya like to be in love?"

"I don't know, probably."

"Didn't you like Nick at first?"

"I like them all. I'm lucky like that."

"But everyone says he's a womanizer, yet I've never seen him with one. Have you?"

"No." Chrissie kept her eyes on the TV. "Probably has them up against the barrels in the back room."

"D'ya think?"

"And there's rumours that he was married once, but I don't believe that."

"Married?"

"Yeah, years ago, but that's only Sil trying to put me off. He's dead jealous of him."

"Why?"

"Money," Chrissie rubbed her fingers together.

"Money, money, money." Mo arrived in, singing the Abba song.

"Jaysus, you frightened the life ouda me!" Chrissie rolled off the couch.

"Someone's in a good mood." Kaye said, attempting to chat, still a little afraid of Mo, but she'd have to try if they were going to be roommates for another three months. "How did work go?"

"Busy, busy, made pretty great tips." She shook her apron, coins jangling. "George is grand, Tina too, Violet and Rose a bit bossy. There's a new one on the counter. The lads in the kitchen are gas. Everything was exactly as you said it would be. How was the teaching?"

"I didn't do any teaching yet." Kaye would've swapped with Mo in a second.

"No? Well I'm wrecked. I'm gonna have a shower and a nap. See yis."

"She's not herself," Chrissie said.

"Probably embarrassed about losing Mrs. Polowsky and tellin' us lies, and then nearly half-killing me," said Kaye. "Also, the immigration thing, she still has that hanging over her."

"It's Polansky." Chrissie pulled her top over her head. "And that's not how Immigration works; they don't call in advance to announce they're coming to deport you."

"Well, don't ask me, I know nothing about it, contrary to what some people might think." She nodded towards the hall. "Maybe she's worried about starting a new job?"

"It's more than that. There's something bothering her. She's very sharp at times."

"Well, I've always found her like that. Didn't she tell me not to step on her territory?"

"No, there's something wrong. I know it."

"Well, nothin' we can do about it now." Kaye gathered up her class notes. "I have to get ready for tomorrow."

She sounded nonchalant, despite the butterflies.

CHAPTER TWENTY-TWO

Taking a deep breath, she tried to relax, tried to look confident, tried to reassure herself of Brother Vincent's conviction that pupils in New York were no different from those in Ireland: that teenagers were the same everywhere.

"Right?" he'd said.

Wrong.

They talked, laughed, sighed, sang, chewed gum, checked their hair and make-up in hand mirrors, perused photographs and gyrated to hip-hop from *Walkmans* hooked to their ears like intravenous drips, all through Kaye's introduction to alphabetical filing. If she asked for attention, they told her she wasn't their mother. If she didn't let them go to the bathroom during class, they threatened to pee on the floor. If she did let them go, Virginia, who was on perpetual hallway patrol, steered them in again. Sometimes she lost control. Some students made such a din, the Mother Superior would knock on the door, and look in, frowning.

"Why don't you lock it, Miss?" The suggestion came from a girl in the back row, who was painting her nails a black cherry colour. "In case that awful nun comes in."

"You should stand up to her," said a long, lanky lad whose sprawled legs into the aisle forced Kaye to jump over them every time she walked up and down, handing out index cards.

"Are you scared of her, Miss?" A mousy little girl in the front squeaked.

Scared?

Pearls of perspiration beaded her forehead; salt stung her eyes, while she read from a textbook. Streams of sweat trickled down her legs, her back and abdomen. Raising her hand to the chalkboard revealed wet armpits.

Kaye wasn't scared. She was petrified.

In the staffroom, she poured coffee for the English teacher, Mister Al, before anyone else, just because he was right behind her.

A nun with her hair cut close to her scalp sighed. "You're not in the old country now, you know."

"Oh, I know," Kaye said and gave her a strained smile.

"I'm afraid you're too stressed," Sister Virginia said. "Don't make yourself sick."

She was already sick, and every day, got sicker and sicker. Sick with dread and trepidation every time she ascended the twenty-eight steps to the carved door. Sick with worry. Sick from counting the hours until two o'clock. Sick that she wouldn't be able to control the class; that her plans wouldn't work; that she wasn't prepared; that they'd ask her a question she couldn't answer. Sick from lack of sleep, from carrying her work around, bogged down by a heavy bag straining her shoulders.

Her heart was heavy too. She dragged herself into bed each afternoon, drew her sheet over her head, longing for the darkness, and a handful of hours alone. Needing to soothe her furrowed brow, her aching jaws, her tensed lips, her foghorn voice from the shouting and the chalk dust. Craving silence, she pulled the comforter up around her ears. Here there was no noise, no chatter, no questions, or comments, no one seeking attention.

Don't smile until December? Easy.

On the Saturday, homework had to be marked; classwork appraised and evaluated. For each pupil, Kaye struggled to come up with a fair grade. She'd put Burger Heaven off for another week. At least that meant she wouldn't have to work with Mo, not yet anyway.

Chrissie busied herself with laundry all morning. "Want any done?" She fixed five white shirts over the bath.

"Nah." Kaye would never let anyone wash her clothes.

"Comin' for a manicure?" Chrissie whispered through a slice of doorway.

"Nah."

"Want anything from *Foodtown?* Anything for dinner?"

"Nah." Kaye made a sandwich and planned lessons on the home keys and words she would need when they became familiar with the keyboard. It was best to have students type immediately; give them something practical to do, again, to motivate them, the typewriting teaching manual advised. But nothing had prepared her for this. Not the teaching practice in the Tech, not the prissy Inspector who hadn't taught in thirty years and had tried to quieten them with a *Ciúnas!* - who'd told her to relate Bray to Shakespeare's Denmark.

What do these pupils relate to, she looked around her classroom, and hadn't a clue.

She slept in fits that afternoon. Dreamt about Liam. Woke up. Drank tea, munched crisps, ticked the right answers, circled errors, and walked the wooden floor trying to come up with next week's plans. Slept again.

It was still hot despite America news shows declaring summer was over. Don't wear white after Labour Day, cried the fashionistas.

"Comin' down to Celtic House?" Chrissie phoned her later.

"Nah, I have tests to correct."

When she could've had Chrissie to herself, she couldn't.

"Forget about it," said Chrissie.

"Forget about what?" Kaye asked.

"G'way from me." Chrissie was giggling "Sil's tryin' to cop a feel," she said.

So much for the grocery shopping. And having Chrissie to herself.

Then Mo arrived home, making straight for the shower, reappearing a few minutes in a lavender towel.

"Andy said to say hello." Mo briskly dried herself revealing rolls of flesh.

Used to the nakedness now, Kaye found herself, instead of embarrassed, delighted to see Mo getting doughy around her tummy. About time all those take-aways and lack of exercise took its toll on her too.

"How was today?" Kaye asked her. "Did I miss anything?"

"Nah, it was quiet. But it's nice being off at seven on a Saturday."

"And Melissa? How's she?" Kaye was trying hard to get rid of that niggling feeling that Mo would try to monopolise Melissa. Hijack another one of her friends.

"Nice, yeah, a pisser." Mo tied the towel around her. "I'd better get dressed."

Kaye was left alone with her Teacher's Handbook.

"So, are you coming down to the Celtic?" Mo reappeared in her underwear.

"Nah, I have to prepare for next week." Kaye sighed.

"That's right, you do." Mo sprayed *Sure* all over the place.

"I'd love to go for one," Kaye said. "But sure I won't stop at that. And then I'd have a hangover tomorrow. Can't have that."

"No, we can't have that." Mo dragged on a pair of shorts and a tank top and patted down her hair, not giving a hoot how she looked. Low maintenance, Melissa would say. She grabbed her keys from the hook inside the door. "Have to run; Andy's waiting for me downstairs. Ta–ra. And Kaye."

"Yeah?"

"Don't fuck this up, remember, teaching is a vocation."

What had she ever fucked up before that Mo knew about? Teaching a vocation? All the times she'd prayed not to get a vocation. When Miss Brennan had terrified them that if God called you, you couldn't say no. He'd come in through the keyhole after you. Kaye had pleaded with Him not to call her. Her mother said it was the shoes.

She ran water into the kettle, made a cup of *Chocful o' nuts* instant coffee, and humming along to the salsa music outside, she took out a writing pad and started a letter to Olivia, who still didn't know she had decided to stay. They hadn't spoken since June, the longest since they'd met. Calls to Ireland cost a dollar a minute, so were limited. Except when it was five o'clock in the morning after the pub.

She described the apartment building and 4D, the Bodega and the candy floss houses, the Terminal and the taxi drivers, the bartenders, Burger Heaven, and Pope Pius High. She didn't admit that she hadn't got the hang of the teaching yet. And only as a postscript did she send her regards to Liam. The words looked forlorn on the paper, like they would have sounded if she'd uttered them out loud. She placed the pages in an envelope, licked the flap, put her head on the table and fell asleep.

She's sitting on a tall chair on Florence Road, in front of the Church. He struts out of a shop, on stilts. Her heart stops, the breeze lifts his fringe. They're the same height now: higher than anyone else; higher than the whole town. 'Liam' she shouts. He looks left, right and crosses the road. As he ambles past, straddling Main Street on his stilts, she realizes it's Nick.

In the Terminal on Sunday, everyone fussed over her, as though she'd been away for weeks.

"How's the teaching going?" Nick asked.

"Grand," she told him. "Thanks to you for getting me the job."

"Not at all, it was all you." He whizzed away.

"Tell me." Izzy grabbed her in a bear hug. "How's it goin'?" She was sporting new glasses with clear lenses and gold frames, revealing new sparkling green eyes.

"Grand, grand."

"How's Florence Nightingale?" Pete was beaming, as usual.

"She's a nurse, ya eejit." Chrissie glared at him.

"Oh, so it's Mary Poppins I'm speakin' to?" Pete poked his chin with a forefinger.

"She's a nanny, ya gobshite." Chrissie rolled her eyes.

"How about *The Prime of Miss Jean Brodie*?" Kaye suggested.

"Ah, I'd say yer in yer prime all right." Pete rubbed his hands together.

"And Maggie Smith never looked this good." Nick glided by, pointing a finger at her.

"Yis have me lost now." Chrissie folded her arms.

"How are the Muppets?" Kaye flung her arms around Sil and Seanie.

"For yer information." Seanie squinted at Chrissie over the top of his specs, "Maggie Smith played Miss Jean Brodie in the aforesaid movie."

"He didn't go to a high school in the mountains for nothin'," said Sil.

"How did you survive a whole week without this?" Nick winked.

"I don't know." Kaye smiled at him.

Cliona Kenny, who had won a talent competition on television at home, was tuning her guitar; a leather-clad lad setting up the sound system. Part of her prize had been gigs in New York. Kaye was sure poor Cliona had imagined something fancier than the Terminal. But if she was disappointed, she didn't show it, and belted out Mary Black and Maura O'Connell tunes, every bit as good as the original.

Sil pulled Kaye out to jive to *Past the Point of Rescue*. As they twirled around, the shabby ceiling spinning above them, all she could think about was Pope Pius High, Sister Virginia, the Farrah Fawcetts and alphabetical filing.

"I'm findin' it really hard," she gasped.

"Ah, we're getting old, girl." He wiped the sweat from his forehead with the back of his hand. "I'm not the twinkle toes I used to be."

"I mean the teachin'." Kaye caught her breath.

"Oh that. I admire you girl." Sil downed half his cider. "You have balls. Right Nick?"

"Sure," said Nick. "I've been through the system here and even I wouldn't try it."

"Fair play to ya, altogether." Sil drained his drink.

"Hang in there." Nick knocked on the counter and was away again.

Kaye scuttled off to the loo to exhale in comfort.

"So, how's it really goin'?" Izzy was washing her hands.

"Oh, not that great." Kaye wet the bits of frizz at her ears. Her cheeks were pink from dancing and mottled with freckles.

"You're not there a wet week, girl." Izzy's green eyes were popping out of their sockets. Kaye hadn't realised they were that green. "It took me months to get used to it."

"Months?"

"Shure it's the hardest job in the world, girl." Izzy slumped against the sink. "You're thrown in at the deep end, to a bunch of blackguards bent on making your life a misery. There's nobody to help, to train you, to take over when times get tough. And there's no thanks for any of it. If the kids do well, they're great; if they do badly, it's your fault."

Kaye checked her new pink stretch jeans in the mirror. She looked very American in a navy sweatshirt and pink Timberland boots too.

"You shouldn't wear pink, girl," Izzy said to her.

"Wha'?"

"It's not your colour." Izzy looked her up and down. "I'd say you're more an autumn."

"What are you talking about?"

"*Color Me Beautiful*. They tell you what colours to wear, not just clothes, but make-up too. They tell you what suits your skin."

They tottered back to the bar where Nick was polishing a glass, his shoulders straining against his shirt.

"And if you don't like this job, you can always leave and find another school, there's plenty of them out there," Izzy told her.

"Ah, there's not much point chopping and changing now, sure I'm going home in three months." She'd stay where she was and make the most of it.

She would consider changing her colours though.

Cliona was tweaking the guitar. Her nails clipped like Liam's, strumming the strings, her hair hanging over her face, like his.

"And now we have a request for Kaye? Kate? Katie?" Cliona

announced.

"Go on Kaye." Chrissie shoved her towards the stage.

"Give 'em socks, Katie." Pete took her by the hand and escorted her to the podium.

"What key love?" Cliona asked.

"You'll just have to follow me," Kaye said.

"Give her an F." Seanie shouted. "That works every time."

Mo shot him a look.

Nick arrived from the other side of the bar. Maybe she shouldn't wear pink? Taking a deep breath, she launched into *Red is the Rose*.

Chrissie and Tim waved two dishtowels, their eyes like marbles. Izzy swayed on a stool, glass in hand. Seanie and Sil waltzed, Mo sat with her arms folded. When the song was over, Kaye grabbed her bag and waved goodbye. She had that sinking Sunday-night feeling from her schooldays, except this time, she was the teacher. But, as she scarpered out the door, Cliona spoke into the microphone, "Well done, Kaye," and everybody cheered.

"Awesome." Nick roared.

"Bring me home," she pleaded with Andy, her heart heavy at having to leave.

"You looking good." He pecked her on the cheek. "Pink is me favourite colour."

"Andy! You sound like me!"

When the students progressed on to office machinery, things calmed down. More occupied, they spent less time distracting one another. She used continuous assessment to threaten lower marks if they didn't co-operate. Impressed them by computing simple problems on a piece of paper, or in her head in less time than they did on the calculators. Thanks to Miss Brennan's mental arithmetic lessons.

"How d'ya think people managed before calculators?" she asked them.

"There was no math, Miss?"

After a month on manual typewriters, they graduated onto electric.

One day, Sister Virginia entered the room. Kaye greeted her. The nun sat at a desk. Kaye took a deep breath. It was a class observation.

She picked up a long stick and turned to the board. "Heads up, eyes on the chart, fingers on the home keys." She paused.

"F–R–F space, J–U–J space," she chanted, as twenty-six sets of fingers beat out the rhythm. "D–E–D space, K–I–K space." She tried to ignore the shake in her voice, the perspiration on her brow. "S–W–S space, L–O–L space." All eyes were on the chart. "A–Q–A space, semi-colon, P; semi-colon."

She walked up and down the aisles, repeating the drill until they were ready to advance on to words. All was going according to plan until, snap. The lights went out, the burr of machines died, and an eerie silence descended. Twenty-six sets of fingers were still, twenty-six pairs of eyes stared straight ahead. Virginia nodded to continue.

She can't be serious.

She was.

For the next forty-five minutes, twenty-six pairs of hands tapped out keys that refused to budge, and twenty-six pairs of eyes beseeched her, as she called out the letters. They typed far–fed–war–wed–jar–jaw–queue–quest, semi-colon, as other classes vacated the school. They tap-tap-tapped, as Kaye paraded up and down checking blank pages. They gaped at the chart, their fingers hopping off the keyboard, wrists perched over the spacebar.

Finally, the bell rang. Kaye placed her notes in a folder, the textbooks in a cupboard.

The students filed out and she followed Sister Virginia to her office. "Just a few things need going over." Her smile was syrupy. "First of all, you'd be better off selling shoes."

What? Hadn't she done fantastic, despite all the odds. Kaye concentrated on a Betsy Clarke poster on the wall. I WANT A HUG written above a cuddly blue bear. You'll be waiting.

"Maybe you could help me?" she heard herself say.

"Excuse me?"

"You have so much experience," Kaye began. "Maybe you could give me ideas. Show me how to be as good as you are? My previous employer made me the best waitress in New York; maybe you could make me the best teacher?"

"Well, I don't know."

"It's worth a try. God loves a challenge." Where was she getting this shite from? Too much Oprah. "Perhaps I could sit in on your classes when I'm free?" Kaye held out her hand.

The nun eyeballed it, hesitated, and then took it limply.

"We'll see," she said.

CHAPTER TWENTY-THREE

The summer faded into autumn. Two couches were hauled up the stairs from the sidewalk, and a rug for the living-room floor. Auntie Lou sent lace curtains with strawberry motifs for the kitchen. Strawberries were the theme that year, she said. And Kaye bought red linoleum for the floor, her gift to the girls for letting her stay, which she carried over her shoulder all the way along South Broadway.

The sky retained its vivid blue. Gone were the short grey days of an Irish October. Van Cortlandt Park was a myriad of falling leaves, must be why they called it the fall, she decided. Orange, brown, sienna, and rust, even pink and green, every shade of green imaginable.

Whereas, at home, it was just green.

She joined a gym called *Living Well Lady*, which added another hour onto her stressful day. Afterwards, she waded home every day through a leafy carpet, anxious for a cup of tea and Oprah, and maybe a chat when the girls came in. For, as the teaching got easier, she felt more in the mood for chatting again. One evening, with leaves rustling under her feet, she recalled the previous night's dream, as she walked. Like all her dreams here, it was of home. Never America.

She and Olivia are walking down Killiney Hill. It's dark. They cannot see their way. Olivia is scared. Kaye has to push her. They pick tomatoes and go into a house. There's music playing and Kaye starts singing. She's scooped up by a roller coaster soaring to the sky. It stops, leaving her suspended, upside down. Hanging. Terrified. She starts talking to a row of women in front of Auntie May's house in Kilcoughlan. They're laughing. She describes her perfect man to them: he's wearing a white shirt, and black trousers.

She told Chrissie about it when she got home.

"I don't know how you remember all that stuff," Chrissie said.

Kaye didn't know how she did either.

"The minute I wake up, I forget them." Chrissie placed two mugs on the table and dropped a *Barry's* teabag into one of them. "By the way, that's the last one, so we'll have to share. Who's comin' over next, so's we can get them to bring some?"

"Em, Bren?"

"Good, must make a list of what we want. So, how was your day?"

"Actually, it wasn't too bad," Kaye was flicking through a pile of mail she had picked up from the metal box. "I'm getting used to it, I have to say, and in a good mood, for a change." She perused a flimsy blue one with PAR AVION stamped across the front. She turned it around to look at the back. "What were ya sayin' about dreams?"

"Just that I forget them the minute I wake up. I get the feeling that I was somewhere nice, or that something lovely was happening to me, and I want to fall straight back asleep again just to recapture it. Ya know what I mean?"

"Yeah. That happens to me too."

"As for Mo," said Chrissie. "She keeps me up half the night yappin' in her sleep. Takin' orders and mouthing off the burgers, even roaring into a microphone."

"I'm glad she's getting into the swing of it." Kaye inserted her fingernail under the flap and tore open the envelope. "She's really cool to work with too. Gets on great with Melissa, but not in a creepy, trying to take her away from me, sort of way. Has us all working one big station and pooling our tips, which makes … much … more … sense …"

"Didn't I tell ya? What's that?" Chrissie squinted at the envelope.

"It's from Olivia."

"Wow!" Chrissie snatched it off her. "That's weird. And you only dreamin' about her."

"Yeah." Kaye grabbed it back and escaped into the hallway. "Think I'll go lie down."

"Do, and I'll give you a shout for dinner."

Kaye lay on the blue plaid comforter she'd bought in Alexander's on Lexington Avenue. She loved getting letters and had been writing them since she was seven.

Olivia was surprised that she'd decided to stay. The apartment sounded great, the new job and the friends. Olivia was delighted for her. IT'S JUST AS WELL YOU DIDN'T COME HOME, AS THERE PROBABLY

WOULDN'T HAVE BEEN ANY CLASSES FOR YOU. THEY'VE CUT BACK DRASTICALLY ON PART-TIME HOURS. THE FRIDAY NIGHT GROUP IS STILL IN FULL SESSION. KAYE TURNED THE PAGE AND SAW THE WORDS: I'M GOING TO MEET MY FATHER SOON, IN LONDON. YOU KNOW HOW I'VE ALWAYS WANTED TO. LIAM IS COMING WITH ME FOR MORAL SUPPORT.

Kaye put it down and exhaled. In all the years she'd known her, Olivia had never once mentioned wanting to find her father. And Liam going with her? Why hadn't Kaye been told before? Wouldn't this have been planned before she left?

"Everything all right?" Chrissie was at the door.

"Yeah." Kaye handed her the letter.

"I knew there was something sneaky about that one." Chrissie flung the pages in the air when she'd finished reading. "She was always sorta – what's the word? – conde."

"Condescending?"

"That's it. D'ya think there's something going on between herself and Liam?" Chrissie sat down beside her.

"Nah."

Sneaky?

Olivia used to stray off with other House Children from time to time, or new friends in the flats where she went to live with her mother, colleagues in the Tech, but she always came back to Kaye. And she'd always supported Kaye where Liam was concerned. For that, Kaye had been grateful. And wasn't it Olivia who'd encouraged her to continue her studies, who got her the hours in the Tech teaching typing and then for her teaching practice when doing the Dip, who had urged her to have more confidence, especially with men?

Sneaky?

She didn't tell her everything, Kaye knew that, and she was obviously closer to Liam than she had pretended.

But sneaky?

"Yeah, sneaky." Chrissie's feet thudded the floor, as she stood up. "And it's obvious now that she was tryin' to get into his pants all along."

Kaye had this image of Olivia tugging at Liam's sweatpants.

"Nah, it's not that."

"Why not?"

"Ah, it's just a feeling I have. He has some sort of problem. He had something to tell me last Christmas, but never got around to it.

I'm sorry now I didn't press him more. Anyhow, they're all part of the group, it's only natural they'd be friendly. I just wish sometimes that I was there with them."

"Then why is she only telling you this now?" Chrissie sat down on the bed again.

"I dunno." Kaye shrugged.

There had been that other letter, where she'd mentioned that Liam had received Kaye's card. Did she know then? Maybe not.

"Maybe it's only come about lately."

"Maybe that thing he was going to tell you was that he was with Olivia?"

"Nah, I don't think so."

"Last Christmas, you say? Why didn't you tell me before now?"

"Oh, you were busy getting ready to go away. And, anyway," she sighed. "It's probably not anything too serious. And if it was a secret, I probably couldn't share it anyhow."

"Maybe it was just an excuse to get rid of you." Chrissie moved in closer.

"Gee thanks."

"Maybe he's just not attracted to you."

"Jesus, Chris, you're startin' to sound like Mo now!" Kaye pushed her away. "He's going to therapy, so I'm hoping he'll be cured by the time I get home."

"Gosh, Kaye, for such an intelligent woman, you can be really stupid sometimes. There's lots of people you're not attracted to, like Bren, for instance. So what if someone's not attracted to you?"

"Four years, Chris, I spent four years loving him, dreaming about him, thinking about him every second of every day. I'd hardly get over him in four months."

"Four months? Last Christmas was ten months ago."

"I'm counting four months, since I left home."

Was there something going on? Did the gang in the Strand know? The Harbour? Begnet's? The Tech? Had there been pity in their eyes?

"Oh, who cares." Chrissie slid off the bed. "You have a new life here now. Don't reply to that letter. I'll make more tea."

"There's no teabags, remember?"

"Oh, right I'll go get some then." She made for the door. "Teabags and beer. I won't be long." She stopped all of a sudden and looked back at Kaye. "You're gonna have to stop dreaming, you know, and start living."

"I know," Kaye said.

Later, she looked at herself in her new wicker mirror. Her face was thinner; her freckles concealed by *Elizabeth Arden's* flawless finish; her highlighted hair curlier since she'd stopped blow-drying it; her body trimmer from *Living Well Lady*.

But what good was it?

Chapter Twenty-Four

They went down to the Terminal to meet Bren after organising Andy to taxi him in from the airport.

"I'm fucked," he said, as he hugged them.

Seanie and Sil were seated in their usual Muppet positions. Nick popped open a round of cold beers and Pete insisted on shots of *Fuzzy Navels* – peach schnapps with orange juice. The jukebox was cranked up and though it was mid-week, the bar was humming.

"Jaysus!" Bren looked around in amazement. "Yid never see this many in the pub at home on a Wednesday night. Will yis be able for work in the mornin'?"

"Oh, we will." Seanie leered at him. "I'll be up like a bollix with a smile on my face."

"Jaysus!"

"Now we do get the odd 'DMM' warnin'." Sil told him. "But missin' one day won't matter. We've more money than sense over here."

"What's DMM?"

"Don't miss Monday!" Sil and Seanie tipped glasses and downed their shots.

"D'yis not have sick days?" Bren's eyes were open wide, like flying saucers.

"Ya must be jokin'."

Kaye pinched Bren on the arm. He was here, in the Terminal, beside her, in the Bronx. Not only was he her badminton partner, but their social organiser in Begnet's, playing football and hurling too. It was Bren who organised the day trips to the beach at Brittas Bay and picnics on White Rock; the end-of-season parties; the buses for 'away' matches; the excursions into Croke Park; the fancy dress at Halloween; Karaoke 'n' Kurry on New Year's Eve and the black-and-white pub crawl.

"Black and white?" Seanie's specs were steaming.

"We dressed up in black and white and went on a pub crawl through the town. Chrissie came with us."

"Jeez!" Pete clapped his hands. "That sounds like a pisser!"

No reaction from Nick.

"We brought the traffic on the Main Street to a standstill." Chrissie told them. "One lad in a Ban Garda outfit took names from stupid drivers."

Kaye butted in. "Crispy was a vampire and she had a white glove stuffed into the top of her black fishnet stocking." She spluttered. "When I asked her what it was doing there, she said yer man's hand got caught in the rush."

Chrissie gave her a look. Kaye supposed she didn't want Sil to know too much about her personal life at home. A man's glove in her fishnet stocking? Kaye felt bad now for mentioning it, for looking for a laugh at Chrissie's expense.

"Who's hand?" Sil asked. "And who's Crispy?"

"Chrissie, that's what Gary called her when they were small. And it was nobody's hand. It was just a joke. It could have been anybody's!" Kaye tittered. Oh, God, she was making it worse. Was it a case of attention, attention?

"Ya had to have been there." Bren told the lads.

"Well, I wish I had been." Pete uncapped more bottles. "Sounds like a cracker to me!"

Turning to Kaye, Bren said, "Ya didn't look too bad yerself in yer French maid's outfit."

"Ooooooh, I'd really like to have seen that." Pete licked his lips.

There was no sign of Nick at all now. He must've been somewhere in the shadows. Keeping his distance.

"And you, punk rocker, sticking your spiky hairdo under me lacy apron." She hit Bren on the head with a beermat.

"Did I tickle yer fancy, Katie?"

"Ya mustn't have. Didn't I frisk ya with me feather duster?"

"I have to go." Seanie slid off his stool. "Not able for all this excitement."

"Me neither," Sil followed him.

"Don't bang the door behind yis," Bren called after them. "Hey Pete," he roared up the bar. "Any chance I can cash one of these itinerant cheques and buy a real drink?"

"He means a travellers' cheques." Mo explained.

"I know what he means, don't worry." It was Nick who reappeared with the drinks. "These are on me." He looked at Bren. "Keep your money." He knocked on the counter and returned with a pint of Guinness for Bren, winked at Kaye, and was gone again.

"Jaysus, girls, what are yis doin' here?" Bren gaped around. "The stuffin's fallin' outa the chairs, for feck's sake!"

"So what?" said Chrissie.

"It's not that bad." Mo insisted.

"Ya get used to it," added Kaye covering a lump of stuffing with her bag.

"And the music's crap." Bren jerked his head at the jukebox. "Wolfe Tones? Clancy Brothers? Sure, nobody listens to that shite anymore."

"They do here," said Chrissie. "So, shag off with yerself."

"Will I play Madonna?" Kaye took a dollar bill off the counter.

"Not unless you want to," said Mo. "Don't do if just for him."

"And all yis talk about is drink. And money."

"Feck. Off. Now," said Chrissie.

"Are you for real?" Mo snapped the dollar from Kaye and took off in the direction of the jukebox.

"D'ya think so?" Kaye scrunched her nose at Bren.

Chrissie eyed her sideways. "Don't be worryin' with the likes of him." She dodged a smack from Bren. "And he only in the door. His ass not warm in the seat."

"It's arse, Crispy, arse. An ass is a dunkey."

"And dunkey is donkey where I come from." Kaye told him.

Bren looked at her. "Yis are after changin'. And it's not for the better, eider."

Kaye had wanted him to like it here. She'd wanted him to see her happy and go back and tell the others, Olivia, and Liam in particular. Bren who had sat through all the long chats about what she should do about Liam. 'Just ask him where you stand,' he'd say, 'what's the harm in that? What's the worst thing that can happen? Leave no stone unturned.' He'd say.

Now, it struck her that she shouldn't have put him through all that, because he probably did like her. He'd never crossed that line, though. Not once.

She'd make it up to him on this holiday, not by crossing the dreaded line, oh no, but by being nice to him.

"Get me another one of them itchy bellybuttons." Bren called to Nick. "While I have a chat here with Katie." He huddled in closer. "So, tell me then, what is it? Is it the money? Is that why you stayed?"

"Are ya mad?" she said. "Do you know what they pay a Catholic School teacher over here? Chrissie and Mo make more servin' them burgers than I do educating their children."

"Well, there you go, who'd want to live in a society like dah?"

"Well, I'm legal, and working at what I'm qualified for, and ..." She lit a cigarette. "I'm only staying another three months." She took a drag. "Have ya seen Liam lately?"

"Aha!" He banged his fist on the counter, which set Nick into a spin, Pete into the roars of laughter.

"It's all right." Kaye told them. "Bren here is getting' all fired up."

"So, I see." Nick said. "Must be all those itchy bellybuttons."

"Er, yeah." She was glad she had a man beside her tonight, to test Chrissie's theory.

"So that's it." Bren hadn't taken his eyes off her. "That's the real reason, eh?"

"Well, no." She flicked some ash into an ashtray. "Not exactly. I do like it here, really. But the plan is to go home all dolled up and gorgeous and have him fall for me, finally."

"Hmm." Bren tapped his fingers on the countertop. "Doesn't sound like such a good plan to me."

So much for Bren fancying her. She'd tried once before to get him to feel sorry for her, at the badminton party in Enniskerry. But he'd no sympathy for her then, telling her to cheer up and enjoy herself. What made her think he would now?

"D'ya want another bellybutton?" She pointed at his empty glass.

"Ya know what?" He smelt of sweat and aftershave. "I'm bolloxed."

"Let's go then. Wake that one while you're at it." She pointed at Chrissie, her head on the bar, eyes closed. There was no sign of Mo. She was probably in the Short Stop.

"We'll go get some brekkie, and then get you home to bed," she said to Bren.

"Breakfast before bed, are ya jestin'? Shouldn't it be when we get up in the mornin'?" Bren rubbed his eyes and hoisted a suitcase over his shoulder. "Getting me into bed, Katie; now that's somethin' you've always wanted to do."

"Yeah, right." She looped her arm through Chrissie's, dragging her after them.

"Straight home now, Kaye." Pete grinned, and Nick bowed his head at her, just once.

"Oh yeah," she said. "Sure will."

Every day for the next two weeks, when Kaye arrived home from school, Bren had the kettle on and the teabags sitting in their mugs. She didn't bother insisting on the teapot anymore and was surprised at how quickly she'd got used to the teabags. It was the chat she enjoyed most, before the girls got in, telling him bits and pieces from her day.

"I'd say yer a great teacher, Katie," he said one day. "I bet they love ya."

And it was true, the kids were starting to like her. The girls would sometimes, recommend hair products, stop her on the corridor or in the lunchroom and ask her advice on school, home, boyfriends, friends, other teachers. Two had confided in her that they thought they were pregnant, which concerned her for days, but they were only false alarms, thankfully. One of the boys had admitted in homeroom one morning that he'd become a father twice that week. Kaye had tried not to flinch.

One day, she had one of the girls dictate a passage from *Great Expectations*, while the others typed. She had suggested to Mister Al that they correlate their courses - English literature with typewriting. A boom box could be heard in the distance, music blaring. Kaye held her breath, as it got closer and closer, until it was just outside the classroom window. No one else seemed to notice; the pupil continued reading, and everyone else kept their gaze on the keyboard chart on the wall. As the music faded, Kaye exhaled slowly.

Wow, was all she could say to herself.

Another day, Marisol, the Class Captain, had approached her, as she was walking around the athletics track, and confided that she was tempted to go out with a friend's boyfriend. Kaye advised against it: the guy might be a fleeting fancy, whereas the friend could last forever. "Don't do what you wouldn't like done to yourself."

"Wow! You're cool, Miss Butler," Marisol told her. "The whole class says it."

"They do?" Kaye could have sprinted around that track, without catching her breath.

"What did I tell ya?" They were sprawled on the couch, Bren patting her ankle. "Is it time to watch Winnie?" He checked his watch.

"Who?"

"Winnie Oprey, the one you love."

"It's Oprah Winfrey, ya thick." She slapped him with a cushion. "And ya, it's time. Tea!"

The topic was about women taking their friend's boyfriends.

"This one's for you, Katie." Bren handed her a mug, the steam lifting out of it. "And I don't mean the tea." He sat on the couch and stretched his legs.

Kaye rested her head on his shoulder.

According to Oprah and her guests, it happened every day. 'It's a common occurrence,' an expert told Oprah. 'The easiest thing in the world.'

'Why's that?' Oprah asked.

'Because your friend can learn from your mistakes. She's familiar with the ins and outs and behind-the-scenes of the relationship, so she knows what to do when it comes to her turn.'

Oprah and the expert nodded at the audience and into the camera. Oprah's parting comment was that women should not betray women; men were already famous for that.

"That's what I said to the young one at school."

"Winnie should have you on there, Katie," Bren said. "You'd be brilliant."

"Sssh. Listen to this."

The topic had changed to good sex versus bad sex.

"Isn't all sex the same?"

"How would I know?"

"G'way outa dah." Bren poked her in the ribs. "I'd say yer a flyer between the sheets."

"Right!"

As well as Oprah, Kaye was addicted to the programmes that analysed and explored the backgrounds of real-life cases - documentaries like *Dateline*, *20/20* and *60 Minutes*.

'They're all numbers, Katie.'

"I know, Bren."

Not the sitcoms and soap operas that everyone else loved. And, of course, Oprah was her favourite. It was such a thrill to have the TV to herself; not having to share it with Gary and Trish and Mam and Dad.

"It's real ordinary here, isn't it?" Bren said to her one afternoon, the sun spilling in the kitchen window, the strawberry curtains fluttering. "Just like at home, it is." He dunked his teabag a few times and dropped it in the sink.

Kaye slumped into a chair and kicked off her shoes. "Ya didn't say that the first night."

"I know, but I thought it was gonna be a mad place altogether." He stretched his legs out onto the red linoleum floor that he had expertly laid for them. "I was prepared for anythin'. Anythin' at all. Naked wimen walkin' down the road wasn't gonna surprise me."

"In yer dreams." Kaye sprung open the refrigerator door with her toe and reached for the packet of *milk chocolate goldgrain* biscuits he had brought over.

He lifted her foot onto his lap. "But d'ya know what ya'd miss?"

"What?"

"Not meetin' anyone ya know."

"I love that about it!"

"Ah, Katie, ya can't beat walkin' around Bray on a Saturday afternoon and stoppin' every five minutes to chat someone."

"I don't miss that at all. I love bein' anonymous here."

"Why?" He massaged her toes. "Did ya commit a crime or something?"

"No." She swished him away. "I love that nobody knows me here. I could walk down Fifth Avenue in me knickers and no one would notice."

"Ah, I don't believe that." He dropped one foot and took up the other. "I'd say you'd still create a bit of a stir." He kneaded her ankles, pummelling the pain.

They spent the next few days sightseeing. Each of the girls had a favourite spot to show off to Bren. Even Mo, who took them to the Twin Towers and South Street Ferry Seaport. He pressed his whole body against a window in the World Trade Center, arms spread-eagle, and Kaye had to step back, she was that afraid of heights. She had chosen the Statue of Liberty, but the spiral staircase made her dizzy, or was it the itchy bellybuttons from the night before?

"Jaysus! You've a great arse, Katie." Bren roared up at her. "This is the best sight I've seen so far."

"Just as well. You've had your head up it for the past hour."

Chrissie took them on the Circle Line.

"If I see one more bridge," Bren said. "I'll puke."

"Well, Manhattan is an island," Mo reminded him.

Chrissie thrust her HEAR NO EVIL, SPEAK NO EVIL, DATE NO EVIL chest into Bren's face.

"Shouldn't it be 'see no evil'?" He was befuddled.

"No, eejit. It's DATE. Not dat you'd know much about it. Can't even spell it."

"Ah, now, Crisp." He enveloped her in a hug. "Don't be so hard on me."

Kaye brought him to FAO Schwarz so's he could get presents for his nieces and nephews. He insisted on having his picture taken with the clown who greeted them at the door, hurling the camera at Kaye. She snapped them underneath the revolving stage with giant stuffed animals rotating to the sound of *It's a Small World After All*, Bren and the clown chatting their heads off.

"He's from Kilmacanogue." Bren bounded up the escalator after her. "I went to school with his sister."

"Now are ya happy?" She grinned, as he hopped onto the giant piano from *Big*.

CHAPTER TWENTY-FIVE

What were they going to do with Bren during Izzy's bridal shower? Kaye didn't want to dump him in the Terminal with Sil and Seanie, who hadn't been that welcoming, Nick, neither. Probably thought he was a smart Alec from Ballybrack.

"Yis are gonna have a shower?" Bren shrugged. "So what?"

"We're goin' TO a shower." Chrissie roared at him. "It's a party given for the bride-to-be by her girlfriends, before she gets married to an eejit like you."

"By her girlfriends?" Bren ducked a swipe of the dishcloth. "Excuse me."

Chrissie wiped his face with the slimy, wet cloth, then linked him out the door and into a cab.

"Don't miss us too much." They dropped him at the Roaring Twenties on Bainbridge Avenue and then tottered up the street to the Greentree in their high heels, clutching various packages that contained pieces of a salad set.

They had assumed it would be like a hen party at home: a night out for the bride's friends. Mo had informed them that American showers were more elaborate, and a present would also be expected. So, they chipped in for a glass salad bowl with six glass plates and a giant wooden fork and spoon that Kaye had bought in the Chinese shop.

They found Izzy, hair blow-dried, in new Nana Mouskouri glasses, enthroned under a pink umbrella, decorated with fake wedding bands, diminutive brides and grooms and garters.

"This was no surprise for her." Chrissie whispered. "She's all dolled up."

"Must be that Color Me Beautiful crowd she went to," Kaye whispered.

"Colour me dog," said Chrissie.

Kaye spluttered her drink, as Izzy proceeded to open gifts, discarding wrapping paper and coloured string, and cooing as each package was presented to her, one by one by her six bridesmaids. They binned the paper, saved the cards and envelopes in an ivory silk bag, stuck the rosettes onto a paper plate and recorded the bride's comments in a notebook.

"They'll be read out later," Mo whispered, "as if it's the two of them talking on the wedding night."

"Would they like a copy of the conversation the night I was with him?" Chrissie said.

"Stop it," said Mo between clenched lips, and Kaye gulped.

They were soon silenced, as microwaves, silverware, crystal, dinner sets and a picture of a dining-room suite, too big to bring to the party, accumulated at Izzy's feet. At home, the gift would be a rolling pin or dishtowel, a bar of soap in the shape of a penis. When Izzy held up the salad bowl, there was a murmur around the room. The girls slunk in their seats.

"I thought you knew all about bridal showers?" Chrissie narrowed her eyes at Mo.

"I never was at one as lavish as this." Mo frowned. "I suppose a salad bowl was cheap."

"You suppose?" Chrissie glowered at her.

"Ah, to hell." Kaye sat up in her chair, pretending not to care, delighted to see some friction between her two flatmates. "We'll make up for it with the weddin' present."

After the gift opening ceremony, Izzy had to parade around the restaurant with the plate of rosettes on her head, as her comments were read out, as Mo had predicted: *I've waited three years for this - Oh! How cute! Where did you get it? - My God! It's enormous, I'm afraid to touch it in case it breaks -Ah, a little pussy, so cute. You're just too good. You shouldn't have.*

Kaye couldn't imagine Tim saying anything remotely intimate to Izzy on their wedding or any other night. She was glad when the gift session was over, and the lights lowered, Indian sitar music replaced Christy Moore on the tape recorder.

A built-like-a-brick male gyrated across the stage to Izzy, who was back under the umbrella. Sleeked in oil, he peeled off leather, suede, leopard skin and plastic underpants, prancing in front of the bridal party, until all he'd on was a gold thong. For the finale, he stuck a birthday candle in the zip and his hand on Izzy's head, coaxed her to blow it out, as women of all ages and sizes stood on chairs, stamping their feet, jangling jewellery, shouting, 'Get them off ya' at the stripper. Some of them tucked money in his thong and tried to pull the candle out of his fly. The girls sat speechless, even Chrissie who had intimated what she'd like to do to his oily abdomen. The three of them, and Izzy, who hadn't uttered a word, were the only ones in their seats when it was over.

"What about a singsong?" said Chrissie, "to calm yis all down?"

After much cajoling, Kaye sang Mary Black's *Katie*. There used to be silence in the Strand, as soon as she started, but not in the Greentree on Bainbridge. Women laughed, talked, ordered drinks, banged doors, and roared across the room throughout the song.

"Never," she said to Chrissie, when it was over, "never ever make me do that again."

Afterwards, they tipped it down to the Twenties to meet Bren. It was full to the brim and there in the middle of the crowd, was Billy.

"Katie Daly!" He hugged her. "You're still here."

"I am." She gulped when he let her go. "A fully-fledged high school teacher too."

"Be Jaysus." He grabbed her shoulders. "I knew you weren't just a pretty face."

"Down there for dancin'." She pointed at her feet.

"What brought yis to my neighbourhood, anyhow?"

"We're on our way home from a shower, with strippers and all."

Billy guffawed. "Oh, I'd say you enjoyed that, Katie?"

"Well, it was a bit embarassin' in front of a throng of women screamin' the house down." Kaye scanned the bar for Bren. "Anyhow, any sign of you getting married?"

"Not at all, although I'll probably have to get the skates on soon. The quare one is puttin' pressure on me. How about yerself?"

"Nah, it's hard to find one around here." She sighed.

"Well, ya must be very fussy. Sure, isn't this place packed with them?"

It was. Like every other bar in the Brohx, every night of the week.

"Mother's milk." Bren came towards them, raising his glass of Guinness, licking the creamy froth from his lips. "Can't beat it."

"Ya got that right." Billy lifted his hand for a high five, and Bren met it slap on, as if he'd been doing it all his life. "And this is one of the best places in the Bronx for it," Billy continued. "Not as good as home, mind you." He indicated to the barman for two more. "They say the further you get from the brewery, the worse the Guinness is. But this," he raised his glass, "is not bad. One good thing to come out of Dublin." He threw his head back.

"What about the wimen?" Chrissie poked him in the side, inclining her head at Kaye.

"Oh, there's nothin' wrong with the wimen neither." Billy shook laughing. "Sure we were all dyin' for a Dublin woman."

"I'll drink to that." Bren, on tiptoes, draped his arm around Billy.

"Kaye had all the lads in Kilcoughlan gone mad when she came down on her holliers. They'd be queuing up at the carnival to dance with her." Billy pointed his glass at her.

"I'd well believe it." Bren's wink turned into a blink and ended up with his two eyes twisted into his nose.

"I must go down the country, so," Mo said with her usual sarcastic edge.

"Yeah, you should." Kaye put a finger on her chin. "Or don't you have enough men?"

"I used to be mad jealous." Chrissie nestled into her.

"Yeah, right." Kaye pushed her away.

They stayed there until Bren got his fill of Guinness and it was he who suggested going back to the Terminal for the last one. Kaye smiled. Everyone soon caught on that a night out in the Bronx wasn't right without ending it in the Terminal: the last port of call.

"So, have ya shifted here?" Billy hugged her goodnight.

"Ah, the odd one here and there," she said. "I'm saving myself for someone at home."

"Lucky lad." Billy sauntered away.

One morning, her lips refused to cooperate when she tried to apply lipstick in the cloakroom. Oh, no, please don't let it be. As the day wore on, her words were starting to jumble. Oh, no, it couldn't be, could it? Not now when everything was going according to plan. There was nothing she could do until the school day ended. By then, her eyes had started to blur.

"What's wrong with your eye?" Bren asked when she walked into 4D that evening.

And then, she knew.

"Facial paralysis," she screamed. "Facial paralysis."

"Facial wha'?" Bren's mouth remained open.

"She had it before." Chrissie frowned. "I remember."

"Bell's Palsy, Bell's Palsy," Kaye ran around the room, holding onto her face.

"What are ya talkin' about?" Bren grabbed her shoulders.

"I have to get a doctor, a doctor." Kaye fled to the phone.

"Wait 'til Mo comes home," said Chrissie. "She'll know what to do."

But there was no time to wait. Kaye rang Izzy to make an appointment with Doctor Fingers, and then Andy for a cab.

Chrissie guided her downstairs and into the car. Bren leapt in beside her. Soap powder wafted up from the basement, as they pulled away, leaving Chrissie at the kerb. For the whole journey, Kaye lay back in the seat while Bren chatted to Andy, who eyed her through the mirror, as he overtook, and swerved in and out of traffic.

"Please hurry, please hurry." She implored him. "I'll have to go home," she cried. "Get electric shock treatment."

It was all coming back. The thrice-weekly trips into Doctor Steeven's Hospital in Dublin. Her jaws twitching for hours afterwards. Getting off school and a 99-ice cream in Woolworths. Olivia coming up to the house one night with her Ma's make-up bag, showing Kaye how to use pan stick foundation, blue eye shadow; how to move her eyes up and down, as she applied mascara and eyeliner. "You look lovely," she had said standing back to admire her, never mentioning the one eye bigger than the other, the lips curving onto her left cheek.

"Are you a nurse?" Dr. Fingers prodded her face.

"No." Kaye was perched on a bed, holding a nurse's hand. "I had it before."

"Smart lady," he said. "For coming so soon. And don't worry, there'll be no electrodes in your face this time. It's America, it's the eighties and we've a miracle cure."

"Steroids?" Kaye studied the prescription.

"I heard tell of them for pumping muscle," Bren said. "But other than that?"

On the way home, Kaye slumped back in the seat again, Bren's arm draped over her. Andy, who'd insisted on waiting, still peering at her through his mirror.

"Steroids cure lots of things." Mo told her later. "But there are side effects."

"Like what?"

"Well," Mo took her time. "There's weight gain, facial hair, a moon face."

"Ah, Jaysus! A MOON FACE? As if it's not round enough!"

The others tittered nervously.

"Holy water from the Shrine of St. Philomena of the Bronx," said Izzy arriving in with a small, glass bottle, with a blue cap. "The patron saint of faces."

"Can ya get me some too?" Chrissie wanted to know.

"Or you could do this nine-day novena to St. Jude for hopeless cases." Izzy produced a crumpled prayer card from her jeans pocket. "Your request will come true on the ninth day."

"Could we do it to win the Lotto?" Chrissie grabbed it out of her hand.

Kaye slipped into bed and tucked the blue plaid comforter under her chin.

"Well, it won't be hopeless anymore, if St. Jude gets at it." Izzy insisted.

"I don't believe in that stuff," said Mo. "Just take your medication and you'll be grand."

"I will." Kaye looked at their concerned faces, as they eased out of the room mumbling about tea and her needing to rest and seeing her in a while.

She phoned Sister Virginia the next morning, told her "I won't be in today. I'm sick."

"And what is wrong with you now?" The nun sighed.

"I have Bell's Palsy." Kaye replied. "And my class plans are in my desk drawer."

"God bless you." The phone clicked and Kaye lay back in bed.

Bren brought her tea and toast, coaxed her for walks through Van Cortlandt woods, encouraged her facial stretching exercises, doused her cheeks with Izzy's holy water.

"You'd make a great nurse," Kaye told him.

"A night nurse, that's what I'd be good at, Katie, night nursin'."

Kaye couldn't help laughing, despite her crooked mouth.

With sunglasses to protect her weeping eye, and the fuchsia dress loose on her hips, she set off for Izzy and Tim's wedding. Bridesmaids strutted up the aisle in daffodil yellow, followed by the bride in ivory silk, hair smooth and shiny, teeth porcelain, eyes two pools of sparkling jade. Chrissie had been warned to stay away from the altar when Tim was saying 'I do.' But once outside the church, she whispered. "I hope you get lucky tonight." Izzy shot her a look.

At the reception, the band started before the meal and the girls didn't know whether to dance or wait for food. Kaye got heartburn from all the free champagne. The line for the loo was miles long, despite two, even three girls sometimes using the same cubicle. Kaye could never understand women who piled into a toilet and peed in front of one another.

"Oh, I'd say they're at more than that." Bren waltzed her around the floor.

"What d'ya mean?" She ducked in and out of his twirling arm.

"They're not powdering their noses. They're puttin' the powder up their noses."

"Nah, Americans, maybe, but not the Irish. Definitely not the Irish."

CHAPTER TWENTY-SIX

O n his last day, Bren and Kaye stopped into the Terminal for a Bellybutton.

"Two fuzzy navels," she said to Nick, trying not to smile, to keep her lips straight.

"I hear you haven't been well." He sounded concerned. "But you must be better because you look great." He added, pouring the shots.

"Thank you," she said. "Yeah, not too bad now."

"He has all the lines." Bren whispered, as soon as Nick was out of range. "He should bottle them. Bottle them. And then, we could sell them and make a few bob."

"You don't think he means it?"

"I don't know." Bren downed his drink. "I can't make him out." He banged his glass, then shouted up at Nick, "I'll have another one for the ditch."

"Coming right up."

Nick was back pouring again.

"How about you, Katherine?"

"Sure I might as well."

Bren clinked her glass. "Ya know what, Katie?"

"What?"

He leaned into her, a whiff of peachy schnapps on his breath. "You know I always liked ya, didn't ya Katie?"

"Ah, Bren." She put her head on his shoulder. "You know I like you too. You're a nice guy, a good friend, always been there for me. You're too nice really, but you know." She lifted her head, glanced down the bar. "You know I like Liam. You and I can only be friends."

Like what Liam had said.

Bren paused, then vaulted off his stool. "Too nice. Nice." He looked at Nick. "That's all I ever hear, I'm too nice." He made for the men's bathroom.

"I hear ya, man." Nick pointed a finger after him. "I hear ya."

Yeah, right.

"What's up with Romeo?" Nick asked her.

"Nothin'." She fiddled with the stem of her glass. "Doesn't want to go home, that's all."

"Like the rest of us."

"Not me. I can't wait to get back."

"Are you gonna miss *him?*" He tilted his head at the restrooms.

"I am, actually."

"Come for a walk with me after he's gone, I'll be finished soon."

A walk?

"OK."

"I'd better head," Bren said when he returned, swinging his suitcase over his shoulder.

He held out his hand to Nick. "Thanks a million, man; you're a legend."

"You're welcome. Come back and see us again sometime."

"Oh, I will. Tell Pete I said goodbye."

Bren took Kaye's elbow and veered her out the door towards Andy's Oldsmobile, where he flung his case into the boot. Then, before she even knew what was happening, he pressed his lips against her slightly out-of-sync ones in a long, slow kiss. Then rested them on her neck and squeezed her with both arms.

"I've wanted to do that for years." He whispered.

As she steadied herself against the bin where Mo had heaved up her breakfast, peak-time passengers rushed down the subway steps, and taxi drivers hollered above the screech of Beeline buses. A thumbprint of moon smudged the sky over Van Cortlandt Park. Why had Bren done that after she telling him she just wanted to be friends? Kaye was confused, but it had been such a nice kiss, with so much feeling in it, Kaye was surprised.

All this time, Andy had been waiting with the car door open.

Rolling down his window, Bren said, "Why don't you just come home?"

"I will."

She stood on the sidewalk watching the cab disappear amid a confusion of smoke and exhaust fumes into the merging traffic. Then turned around and came face to face with Nick. Denim jacket slung over his shoulder; he was slouched against the rail of the subway stairs.

"That was some smackeroo." He raised an eyebrow.

"Em, yeah."

"You need some fresh air after that." He crooked his elbow for her hand. "Let's take a stroll."

A stroll? That's what Liam used to call it.

The air was warm, the grass crunchy, the park enormous ahead of them. A giant turtle on stone steps marked the entrance.

"They represent new beginnings." Nick told her.

"How apt," she said.

It was easier to talk, walking along, watching the baseball, cricket and soccer games that were taking place; as music blared from the picnic areas; admiring the dogs in the canine playground, while every now and then, Nick greeted someone.

"It all seems to be working out," he said. "Good for you, Katherine, you deserve it."

"I do?"

"Sure, you're good people."

People, not person. Another American expression she liked. She always knew there was more than one of her in there.

"So, what's next?" he asked her.

"I dunno," she shrugged. "I'm here until Christmas. Then we'll see what happens."

"Sounds like you want something to happen?"

"Not really," she lied.

The Pinewood, a small pub beside the Terminal, was more suited for a quiet drink and a chat. She'd been longing to sit at a bar with a man and there she was with her second one on the same day. And both of them had kissed her with feeling.

She exhaled rings of smoke into the dusty atmosphere, discretely pressing her lips together to see if they were still slightly out of line. A man on a galloping horse wouldn't notice, Dr. Fingers had said, and had promised they would improve even more. Her face was still puffed from the steroids but should soon be back to normal. At least, she could kiss. She'd been kissed by one man and was having a drink with another. Something different, Mo had said. And Chrissie's theory had been tested.

"So what thoughts are tangled inside that pretty head of yours now?" Nick waved his hand in front of her face.

Billy had told her once to pretend she didn't think as much as she did; to pretend that she didn't remember as much. It unnerved men, he said, made them feel uneasy. 'So what?' Chrissie had scoffed, well able to play the game. For it was a game, Billy said. A game Kaye had never learnt how to play.

"Are they about your guy at home?" He took his eyes off of her for a second, as he swigged his beer.

She'd forgotten about that, forgotten she'd told him Liam was her boyfriend.

"Em, ah, yeah, sometimes." She took a sip of her vodka and lime, a gimlet it was called. She loved all the different names for the drinks here; it made them seem more exotic.

"Actually," she said, "he's not really my guy. But I'd like him to be."

"Oh, I thought you two were an item?"

"No, no, what made you think that?"

"Well you said … oh it doesn't matter … I thought." Nick held up his empty bottle to the bartender. "I must've picked you up wrong. And what about him, how does he feel?"

Outside the window, the evening dimmed, and headlights beamed on Broadway, the moon no longer a blotch, but a bright copper penny pulsating.

"I don't know," was all she could say to Nick's reflection in the mirror behind the bar.

According to Olivia, Liam had been in therapy since January, sitting in a chair, not a couch, talking to a woman, not a man, for a whole hour every week; a box of tissues on her desk and a timer ticking out the minutes. Kaye would love someone listening to her like that, she said, uninterrupted. As she spoke, Nick never took his eyes off her, nodding at appropriate places.

"I think it's time to let him go," he said when she had finished.

She sighed. "Everyone is telling me I have to change."

"You don't need to change, your thinking does." He tapped his forehead. "Replace negative thoughts with positive ones."

"Does it work?"

"Worked for me." He rested his hand on the counter, blue veins snaking through it, the nails clipped square, and clean.

Should she just get off with him again? Chrissie and Olivia would. Mo too.

"So, anyhow," she said. "I'm hearing all these rumours."

He straightened up. "What rumours?"

"Well, I keep hearing that there's something you're hiding, but nobody will tell me what it is." The vodka was talking now. She had lost track of how many she'd had. Lost track of the time. Still, she ploughed ahead.

"Hiding?" He squeezed his forehead. "I'm not hiding anything."

"Well, aren't you married?"

"Married? Oh yeah, I was, years ago, to a girl from Guatemala."

"Guatemala?" She fumbled for another cigarette, lit this one herself.

"And we have a daughter."

"A daughter? Are you … are you still with them? Your wife and child?" The words sounded strange.

"She upped and left before the kid was a year old. Went back home."

"And are you in touch with them?" She didn't know whether to believe him or not.

"No."

"Why not?"

"Last time I went there, her brother met me at the airport, said to leave them alone."

"That's terrible."

"Maybe they were afraid I'd kidnap the girl."

"Kidnap? Why would you do that?"

"People do it all the time here. Parents take their children from one another."

"They do?" Kaye had never heard the likes of it.

"Yeah, you see their pictures on the backs of milk cartons every morning."

"You do?" What a strange place to put pictures. "Still," she said. "You should keep in touch with the girl, send her birthday and Christmas cards."

He winced. "Her Mom wouldn't show them to her."

"You don't' know that. And then, when she's older, she'll know you cared."

"Maybe," he shrugged. "But I'm not about to do anything anytime soon. Unless I get a divorce."

"You're not divorced? Why not?" Kaye was finding this harder to believe.

"Never got around to it," he shrugged. "Didn't seem much point, paying those lawyers thousands of dollars, and if I'm not going to get married again, what's the point?"

"I suppose."

Melissa was right. You never knew what people were going through. *There's no art to find the mind's construction in the face.* Duncan said to Macbeth.

She badly wanted to give Nick a hug.

"Let's go get some breakfast." He tossed a wad of notes on the counter, slid off the stool and placed his jacket over her shoulders.

"Don't flit from one to another, like me," he said, as he opened the door for her. "Don't build a fence around your heart, like I did."

A fence? The other one had a wall; this one had a fence.

"You're too nice, Katherine," he added, as he slotted his fingers into hers. "Too nice for a one-night stand."

Too nice? Now she knew how Bren felt. It was a compliment of sorts but being nice never got her anywhere either.

They sat at the counter in the Short Stop and ordered eggs over medium, crispy bacon, buttered toast, and coffee to keep her awake, for she'd have to go straight to school. She'd been so good up to this: going to bed early, not drinking much, ready to leap out of bed every morning as soon as the alarm went off.

Maybe she'd call in sick?

"Nah, don't be like the rest of the Paddies over here," Nick told her. "Don't take a day off because of drink."

The sun was rising in streaks of pink across the sky. They'd been talking for an astonishing nine hours, which must be a record, as he wasn't the talkative type. They finished their food, wiped their mouths, and slid off the Formica stools, Nick throwing another roll of bills on the counter.

"As for that girl, what's her name? Olivia?"

"Yeah?"

"Sounds like she's been competing with you all along."

"Really?"

"Yes. Sounds like she might like that guy too." He slotted his fingers through hers again and led her out the door.

"You no go home yet, Mama?" Andy had one foot propped against the diner wall.

Olivia competing with her?

"No Andy, I'm going straight to school."

"Watch this guy." His voice was cold, like ice.

"I'm watching him." Kaye stopped at the bottom of the subway steps, turned to Nick. "Olivia is practical, down to earth. She'd have no time for someone like Liam, someone with problems."

"You never know." He shrugged. "Girls like her like to think they can change people."

"But would that be worth losing a friendship over?"

"For some women, yeah. They're not all like you, K for Katherine, Katherine Hepburn." He pulled her towards him.

She raised her eyes to meet his.

He came closer, so close their lips were almost touching.

Kaye ducked. "You're still married, remember?"

"You're right." He straightened up. "I'll talk to ya, K for Katherine." He walked away.

"Just call me Kaye."

CHAPTER TWENTY-SEVEN

The school bell rang, as she hurried along the hall thinking up words for typewriting, and problems for the calculators.

"She's got the same skirt on," one of the girls whispered, as Kaye sat at her desk and began homeroom. Oh God! Her head throbbing, she called out the roll, her voice hoarse, as the names reverberated in her ears.

"Jackie, Juan, Marisol, Melanie, Sean." She ticked them off. "Tara, Tameka, Tawana, Tanya ..." she croaked. "Ty-rone, Ty-rell, Victor, William ..."

After wading through the list, she put down her pen and rested her head in her arms.

"Are you all right, Miss?" asked a concerned voice from the front row.

"I'm fine, Annabelle." She raised her head only to flinch at the pain.

"You look like you didn't sleep last night, Miss." Another voiced piped up.

"Of course, she slept." There was a chorus now. "Leave her alone. Leave Miss alone."

"Do you miss your family? Is that it?" Annabelle persisted.

"Yes," she kept her voice low and sad. "I miss them very much. I'm so homesick."

"Poor Miss."

"That's why she looks tired."

"We love you, Miss."

"You're our hero."

The great thing about keyboarding was that they could type and type, as she sat still, without moving facial muscles or any part of her that might transmit pain to her brain. She snoozed through lunch duty in the cafeteria, the smell of sloppy joes turning her stomach. No one at home would eat messy mincemeat in gravy, on a white roll. Hip-hop and rap music blared, and the students danced. When they were walking, they were dancing; when they were sitting down they were dancing; when they were eating, they were singing, and dancing.

The racket drew the attention of other teachers passing by, but when they saw Kaye hunched over a table in the corner, they waved and walked away.

There was a murmur of sympathy for her in the faculty room. Perhaps it was the effects of the steroids or the aftermath of her Palsy her colleagues suggested. She accepted their concern with a smile, hoping not to alter her expression too much, in case the effort paralysed her face again.

When Mister Al teased her about Dublin applying for European City of Culture with - "Are they opening another pub?" she managed to force a smile, even if she was not in the mood for his shite today.

Finally, she made it to the last class armed with calculations. The plan was that they would solve them while she daydreamed about bed.

That was the plan until, just as she sank into her chair, Virginia slipped in and sat at one of the vacant student desks.

Kaye sprung upright, pain slicing her head. What the hell is she frigging doing? Another class observation? Was she mad? Kaye scrawled the class objective across the chalk board, not knowing where it came from only that ESTIMATES appeared in bold white letters. She checked the homework and revised what had been covered the day before. Introduced the topic and proceeded to give a short lecture on the efficiency of calculating how much something is going to cost before being presented with a bill. She demonstrated solving the problems listed on the handouts, and asked the students to try their own, all the while cruising the aisles.

Goal, instruction, demonstration, follow-through were taken care of. Questions encouraged, which the students posed, and which she answered with aplomb, applying the solution to their own experience, and initiated a class discussion on the advantages of estimating while on a personal shopping trip. Keeping an eye on the clock, she made sure she had enough time at the end to give out a homework sheet, which pertained to the lesson.

When the bell struck, she thought she'd collapse from exhaustion and anxiety. But her pain had subsided, and she could've kissed every Tameka and Ty-rell. She'd nailed it, she thought to herself, as she watched Virginia gather her papers and leave the room.

Outside the nun's office, Kaye wiped her forehead with the back of one hand, her other hand clutching her folders to her chest. Sweat bubbled under her arms; rivulets streamed down the small of her back. Holding her now pain free head high with a confidence she did not feel, she popped it around the Sister's door. "Was that Ok?"

"Perfect." The nun smiled.

Perfect? Everything was perfect.

She slid underneath her comforter, and the flannel fabric was indeed a comfort; 'comforter' a far better word than 'duvet.' What other American words had she picked up without noticing? Events of the previous twenty-four hours bounced around in her brain, but she was snug now in the safety and warmth of 4D, wallowing in its cosiness. Popping a Reba McEntire tape into the cassette deck beside her bed, she chewed over everything from Bren's kiss to Olivia being in competition with her; from Nick's wife to Virginia telling her she was perfect.

Olivia, competitive? Maybe. She often repeated Kaye's opinions, as if they were her own. There was that velvet jacket she'd bought, exactly like one Kaye had. Kaye hadn't said a word, just made sure they never wore them at the same time.

Then there was the night she'd entertained Billy in Peekers, where he'd turned up after an All-Ireland, looking for Chrissie.

"She was chompin' at the bit," he said. "I could've climbed up on her there and then."

"You're so full of yourself," Kaye had scoffed. "Anyhow, she doesn't like culchies."

"Well, she seemed to like this one." Billy had punched his chest.

Reba was singing about looking for a new love story, when Chrissie clattered into the room discarding bag, boots, keys, and an apron full of dollar bills onto the floor.

"Sorry." She plopped on top of Kaye. "I know you hate this, but I'm exhausted from smiling all day."

"How would ya like scowlin' at young ones, and licking a decrepit old nun's arse?"

"Why are ya playin' this slit-your-wrist music? Have ya nothin' cheerful?"

"Bren kissed me."

"Well, it's about time."

"And I had a drink with Nick."

"Yeah?"

Kaye couldn't gauge how Chrissie felt about that.

"And the Virgin told me I was perfect," she said.

"About time for that too. So, what had the bold Nick to say for himself?"

"Nothin'." Kaye couldn't repeat Nick's story, in case it wasn't true, in case he was having her on. And if it were true, she couldn't betray his confidence.

Chrissie clapped her hands in front of Kaye's face.

"Get up and we'll go to Doubleday's, plan our Christmas party, and discuss how I'm gonna tell Sil I don't want to be his girlfriend."

"Oh yeah? What brought that on?"

"Nothin'." Chrissie spring up off the bed. "Just time to move on, that's all, which I keep tellin' you to do. How about Bren, he's always been there for you?"

"Like I said before." Kaye was now talking to her retreating back. "I don't feel anything for him."

She closed her eyes. If Nick was a bit of a lad, wouldn't he at least want a one-night stand with her, if that's what he did with everyone else? Why wasn't he coming onto her? Was she that unattractive? No, think positive.

As for Olivia competing? The together one; who had all the answers; the one who knew what she wanted and where she was going; who didn't change her mind every day.

The one with confidence, especially where men were concerned. Small and petite, yet self-assured, never bothering with style, make-up, jewellery, who would have scoffed at *Color Me Beautiful*. Why would she compete with anyone?

"ARE YA RIGHT?" Chrissie yelled down the hallway.

Kaye put on a pair of high-waisted, loose-fitting jeans and a sweatshirt; smeared gloss on her lips and ruffled her hair. At home, it took ages to get ready. It was another reason she liked being anonymous here. Another reason, next time she had to explain.

Keys, perfume, money, bag. Chrissie held the door open; Reba McIntyre was still looking for a new love story. Kaye slammed it shut.

Me too, Reba, me too.

CHAPTER TWENTY-EIGHT

'I made it!' Kaye exclaimed, when Lou opened the door. "In six months, I've managed to find my way around two American cities."

"Like a native," Lou said. "It's so great to have you, finally, for Thanksgiving." She cupped Kaye's chin in her hand. "You'd never notice a thing," she said. "We have St. Jude to thank, all the prayers I said and the candles I lit."

Izzy thought it was St. Philomena of the Bronx they had to be grateful for. Kaye's mother gave credit to Padre Pio. Kaye didn't care which of them it was, as long as the job was done. She wolfed down a roast beef sandwich Lou had quickly fixed for her and over they went to Doyle's Tavern.

"Tradition!" Lou explained.

Matt could not break tradition and had been there since he'd clocked off work.

"Bartender," he roared when they walked in. "Give these young ladies a drink."

It was the first time Kaye had seen him tipsy. She ordered a vodka and club soda with lots of ice and lime and dumped the straw the minute it was placed in front of her. She'd been off the beer since Bren left, and had shed more pounds - thanks to that, three afternoons a week in *Living Well Lady* and not having to take anymore steroids. She'd also made an appointment with *Color Me Beautiful*.

"You look amazing; doesn't she look amazing, hon? My wife's niece from Ireland everybody," he announced, and his buddies smiled. "Well, I should say New York, that right?" Kaye nodded. "A high school teacher." He beamed.

Kaye kept smiling, slowly sipping her drink.

When Matt sang *Danny Boy,* she wasn't mortified like the first time, but delighted to be there, among people who made her feel special and loved. The night continued, full of fun and craic. No philosophical chats or nuggets of advice or analysis, for which Kaye was glad. Everybody wished them Happy Thanksgiving, before they stepped into the crisp cold air and helped one another home.

Matt looked sheepish the next morning, but still managed to cook them all breakfast and to scoff a whole plate of the rashers and sausages Kaye had bought from the Irish Butcher in Woodlawn. There had been a queue snaking its way along Katonah Avenue to the shop the day before.

They watched the Macy's parade on TV with Anna and Matthew Jr. and a longing for Fifth Avenue nagged at her. How she missed working in Manhattan. Lou prepared dinner, which didn't take that long. Young Matthew had been right about the cans, but Kaye thought it was delicious and Lou chortled at the compliments. After dessert, everyone had to say what they were thankful for. Matt was grateful for his beautiful bride and for this great country of America and his two marvellous American children. Lou thanked the Lord for having a family member with them for the holiday, which Anna seconded; Matthew Jr. gave thanks in advance for Notre Dame winning the football game.

"And Katherine, how about you?" Matt's Irish coffee was still raised in anticipation.

"Well, I'm thankful your hangover got better." There was an uproar of laughter from Anna and Matthew. "I'm thankful you were in a fit condition to cook us that scrumptious breakfast I brought." Matt blushed. "I'm thankful in anticipation of tomorrow's retail therapy." Lou chuckled. "And I'm thankful I have family here to spend this wonderful American holiday with." They all clapped their hands. "More than anything," she concluded, "I'm thankful for the past five months and will carry it all home in my heart."

Kaye and Lou spent the afternoon watching *Lullaby of Broadway* while the rest of them roared and screamed at an American football game on the upstairs television. How Kaye would've loved two TVs at home. All the years she'd had to endure Sunday hurling and football matches, before she became interested in the live variety; Saturday afternoon soccer; rugby, in season; the Horse Show; Wimbledon and the World Cup; Match of the Day on a Saturday night instead of Michael Parkinson's talk show. She would sit at the window willing one of the neighbours to come and ask her to babysit.

"I saw this in the Metropole," Lou sighed. "With a lad from Westmeath. He bought me a box of *Milk Tray* chocolates and I was too embarrassed to eat them in front of my friends."

The two of them couldn't get the lullaby out of their heads for the rest of the night, and every now and then, they burst into a chorus. It was no wonder Lou had had romantic notions of America, when all she'd known of it was from the movies - streets lit up in neon, the clothes, the songs, the glamour. Not a sign of North Broadway or the South Bronx or Kingsbridge Avenue or Fordham Road or all of the places Kaye saw every day on the Number 4 train. Nothing about the hard work and long hours in bars and restaurants and on building sites with no sick days or holidays or lunch breaks or elevenses; the only reward the almighty dollar.

The Food Court was jammed, with shopping bags piled on chairs, in the aisles, under the tables. Kaye finally got to try the famous Philly Steak Sandwich.

The whole city of Philadelphia must have converged on the Gallery Mall for Black Friday, the biggest shopping day in America. 'Fifty percent off,' sales assistants continuously chanted with a smile, even though their feet must have been aching.

As *Jingle Bells* rang out around them, Kaye's tummy fluttered.

"I can't believe I'm going home soon." Her mouth was full of salty meat and crispy fried onions and cheese and gravy and spongy bread roll.

"You're so lucky." Lou sighed. "In the thirty years I've done here, I only made it home for one Christmas, and that was the year my father died. So, it wasn't happy, after all."

Kaye smiled at Lou's choice of words. She'd 'done' thirty years, like she was in jail.

"I felt guilty for all the time I'd missed with him," Lou continued. "For depriving him of his grandchildren. I blamed myself terrible for that. Imagine if Anna and Matthew left me and didn't come back for years? It would be heart-breaking. Yet that's what I did to Daddy." She picked at some French fries.

Kaye kept chewing, her eyes on the sandwich.

"It's different now," Lou continued. "People get home more often.

When the kids came along, we didn't have the money, or they were too young to travel. Then there was school and stuff. Their lives are here, you can't uproot them. But I should've done. After all, he was only in his fifties when I left, the same age I am now. We thought he was an old man. But he wasn't, he was still young. Too young to be a widower. Too young to be left alone."

If Lou didn't stop, Kaye would be bawling. She was glad now she'd splashed out on a nice suit for Mam and a lovely leather jacket for Dad. He'd been dying for one, but thought he was too old. He'd be the trendiest dad on Seafield Green. He'd taken early retirement, it seemed, instead of redundancy, and had received a lump sum. Kaye had conjured up this image of a massive, big lump of money. She was going to be nicer to him, from now on. Trish had said it was her fault they didn't get along, and maybe it was.

"C'mon." She rubbed her hands. "Let's get back to the shops and all those bargains." She stuck out her tongue and licked her now perfect lips, until she had Lou in fits of laughter.

That evening, Anna and Matthew ordered Chinese take-outs. Kaye couldn't believe it and the fridge full of food. Matt went to bed early, without eating anything. Kaye made herself a turkey sandwich with cranberry sauce and stuffing, and packed whatever was left into a Tupperware container to eat on the train the following day. She'd love to have stayed until Sunday, but she had to correct tests and plan classes and sort out the end-of-term exams.

After their 'lap dinner,' they settled in for another round of Doris Day - *Pillow Talk* in which Doris played a girl called Kate.

"You could be called after her," Lou said. "Your Dad loved Doris Day."

"I thought it was Katherine Hepburn?"

"Her too."

"And he shortened it to Katie, because his favourite song was *Come down from the Mountain, Katie Daly?*"

"Well, he did have a girlfriend called Katie."

"He did?" Kaye couldn't imagine her father with any other woman than Mam.

"Yes, she was from Athlone. Took off to Australia. Never heard how she got on."

"Jeez!"

Kaye had never heard a mention of her.

"People here assume that Kaye is short for Kathleen."

"Don't mind them," Lou tut-tutted. "They think we live in cottages with pigs in the parlour." She started singing, *All I Do is Dream of You* along with Doris.

"That's me," Kaye said. "All I do all day long is dream about Liam."

"Still?"

"Yeah? So?"

"Nothing. Oh there's Rock Hudson, he's so handsome." Lou sighed. "Matt used to look like him."

"Really?" said Kaye. "Poor Rock, having to hide his real self."

"Oh, I don't believe all that stuff." Lou flapped her hand again.

"You don't? But he died from AIDS; it's a fact. He was homosexual."

"There was none of that in our day." Lou tut-tutted. "He doesn't even look it. Nah, I bet he got it from a blood transfusion."

"Are you serious?" Kaye looked at her, eyes wide open.

"Yes," said Lou.

"When Olivia and I were in Greece," Kaye told her. "We met these guys from England who were gay. We had great gas with them. One was actually Irish, and he had curly hair too. Was always asking me what conditioner I used. They were lovely."

"Maybe they were." Lou sighed. "But Rock Hudson wasn't like that, isn't it obvious?"

"I suppose." Kaye had to agree. Rock Hudson didn't look at all like the lads in Mykonos, in their mauve dungarees and pink shirts.

She left the next morning amid a flutter of goodbyes and promises to come again soon. "Next time it's your turn." She told Lou. "Come up for our Christmas party."

As the New Jersey billboards flashed by the window, she thought of the last time she had sat on this train, and what had occupied her then, and all that had happened since. And she was glad.

Glad she'd given it a go.

CHAPTER TWENTY-NINE

"The snow gets really bad here."

Mo's backside was all they could see: the rest of her was dangling out the living room window.

"You'll have to get snow boots," she said to Kaye.

"Are ya mad?" Kaye elbowed her aside. Powdery flakes fell on her head like a veil, as she marvelled at the white carpet below. "Me suede ones from Dunne's Stores will be grand."

Chrissie squeezed her way in between them. "I just want an excuse to go shopping."

"It's beautiful now." The flakes melted into Mo's outstretched hands. "But wait 'til it starts mounting up."

"Oh! God, I'll have to ring Mel and cancel tomorrow." Kaye banged her head off the window, yelped.

On the phone, Melissa chuckled. "You kiddin' me? They'll have it cleared by then. Get yourself a good pair of snow boots for the slush."

"Oh! OK."

"See," said Mo. "I was right."

"I know the snow Melissa likes," said Chrissie. "Ask her to bring some to the party."

"Wha'? Snow?"

"Don't listen to Chris. The last thing we need at our party is cocaine."

"Cocaine?" Now, Kaye was totally confused. "No way. We're bad enough without that." Kaye couldn't believe it. "What has gotten into you."

She waited for Chrissie to laugh; to say she was only joking.

"It's great for giving you energy; has ya goin' mad on the dance floor," Chrissie said.

"You don't like dancing."

"So? And as for sex." Chrissie shook her head.

"What about it?"

"They say you can go all night on the stuff."

"Why would you want to do that?"

"Just ask her," said Chrissie. "The Melissa one, ask her about it."

"There's something I might need you to ask her too," Mo said.

"What's that?" Kaye asked, as Mo left the living-room.

Kaye woke to someone sobbing. Her clock told her it was not yet midnight. She sat up, cocked her ear at the window. Then came the sound of footsteps in the hallway. A door banged. Muffled voices. Sobs. She had only six hours sleep left. But the crying continued. She crept down to the bathroom and put her ear to the door.

"What am I going to do?" It was Mo, pleading. "What am I going to do?"

Kaye edged open the door. Mo was sitting on the toilet, moaning, and moving back and forth, clutching her tummy. A pink box lay on the floor, Chrissie waving a white thermometer thing like a wand.

"Are you sick?" Kaye picked up the pink box with FIRST RESPONSE written on it.

"Well, she is now," said Chrissie.

"What's wrong?" Kaye noticed 'pregnancy test' on the box. "Jesus, what's goin' on?"

"It's blue." Mo wailed, her whole body shaking. "It's blue, blue."

Kaye gave Chrissie a questioning look. "What on earth is she talkin' about?"

"It's blue." Chrissie waggled the stick. "That means it's positive."

"What's positive?" Kaye still couldn't take it all in.

"The test, ya gobshite," said Chrissie. "She's pregnant, for feck's sake."

"But ... but." Kaye looked at Mo, who looked away. "I thought you didn't?"

"Well, she did once," said Chrissie.

The three of them crept down the hall. Kaye made for the kitchen, filled the kettle, and turned on the gas. The blue glow flickered. She made three mugs of tea, then hooked two with the first fingers of one hand, grabbed the third mug and a packet of Marlboro with the other. Then thought better of the cigarettes – wasn't there talk of them being bad for expectant mothers? She put them down and snatched a packet of biscuits instead. Then again, the sugar wouldn't be good either. She left them down. Took them up again and the cigarettes as well. Let them decide. She hadn't a clue.

"So," she said to Mo. "What are you going to do?"

"Well, she can't keep it," Chrissie cried. "And ruin her life?"

"I can't." Mo was whimpering now, still rocking back and forth. "I can't bring up a child by myself over here. And there's no way I could arrive home with it. So."

"You don't mean …?"

"I don't have a choice!"

"And what does Seanie think?"

"He doesn't know. And I won't be telling him."

"Sure, what he doesn't know won't hurt him," said Chrissie. "And don't worry, Mo, whatever you decide, we'll be right there with you." She looked at Kaye. "Won't we?"

"Sure," Kaye said, even though she wasn't at all sure.

The three of them sat on the settee, hugging their mugs, staring into space, watching the snow fall outside the window, their gaze fixed on how the streetlights illuminated the milky white rooftops against a silvery sky.

Then Kaye leapt to her feet. "Jesus! I'd better get back to bed."

"Will you ask your friend Melissa how I'd go about it?" Mo's eyes were swollen.

"Yeah," she said. "Of course, I will."

"You're lucky, Kaye, d'ya know that?" Mo's eyes were sad.

"Yeah, I know."

She headed down to Burger Heaven, as soon as the school day was over, looking forward to a *Roquefort* blue cheeseburger with fried onions.

"Bernice didn't show up." George flicked menus into her face, his necktie askew and the strand of hair that covered his bald spot flopping into his eyes. "Any chance you could jump in behind the counter for a bit? We're gonna be mobbed with tree-watchers."

"Who's Bernice?" She had to tie the apron strings twice around her waist.

"Oh Bernice, Bernard, what the hell do I know …" George trailed away, muttering.

Kaye looked at Mo, who was gaunt around the eyes. "Bernard is now Bernice?"

"You got it girl." Tina handed her a rag to wipe the tables.

"You're a pisser," said Violet. She and Rose kept howling and slapping her on the back. "You, a teacher! That's the funniest thing we've ever heard."

Kaye grinned back at them.

By the time Melissa swaggered in, an hour late, she'd made twenty bucks. "God bless America," she said.

"You're a pisser." Melissa stuck a cigarette between her lips.

"So I've been told." Kaye untied her apron. "If Bren could hear me now!"

After burgers and a mountain of fries, they strolled along Lexington to 49th, Melissa's arm casually draped around Kaye's shoulder. As they walked, Melissa gabbled on about the seventy-foot-high tree, how it was the biggest in the world. It felt like cold pins were pricking Kaye's face. She wondered what the wind chill factor was: something she'd never wondered before, just as in the summer, she'd wondered about the humidity. In Ireland, it was only ever raining, or not. Scattered showers, in between sunny spells, and clouds.

As they neared St. Patrick's Cathedral, the crowd thickened. At the Rockefeller Center, they had to jostle their way towards the ice rink.

"It's tiny!" Kaye gaped up at the tree.

"Are you kiddin' me?" Melissa flung her head back. "It's awesome."

"Well, it doesn't look seventy feet, that's for sure." Kaye regarded the tops of buildings nuzzling the snow-white sky. "Compared to everything else around here, it's tiny."

"You Irish are never happy." Melissa looped her arm. "C'mon, are we gonna skate?"

"No way. Could you imagine Sister Virgin's face if I broke me ankle?"

"Bad girl," Melissa tapped Kaye's wrist. "Give the sista her full name." She took Kaye's hand. "Ok, no skating? Then, let's go get some beers."

"OK." Kaye allowed herself to be led into Houlihan's.

They settled themselves on the plush, velvet bar stools. Kaye took in the shiny brass beer handles, the gleaming glassware.

"How are all the men in your life?" Melissa asked, as soon as they got the drinks.

"We–ll, Bren kissed me. Nick told me he was married before. I didn't go home with Andy the last time he asked, but I am going home TO Liam in a few weeks' time."

"And does he know about that?"

Kaye shrugged. "He'll soon find out."

"Janey Mac," said Melissa. "Sorry I asked. If you want my opinion, I'd stick to Bren."

Kaye giggled at Melissa's new Irish expressions. "Why's that?" she asked.

"Because the other two aren't available for intimacy."

"Wow, that's a mouthful! I'm available for dating, they're not available for intimacy? It's hard to get it right."

"It's a pattern. Ya gotta break the pattern. Dump the ones who are not available. Now."

"Liam is available."

"Not emotionally, he's not. He has issues. Isn't he seeing a therapist?"

"Did I tell you that?"

"Yes. There's always something preventing him from being with you, Kathy. Because you're real. You're the only real person in his life, and he can't handle it." Melissa had all this jargon. "Maybe he's gay?"

"Nah."

Melissa would think that.

"We're reading *Women Who Love Too Much* in Psych class. That's you in that book."

"I don't love too much. I don't love enough."

"You do, Kathy, you do. As for Nick. The fact that he was married once is a good sign. It means he's not afraid of commitment. But, if he's not divorced, then he's not available either."

Jaysus! Kaye rested her elbows on the mahogany counter. "Oh what difference does it make, I'm not going to be here anyhow."

Melissa smiled smugly at her.

"Chrissie wants to try cocaine." Kaye changed the subject.

"She don't need that shit."

"Tell me about it!" Kaye agreed. Alcohol, shopping, cigarettes. Melissa was right. Chrissie didn't need another bad habit. "She's changed," she said. "I can't put my finger on it, but she's not the same."

"I guess most people change when they emigrate to another country. Haven't you?"

"Not really. And does cocaine make you better at sex?"

"It gives you more stamina, but from what you tell me, Chrissie don't need anymore."

"And another thing, where would a girl get an abortion in this town?"

"You're not...? Ok, so, which one of them knocked you up?"

"Not me. It's for a friend."

"That's what everyone says, but in your case, Kathy, it's probably true."

"One of the girls . . . did a pregnancy test . . . Where would she have got that from?"

"A pharmacy?" Melissa said. "Over the counter?"

"And how do you ... you know?"

"You pee on it."

"Pee?"

Melissa slid off her stool. "There are lots of clinics in New York. I can get you addresses. But first, I gotta use the loo. Then, let's go catch a movie?"

As the credits rolled at the end of *Broadcast News*, Melissa leaned into to Kaye, "And, the moral of the story is?" She whispered. "When you get the chance to fuck ...?"

"Forget it."

CHAPTER THIRTY

It was the 8th of December, the night they'd decided on for their Christmas party.

"This is the day we used go up to Dublin to do our Christmas shopping in *Hector Grey's*." Chrissie tossed shredded cabbage into a bowl of mayonnaise for some real coleslaw, like they had at home. Not the American shite.

"Ah, and I used to love goin' in to meet yis," said Kaye, as she tipped a packet of Lipton's onion soup into a dish of sour cream for Auntie Lou's dip. "That's when Christmas used to begin for me."

"Isn't it great that you've known each other all of your lives?" Mo stopped sweeping the floor. Ever since she'd made an appointment at one of Melissa's addresses and spoken to one of the doctors and set a date, she'd been in a lighter mood.

"It is," Kaye said.

"Oh, it was great alright." Chrissie winked at Mo. "Havin' to share a bed with her when we were kids, and then later on, her takin' all the nicest fellas."

"Oh, you had a fair few yerself," said Kaye. "Don't worry."

"Well, I still envy you." Mo's eyes had a dreamy look to them. "I don't have anyone that I knew that far back," she said, "not even family. I don't know some of them at all."

"Really?" Kaye had never heard Mo speak of her past before.

"I found it real hard to make friends at school, and never held onto any of them after. Didn't go to my prom or any of the school reunions or anything."

"The debs, we called it," said Chrissie. "Not a fuckin' prom; that's the seafront in Bray."

"I didn't have that many friends either," said Kaye. "Except for Olivia."

"Well, at least you had Olivia." Mo held up the jar of leftover mayonnaise. "Does anyone want a face mask?" She proceeded to daub dollops of it onto her cheeks.

Kaye and Chrissie did the same, and soon, the three of them were clutching their stomachs and laughing at each other's yellow faces, only their eyes and mouths visible.

"She's in much better form, isn't she?" Chrissie said, when Mo ran into the bathroom to wash it off. She and Kaye wiped theirs away with paper napkins.

"Yeah, I hope everything works out. She's actually nice when you get to know her."

"Didn't I tell ya? C'mon. You put on the pasta for a salad, while I fill the bath."

"The bath? Don't think I've had a bath since I got here."

"So that's the smell?"

Chrissie ducked a swipe of Kaye's mayonnaise-saturated napkin. "I'm fillin' it with beer, ya eejit." She explained. "We'll pack ice on top and that's what we'll use when the stuff in the fridge runs out."

"Gosh, you're very smart altogether." Kaye tapped a finger on her temple.

"As ya say yerself, down there for dancing." Chrissie pointed at her shoes and proceeded to step-dance down the hall.

Kaye filled a saucepan with water and tipped a box of tri-coloured spirals into it. At home, the only pasta she'd ever cooked was spaghetti and lasagne. She cranked up the volume on the tape recorder and started to sing along with Whitney Houston.

"I WANT TO DANCE WITH SOMEBODY."

She imagined herself gyrating to it, later. She was toned and gorgeous in her daydream, in the black leather skirt and white fuzzy top she'd bought in *Strawberry*, twirling around, pointing out Whitney's words with her finger.

"What are ya doing?" Mo rushed to turn off the gas under the pot.

"Oh, just practicing for tonight, heh, heh."

Kaye had been leaping up and down the narrow kitchen, her arms flaying, hitting the high notes, higher than Whitney, even.

"I'm shattered," said Mo, flopping down on one of the fold-up chairs they'd borrowed from the Super. "Have been, ever since." She pointed at her tummy. "Tina kept giving me loads of tables today because I was only working lunch. Now, the bloody fried onions and mincemeat for the shepherd's pie are making me gag." She put two fingers in her mouth.

"Muck." Chrissie was back. "I told ya not to make that muck."

"Everyone has it over here." Mo told her.

"Well, we're not everyone."

They were also serving pasta salad, Irish sausage rolls from scratch, chicken wings, Auntie Lou's onion dip, and Chrissie's coleslaw. Melissa was bringing hash browns, which Kaye thought was strange. Weren't they for breakfast? Plastic bowls on the coffee table contained chips and dips; scented candles glowed in the windowsills; a miniature Christmas tree on top of the TV twinkled, paper plates and napkins were stacked on a side table.

"This is so grown up." Chrissie was dressed in jeans and a baby-pink T-shirt with PARTY HEARTY in the shape of a heart, in sequins.

"Déjà vu!" Kaye exclaimed. "You said the same on our first night together in 4D."

A lifetime ago.

"What if nobody comes?" Mo, also in jeans, and a Dublin jersey, sat cross-legged on the couch, nursing a soda water.

"We'll have our own party." Kaye smoothed her ivory angora top over her black leather skirt.

She was glad she'd dressed up; she'd need the practice for home.

The first to make an entrance was Izzy with an onion ring and green bean concoction.

"Mrs. Fingers' housekeeper makes it," she said, handing a bowl to Kaye. "Tim's in the Terminal. He'll be here later."

Then Melissa arrived with a girl called Jill, in tow, as well as a Tupperware box of chocolate 'hash' brownies.

"Are they a couple?" Chrissie jerked her head at the girls.

"Think so." Kaye shrugged, just as George and Tina sauntered in, looking very cosy. Kaye hadn't copped that before.

Billy was on his own.

"Is that quare one a figment of your imagination?" Kaye helped him in with a case of *Coors Light*.

"Now don't be using those big words on me, Katie Daly."

Matt and Lou called from Penn Station to say they were on their way. "Couldn't miss your first ever party." Lou gushed into the telephone, trying to make herself audible over the carol singers. "Is there a bed for us?"

They'd be lucky to get the bath whenever the beer ran out, but Kaye didn't mention that. "No prob, just take the number 1 all the way to the last stop. I'll have a cab pick ye up."

Andy stopped by with a bottle of wine wrapped in silver paper, immediately helping himself to a plate of food.

"How you doin' with the Nick?" He asked Kaye when he'd finished eating.

"Fine," she said. "Can you go get my aunt and uncle?"

"Sure, I'll be happy to bring all the guests to your party."

"Thanks for eating all that green bean and onion shite." Chrissie saw him to the door.

Before long, the apartment was full. Mister Al appeared with a wry smile, an Italian fruitcake called *Pannettone*, and a bottle of Merlot, he called the red wine. Tim brought a few lads from the Terminal; Seanie and Sil contributed another case of beer. The waitresses from 49th Street popped in after their dinner shift.

Izzy twirled Kaye and Chrissie around in a jive.

"I wish I could do that." Mo whined. "Will ya teach me, Iz?"

"I will girl." Izzy's hair was still in place, her jade eyes more luminous than ever; her shoes clattering the floorboards, letting the downstairs tenants know that they had not complied with the eighty percent carpeting rule.

"Don't mind her." Chrissie caught her breath. "She's too cool to jive, Disco Queen."

Is she even capable of jiving now? Shouldn't she have more important things to be worrying about than learning how to jive? Kaye had barely formed the thought when Izzy grabbed the broom and announced a limbo competition, thrusting it at Seanie and Sil to hold for participants to incline under. Chrissie lasted the longest, despite Seanie lowering it as much as possible.

"Thank God I'm good at something." She panted, falling flat on her back.

"I hear you've got loads of hidden talents." Seanie sneered.

Nick and Pete showed up at five o'clock in the morning, with yet another crate of beer. Pete tugged at a string that was dangling between her knees. "What's that?" He looked mystified. "Some girlie thingie I haven't come across?"

"No." She tied it in a knot, stuffing it into her waistband. It was for hanging the skirt on a hanger, but she didn't bother telling him that.

Nick grinned shyly.

When Auntie Lou started *Danny Boy*, Kaye escaped to the bathroom where she sat on the side of the bath, holding a cold bottle of beer to her temple. She was weary from entertaining everyone, and wished she could be quiet and coy and fade into the background, instead of having to be the centre of everything. Olivia was wrong. She didn't love attention; she just had to be the one to keep things going. Ah well! She slithered off the bath, wiped her face with a towel and reapplied her lipstick.

In the living room, Lou was reaching a crescendo with, *until you come to me* ... to rapturous applause.

Tina was dabbing her eyes with a tissue, George's hand on her knee.

"You Irish," cooed Bernice, all dressed up in a dress and lipstick. "I can see you all in your cottages, singing at the fireside."

Billy sang twenty verses of a song about a Thompson gun, inviting them to join in the chorus that began, *Oh Mama!* Even Andy, who had figured he'd get more business in 4D than on 242nd Street, sang along.

Nick surprised her with *Matrimony* and Izzy wowed them with *Patricia the Stripper*, swinging her hips and tugging at her sweatshirt. When there was a mention of pulling off her drawers, Kaye had to close her eyes.

But a pounding on the door had them open, wide.

"The cops!"

"Oh, no."

Chrissie swung the door open to two men in navy-blue uniforms.

"We've had complaints." One of them said grimly.

"Hey Chris," said the other. "We didn't know you lived here."

"Hi yis lads." Chrissie cried. "C'mon on in." She placed beers in their hands, as Mo prepared plates of food.

While the cops were chowing in the kitchen, several guests shuffled out the door.

Andy hid his can under a cushion and mumbled about getting back to work.

When the policemen had finished their beers and food, they made their way out, advising the girls to lower the noise level. "Don't annoy your neighbours, and you'll be fine."

Things started to wind down after that and people starting to leave.

"Interesting party," Mister Al kissed Kaye's hand. "Especially the singing. My ancestors were Irish, you know?"

"Really?"

"Yes, they came over on the *Mayflower*."

"Oh."

George left next. "This was the sweetest party I was ever at." He dabbed his eyes.

"Poignant." Tina air-kissed Kaye on both cheeks.

"What does 'poignant' mean?" Mo whispered.

"Touching," said Kaye.

"Well, she sure got plenty of that." Mo was sweeping the floor again, this time in between the remaining guests who were now horizontal.

Sil and Seanie decided to head for the Shamrock with Billy. "Ya fancied one of the lads here tonight, Katie." He held the door open and looked back at her.

"No, I didn't!"

"I haven't figured out who it is yet, but you had yer eye on someone. What's he waitin' for?"

She gave him a playful slap and had just closed the door, when over her shoulder, she saw Melissa and Jill sneak into her bedroom.

"We're just hiding the brownies." Melissa chuckled when Kaye went in to investigate.

She'd go to the loo again, then pour herself a nice glass of wine. This was always the best part; when most of the guests had gone, and a few diehards kept things going.

The bathroom door wouldn't open. She pushed and shoved but couldn't budge it, gave it a couple of kicks, but no luck. It was like something was lodged against it. Anyhow, the beer was nearly gone, so there wouldn't be much demand for the bathroom. But Kaye needed the loo, she jumped from one leg to the other back to the living-room.

"Ask Izzy if you can use hers," Mo said.

As she walked away, she heard the door squeak open. Looking back, she saw Chrissie tiptoe out, her finger to her lips. Then, a long shadowy figure emerged, and followed her into the bedroom. Nick.

The door to 2B was open, and she heard sobbing from the living room. Kaye was surprised at the mismatched armchairs, the scratched coffee table, the wobbly TV stand, at Izzy slumped on a shabby, stained, corduroy bean bag. Kaye didn't know what to do and was about to dart back out again when Izzy said, "What are you doing here?"

"Em, just using the loo." Kaye staggered backwards. "There's someone in ours."

"Go ahead." Izzy waved her towards the bathroom.

There was a grubby towel on the bathtub, the shower curtain a clear plastic liner.

Kaye couldn't imagine living like this. Even if it was for just a short time, she liked her home to be homely. In 4D, they had peach bathmats and a seashell shower screen, matching curtains; velvety salmon towels fluffing out of wicker baskets, gold soap and toothbrush accessories. This toilet wasn't what she would call pristine white, but she sat on it anyhow and contemplated the floor.

Nick. And Chrissie?

Back in the living-room, Izzy was still crying.

"It's Tim and that cousin of yours. They're at it."

"At what?" Surely Chrissie wasn't still messing with Tim?

"What d'ya think?" Izzy screeched. "Tim was clean there for a good while, and as soon as he saw that one, he was back on it again like gusto."

"Back on what?"

"Oh, don't act so dumb Kay, Katie, Kate, whatever yer feckin' name is."

"Jesus, Izzy, I don't know what you're talking about." Kaye scrunched up her face in disbelief. "I'm tired and drunk and dyin' to go to bed. I can't wait to get home to my boyfriend at Christmas. Chrissie was with Nick earlier, and here you are accusing me of knowing she's fooling around with Tim. And I haven't a clue whether they are or not." Not entirely true. "Chrissie's not the same. I've known her all my life and she's never been like this, and I don't know what to do anymore, to be honest."

"I didn't say they were foolin' around, ya eejit." Izzy's tone was nasty. "They're coke buddies, ya fool."

"They're what?" Kaye was getting more confused by the second.

"They're doing cocaine, ya clown." Izzy was furiously tapping her nose with her finger.

"Whaaaat? No way?" Kaye laughed at the idea.

Chrissie had only been thinking about it, not doing it. Izzy was going mad. Then again, there were her new allergies, Chrissie had never had them before. Kaye had thought she was just trying to be American. But wait, there was Tim's runny nose. His big eyes.

"No, no, no. No way." She shook her head furiously.

"What about all those visits to the bathroom?" Izzy's voice was quieter, her cries a mere sob. "The persistent chatter. The pupils dilated like marbles. And the money. How come she never has any, and she making loads of it below in Hamburger Haven?"

"Burger Heaven?"

"Oh, who cares what it's called?" Izzy was shrieking again. "You're so precise. Always have to be right. A typical teacher, you are."

"Aren't you?"

"No, I'm only a classroom assistant. I came up the hard way; had to study like fuck in school and still didn't even get a grant to go to university. That's how typical I get. I'm not from D4 or D8 or Southside or Seagreen or wherever the fuck it is."

"Seafield," Kaye said. "And, ya know what? I've had enough. I'm goin' back upstairs. If I see Tim, I'll send him down. I don't know what he's at, but I'd be surprised if Chrissie was up to anything. She likes the craic, the having fun kind. Nothing more."

"Huh." Izzy followed her up the stairs. "Oh, she likes the crack alright; ye Dublin girls; ye think ye have it all sewn up."

"What on earth…" Kaye was about to push in the door to 4D when Tim popped out like a jack-in-the-box, bleary-eyed. Behind him, in the hall, stood Chrissie, looking sheepish.

"What's goin' on?" Kaye asked her. "Izzy's in a state. She thinks you and Tim are doing coke. Is that true?"

"No!" Chrissie's eyes flitted to the floor, her normally pale face flushed pink.

"Tell me."

"It's just for the craic," Chrissie said. "It gives me heaps of energy, makes me stay up all night. And I have loads of confidence when I'm on it." Then she whispered, "And the sex."

"Sex?" Izzy, who had been behind Kaye all the time, shrieked and lunged at Chrissie grabbing a clump of her copper bob.

Tim stumbled at the top of the stairs and was about to keel over.

Kaye grabbed him by the shirt and propped him against the wall.

She wouldn't mind letting him fall, but the cops would be called, and there'd be a mess and she wanted to go to bed. Somehow, she managed to wrestle Izzy away from Chrissie and prop her up beside him.

"Let there be no talk about drugs. We're Irish, we drink; we have a good time. Izzy, Tim." They looked at her. "You're lucky to have found one another, not like us."

She swept her arm around. Saw Melissa. "Thought you were gone?"

"I came back for my Tubberware." Melissa told her.

"Tupperware? Oh, yeah, bye." Kaye stepped aside to let her pass and bumped into Jill.

"You go girl." Jill exclaimed. "What a woman; what a waste; if only." Chrissie cocked an eye.

Next, Lou came out waving a brownie. "Can Matt and I have tea and a biscuit before we go to bed?"

"No." Kaye snapped it out of her hand. "I'll get you nicer, Irish ones. Go back inside." She crumbled the brownie and threw it out the landing window onto the fire escape. "We'd give anything to be in your shoes." She turned towards Izzy and Tim again, which wasn't entirely true, but she was on a roll. "If anyone wants rehab, I'll get the address from Mel." She heard Melissa chuckling downstairs,

Kaye pushed Chrissie into the apartment, kicked the door shut and slumped against it. "What a load of shite." She glanced into the kitchen. There was no sign of Matt and Lou. "I'll sleep here." She leapt on the couch. "By the way."

"Yeah?" Chrissie was on her way out into the hall.

"Was Nick in the bathroom with you?"

"Yeah, warnin' me off drugs. Trying to scare me. Said he saw a friend go down a black hole. Another overdosed. He's on a mission to save everyone, Saint bloody Nicholas. Why do you want to know?"

"Just wonderin', that's all."

CHAPTER THIRTY-ONE

The winter sun spilled into the living-room. Kaye tried to straighten her legs, but the coiled springs prodded her shoulders, her spine. So much for fitting into the couch. She had that empty feeling again. It was like a loss, like when something was over or gone altogether.

Matt and Lou bounced in, causing her to sit up with a start.

"Don't move," said Lou. "I'll make a quick cup of tea and we'll be off."

"Stay where you are," Matt said to Kaye. "You had a harrowing night."

"I did? Oh no." She swung her feet onto the floor. "Ye have to stay."

She'd bought food from the Irish butcher and was damned if she wasn't going to cook it. "I'll make ye breakfast. It's all arranged." She dashed into the kitchen. "Be ready in a jiffy."

Soon, rashers were grilling along with black and white pudding; sausages sizzling on the frying pan; eggs scrambling in a saucepan and toast burning.

Toast burning?

"Oh no, the toast!" Kaye rushed to the toaster, singeing her fingers trying to retrieve the crunchy bits.

"Don't worry," said Lou, "I like it that way."

"Dad too."

"Well, he is my brother. It runs in the family." Lou swallowed a mouthful of fluffy, creamy, scrambled eggs. "These are divine." She gushed. "Never tasted eggs so good in a long time."

"The way I learned in Miss Brennan's cookery class in national school." Kaye sat down beside her. "With milk, a knob of butter and tons of pepper. Cooked in a saucepan."

"Delicious." Matt spoke through a mouthful of toast.

"In Burger Heaven, Fernando whisks the eggs straight onto the grill." Kaye passed around a dish of sausage, bacon, black and white pudding. "They don't taste this good at all."

"Well," said Matt. "You handled last night's crisis with aplomb."

"What crisis?" Lou looked startled.

"There was a slight fracas on the landing, that's all, but your niece sorted it out." He winked at Kaye.

"That's right," she said, not so sure things were sorted.

"You're the glue, Kaye." He continued. "The glue that holds this whole place together."

"I am?"

"I don't know what you two are on about," said Lou. "But I had a great time. It was a good old-fashioned party like long ago, with singing and dancing, and shepherd's pie. And now this scrumptious breakfast. I feel like I've spent the weekend in Ireland."

"You probably would've settled much easier if you'd come to the Bronx," Kaye said.

Matt arced his brow at her, as if to say, 'don't go there'.

"Maybe you're right." Lou sighed. "But now I have you here, so everything's alright."

"I'm leaving, remember?"

"Oh, you'll be back. You've got so much going for you here." Lou stood up and began clearing the table. Took the dishes into the kitchen. Soon, the tap was running.

Kaye turned to Matt. "I'm going home, to snare this man once and for all."

Matt shook his head. "Just be careful, ok? What is it you really want? Think long and hard. Not him, I'd say, but what he represents, perhaps? You might be making assumptions, about what your life would be like with him?"

People were always telling her not to think. Matt had been on her side. Why was he saying this now. And where was Lou when she needed her? She'd heard her wander down to the bathroom, as if Kaye and Matt hadn't been talking about anything important at all.

"My yoga teacher says assumptions cause all the trouble."

"She got that right."

Kaye sighed. "I have that Sunday feeling today. Like years ago, coming home from Kilcoughlan after a holiday, or returning to school at the end of the summer. There's a hollowness inside. As if everything is over."

"Well, an occasion you were planning and looking forward to, has ended." Matt raised his shoulders. "Those childhood feelings are stamped on our memory."

Lou came into the room with their bag. Within minutes, Kaye was bundling them out the door, amid hugs and kisses. After they'd left, she felt hollow again, empty inside.

"It's the alcohol," Chrissie said when Kaye brought her in a cup of tea, really wanting to chat.

"Alcohol?"

"Yeah, it's a high, like any drug, there's a comedown after it."

"Drugs?" Kaye raised her eyebrows.

Chrissie lowered her ocean-blue eyes.

Coming down from alcohol? Kaye had never heard of that before. Then again, she'd never drank as much as she had in the past six months. Before this, the only thing that had made her feel empty was Liam.

There was no Oprah on a Saturday, but the two female stars of *Cagney and Lacey* were just as feisty and full of smart remarks.

Half way through the show, Mo burst in the door, and stood there by the sofa, staring vacantly at the screen.

"What's up?" Kaye asked her.

"I'm going home for good, that's what's up. I'm going back to Jim."

"What brought this on?"

"What am I doing here? Seanie's an ass. I'm workin' my tits off. Then, there's the situation." She pointed at her stomach. "Once that's done, I'm going to start anew."

Kaye couldn't believe she'd left the situation until last.

"Are you going to tell Jim?"

"No."

"You've had a light-bulb moment." Kaye told her.

"Huh?"

"Your sudden realisation – Oprah calls them light-bulb moments. You know when the light suddenly goes on in your head."

"Oh, right," Mo said, but Kaye knew she didn't get it at all.

"So, when are you going?"

"At Christmas, with you."

She left the room, only for Chrissie to come in, as if on cue. She was showered and dressed, and all made up like when she lived at home. "I'm going to meet Billy later," she said, "and if he wants me, I'm going to be his girlfriend again. I want him to mind me. Last night." She hesitated, then sat down beside Kaye. "Last night is not what I want."

"Billy?"

"We got talkin'. Things aren't going great with the girlfriend. And all of my pain with men began after Billy left Ireland."

"You mean what happened with Ken?"

"Yeah, and others."

"But what pain? And what others?"

"Men, in general. There were times when I said 'no', and they didn't listen. Like, em, they didn't force me or anything, I just gave in. I often had sex when I didn't want to."

"Really? How come I didn't know all this?"

Kaye realised she hadn't always been there for Chrissie. She'd been so taken up with her studies in UCD and her own problems, like Olivia, and Liam. Especially Liam.

"Ah, I didn't want to talk about it," Chrissie said. "But now, I'm going to ask Billy if he'll mind me, because I can't do it by myself."

"Good for you," Kaye replied. "I'm glad."

Everyone seemed to be getting what they wanted, except her.

On Sunday, the three roommates watched a full afternoon of *The Thorn Birds*, devouring pizzas, and cokes, and Haagen-Dazs chocolate-chip cookie dough ice cream. And as day faded into night, they snuggled into the couch, drawing a blanket up to their chins, chatting and watching anything that came up on the screen, until it was time for bed.

"See me in my office." Sister Virginia apprehended her, as she entered the large, airy, entrance hall.

"Sister Clare is better and is taking your first class today. She will be back full-time after Christmas," she said, as soon as Kaye sat down.

Great, thought Kaye, good for Sister Clare.

"But Albert is going to need help in the English Department." She shuffled some papers. "And we were wondering if you'd like to take up a position there."

A position? Teaching English?

"It pays a little more, a monthly salary rather than a daily rate."

Bren was right – it's all about the money.

"There's a contract." She pushed a sheet of paper across the desk. "Which is reviewed every year for three years, and then you qualify for tenure."

Tenure?

Was Kaye supposed to sign right there and then?

"Or would you prefer to think about it?" Virginia pulled the paper back. "We were very impressed at how you linked the English and typewriting classes; at how much time you spent observing Al's classes. You showed great interest, and initiative."

"Oh good," Kaye said, still looking at the contract now over on Virginia's side of the desk. "I will think about it, if you don't mind. And get back to you."

"Sure. Take your time. You can give me your answer a week before term commences in January."

"Thank you." Kaye shook the nun's hand.

On the empty corridor, she could hear a drone of conversation from the classrooms, her own particularly quiet, except for the tap-tap-tap of the typewriters. She'd met Sister Clare a few times and was always fascinated at how a snarled little old lady in a black frock could demand such attention, and respect, from an unruly crowd of teenagers.

It was ironic. Just what she'd always wanted – a job as an English teacher – just as she was leaving.

Well, one of the things she'd always wanted.

What was the universe trying to tell her?

She escaped to the staffroom and lit a cigarette. Coffee wafted from a pot on the hob. 'Wake up and smell the coffee,' Oprah was always saying. In New York, it was everywhere.

Mister Al came in and grabbed the pot. "Want some?"

Kaye held out her cup. "Sister Virginia said you might be needing help after Christmas."

"Might?" He looked at her. "I actually am. Are you interested?"

"No, unfortunately I'm going home, but I would've loved it otherwise."

"Oh, I didn't realise that." He started to pour. "I thought there was no work over there; that that's why you all lived in cottages with straw roofs, pigs in the kitchen or somewhere."

"Oh, no," Kaye tried not bristle. "There's work, and there's houses, with roofs and all. No pigs, except on the farm."

"I'm just kiddin'" He smiled. "And by the way, I really enjoyed your party the other night."

"Oh good. Thanks for coming. Now." She drew her cup away. "We'd better not let Sister Virginia see you serving me."

"Don't worry about the good sister. I got her." He started to walk away.

"By the way?" Kaye asked. "What does tenure mean?"

"If you qualify for tenure. You can be made permanent."

"Oh, ok."

"Think about staying." He stopped at the door. "It would be great to have you."

Before the bell rang, she dashed to the loo, put on some lipstick, smoothed her skirt, and damped down frizzy bits of her hair. Not bad, she said to herself in the mirror, and for a moment let herself imagine it -an English teacher in a high school in New York city. Then returned briskly to her classroom, her anxiety from Saturday in danger of returning.

The students filed in, one by one, and opened their bags quietly.

"I'll hand out the books, Miss," one of them said.

"I'll close the door." Another piped up, as the rest of them took their seats.

A girl called Marisol pointed to Kaye's bag on the floor. "There's a saying in Puerto Rico, Miss - bag on the floor, money no more." She placed it gently on Kaye's desk.

"Thank you, Marisol."

"Turn to page thirty-two," she said to the rest of them with as much authority as she could muster. "Today's lesson is on profit and loss."

CHAPTER THIRTY-TWO

She got off the bus on McLean Avenue. Mingled into the pale Irish faces, freckled like hers, and tinges of reddish hair. Dark coats with colourful hats, and scarves streaming like rainbows behind them. Pickup trucks trundled by – Shamrock Furnishings, Shannon Electric, Liffey Valley Removals. In *Death of a Salesman*, Willy Loman gets lost in Yonkers. She had read the play in American literature class, not knowing it was an actual place.

Mo was standing outside Tully Travel when she got there, and the two of them burst through the glass door, eager to book their flights home. Six hundred dollars, Kaye counted out in tens, and twenties, for a round-trip ticket from JFK to Dublin, Ireland. There was also a Dublin in Massachusetts, Ohio, California and Georgia, the travel agent told them in that Irish American accent that Lou and Matt had.

They celebrated with dinner in McKeon's.

Mo went straight to the jukebox, played Randy Travis, *I'm gonna love you forever.*

"Cheers."

They clinked glasses before demolishing their meal - Prime rib, roast potatoes, gravy, mushy peas. A real Irish Sunday dinner, on a Monday, washed down by a bottle of red wine.

Kaye told Mo about Sisters Clare and Virginia but not the new job prospect.

"When I was training, the nuns ruled with an iron fist too," said Mo. "Yet, they say the hospitals at home are screwed up now without them, with bugs and things."

They tucked into bowls of sherry trifle for dessert and ordered Irish coffee for afters.

"Should you be drinking?" Kaye asked.

"Sure, what difference does it make now? It'll soon be gone."

Kaye couldn't get over how she could pretend to be so nonchalant.

Alison Kraus was singing now, *That makes one of us.*

"Its gas that you like the country music too. Years ago, it was all the rage at the carnivals down the country but wasn't considered cool at all in Dublin."

"Oh, my Tipperary father played it all the time at home." Mo replied. "Irish country mainly, like Big Tom and Larry Cunningham, but I much prefer the American stuff."

"Me too." Kaye swallowed a blob of creamy custard and raspberry jelly, enjoying another nugget about Mo's family. "Did your dad like the American stuff too?"

"Well, mainly Merle Haggard and Johnny Cash, the older ones. We often talked about going to Nashville, but . . . now we don't talk so much anymore."

"Oh." Kaye could've kicked herself. She didn't want to piss Mo off with questions, they were getting on so well. "Will ya miss it here?" And there she goes, asking another one.

"Oh, I'll miss it big time, but I'm doin' the right thing. Seanie showed his true colours, dropping me like a hot bun, when I needed him most. Jim would never do that."

Didn't she drop him?

"And what about the ... you know."

Mo shrugged. "I'll just have to get it over with, forget about it, and move on."

"I used to hate that expression," Kaye said. "Now, it doesn't sound so bad."

"It's always good to start a new chapter."

"Or go back to an old one?"

"Something like that. You're lucky," Mo said. "You're smart, and principled, and you think things through. You're interested in people, and you make connections."

"I do?"

"Yes, and you'll never be in the state I'm in now."

There had been Yanis in Greece and Patrice in Paris, then Andy; Kaye could've easily ended up in this state; maybe it was luck, but she'd better not push it.

"Well, I wouldn't be as calm as you are, that's for sure."

"That's because I went through it all before." Mo reached for her coat.

Kaye had one arm in the sleeve of hers. "Huh?"

"I had a baby girl when I was eighteen."

"What?"

"Put it up for adoption." Mo kept her eyes on her coat. "My parents threw me out and I had to stay in Jim's house. That's why we keep in touch."

"It's Jim's?"

"Yes. It was the worst pain I ever endured; since then, I've felt nothing; I'm numb."

Don't judge them 'til you've walked two moons in their moccasins. Melissa was right.

Together, the girls slipped out into the night. When cheers erupted from a pub next door, they arched eyebrows at one another.

"Monday night football?" said Mo.

"Why not!"

They pushed through another thick wooden door into another Irish bar, where another gang of lads in Timberland boots and denim jackets sat at a circular bar, stacks of money on the counter, swilling bottles of beer, cigarettes pinched between their nicotine fingers, screaming at a gigantic telly on the wall.

The girls rushed in to join them.

A shot of adrenalin rushed through her, as the bus swung into the open-air Cross County Mall in Yonkers. Awaiting her was Macy's, the GAP and TJ Maxx – with jumble sale prices, except everything was brand new.

Sweatshirts for Trish and Gary, a pair of jeans for her father to go with the leather jacket, and a blouse to match her mother's new suit. Christmassy tea towels, dishcloths and placemats piled up in her bedroom. Earrings for Olivia, and for Chrissie and Mo. Sheets for Auntie May; a Yankees' jersey for Bren. And Liam? She hadn't got anything for Liam, yet.

"Don't forget the postman." Chrissie teased her when she came home laden with bags and a new suitcase to replace the ragged old rucksack that had made the journey over.

Mo smiled at their banter, her eyes sad, not cold, like Kaye used to think they were.

"How do you do it?" Kaye asked her one evening.

"I don't think about it," Mo replied.

By the time the Terminal Christmas party came around, the pallor was gone from Mo's cheeks. Nobody seemed to notice a thing.

There was shepherd's pie, again; Cliona Kenny and her band; again, Nick and Pete behind the bar, as usual; Seanie and Sil on two stools inside the door. Some things never change, thought Kaye, as she made her way through the crowd. Except that all the drinks were free; Izzy and Tim sat lovey-dovey at a small table beside the football machine, and Andy had taken the night off.

Paper garlands replaced the shamrocks on the wall. Bing Crosby on the jukebox instead of Paddy Reilly. Chrissie kept playing *I'll be home for Christmas*, even though she wouldn't. They weren't officially an item yet, but Billy had accompanied her to a Narcotics Anonymous meeting. That is, he left her at the door and waited until she came out.

"It was such a relief." She told Kaye. "To be talking to people who knew exactly what I was going through."

A ton of guilt unloaded itself onto Kaye's chest.

"And Billy has been such a brick." Chrissie added, and Kaye wondered would she ever be able to say that about anybody.

"Ya lucky devil," Sil said. "I'd give anything to be going home for Christmas."

"I wouldn't have stayed unless I could go home."

"Somehow that makes sense," Sil said.

"I could care less." Seanie slugged his beer. "Sure there's no one at home, they're all here." He waved his hand around the bar.

Kaye hadn't seen him talk to Mo at all.

She and Chrissie had left 4D early one frosty morning and Nick had driven them all the way over to Bay Ridge, in Brooklyn; waited there all day and had them home before nightfall. 'That's what I call a nice guy,' Melissa had said, and Kaye agreed.

She continued up the bar to where he was stationed.

"So," she said to him. "Are you all set for Christmas?"

"I'm off to Guatemala."

"Whaaat?"

The tealeaf eyes moved towards hers.

"I sent a card, like you said. Next thing, I got one back, just like you told me I would."

A pity it hadn't worked out the same way for her.

"I'm staying in a hotel, near where they live." He glanced up and down the bar. "My wife and little girl. She's six now, so that'll be fun."

He looked up at the ceiling. Kaye's eyes followed. A sprig of mistletoe was dangling above their heads. Nick lowered his eyes, leaned in, and then, his lips pressed hers, softly.

Just lips.

"By the way," he said, as she moved away. "Is this the letter you were looking for?"

She recognized the crumpled ball of notepaper, Liam's handwriting, the lined pages, circles around some of the words.

CHAPTER THIRTY-THREE

I t was another cold morning, although bright this time, when the girls, all the three of them, Chrissie going along for the ride, climbed into the limousine that was taking them to Kennedy airport. A parting gift to Mo from Mrs. Polanski, whose day nurse, it turned out, had been the one who reported Mo to Immigration.

When they pulled away from 6125, Kaye glanced back at its wrought-iron stairways and barred windows and a wave of loneliness washed over her. Cruising by Van Cortlandt, she saw the cab drivers slouched outside the Terminal and commuters queuing for the bus, and knew they'd be right there, whenever she came back again.

But the feeling passed when the driver started to regale them with stories about the famous people he had carried - movie stars like Dustin Hoffman and Barbra Streisand. Before she knew it, the sprawling airport was in sight, and then it hit her. She was going home.

Lines and lines of lively Irish faces queued up at the Aer Lingus check-in desk, a sea of sweatshirts, baseball caps, sneakers and shopping bags, voices animated in a myriad of accents.

"Shouldn't the earth belong to all of its inhabitants?" Kaye said to no one in particular. "Whoever decided on borders and boundaries?"

Chrissie stopped humming *I'll be home for Christmas* 'to eye her up and down. "I hope you're gonna put on some make-up and change in Shannon." She regarded Kaye's sweat suit. "You can't face your family for the first time in six months in that get up!"

"At least it's coral."

Color me Beautiful had made so much sense; everything in her new wardrobe matched, at last, and her palette included all of the shades of autumn.

"I know I haven't been the best roommate in the world," Chrissie said to her when Mo was checking in. "But I think you're doing the right thing, giving it one last go with Liam."

It was what she'd wanted all along, Kaye realised, her heart filling, Chrissie's approval.

"But, just in case," Chrissie said. "And I don't want to jinx anything. But, just in case it doesn't work out, you're always welcome to come back. There's a room for you in 4D no matter what, and you know Billy loves you too."

Now Kaye's eyes were welling up.

"No tears." Chrissie hugged her awkwardly. "This is supposed to be a happy occasion."

As soon they got on the plane and the air hostess announced, *Céad míle fáilte*, Kaye was home. When they soared into the sky, over the sea of twinkly stars that was Manhattan, she said, "*au revoir*," and turned to Mo who had tears spilling down her cheeks.

"It's like I'm leaving part of myself behind." Mo sobbed into her sleeve. "Which, I am."

"I know." Kaye returned to the blinking lights below, not knowing what else to say.

"I didn't see the half of it." Mo's head squeezed in beside her. "I was never Upstate, in the Catskills, or out on Long Island. I was never even in *Lucky Cheng's* in the Village."

"You'll be back, on a holiday, surely?"

"Ah, it won't be the same. You can never go back."

"You are now?"

"Oh, Kaye." Mo sighed. "Don't analyse everything. Don't make me think so much."

Well, people can't drift through life, Kaye thought to herself. Or was that what going with the flow meant?

The drinks' cart arrived. They ordered two screwdrivers and the hostess smiled.

"You're so lucky, you have a choice, whether to stay or not." Mo sighed. "But, if you do come back, don't spend all your time in the Terminal," Mo said. "See some of America."

"I saw Philadelphia, didn't I?" She tipped Mo's glass with her own. "And Manhattan, Long Island, even Fire Island, remember?" She recalled a weekend with Melissa, where everyone was gay. Except Kaye. "We had some great craic, though, didn't we?"

They made their way to the back of the plane for a cigarette. Some of the passengers were singing already, getting the party started. After dinner, a movie, and spurts of sleep, the pilot announced their descent into Shannon airport, in County Clare – Nick's County.

"Jesus! It's so green." Mo exclaimed.

"The Americans got it right," said Kaye. "It IS the Emerald Isle."

People made straight for the bar, and by the time Kaye and Mo exited the bathroom, fully made-up, the lads were supping pints of Guinness, and it only five o'clock in the morning. The girls were content with a cup of tea: real Irish *Barry's* tea made with real Irish water, and a packet of *Tayto*, before they boarded the plane again.

The excitement was palpable on the short journey to Dublin, and when they landed, there was a rapturous round of applause. Something else they'd picked up in America.

Kaye's new suitcase was bulging, as she hauled it from the carousel and then rushed through the glass doors to the Arrivals Hall where her parents stood waiting.

And for the first time ever that she could remember, she hugged them.

"You look smashing." Mam had stiffened, but there was a shrill in her voice. "And except for that lazy eye, you'd never notice a thing wrong with your face."

Lazy eye?

"Will ya stop it, woman," Dad said.

Kaye noticed Mo and Jim embrace, mutter monosyllables, slouch out of the airport, not saying another word. None of Mo's family had been there to meet her.

The car spluttered out of the sleepy airport, which was more like a village than the sprawling metropolis that was JFK. A giant Santa on a sleigh, drawn by two reindeers, lit up the pre-dawn darkness. They crawled at forty miles an hour through Santry, Whitehall, around by the red church to Killester, into Fairview and over the bridge to Ringsend, her mother remarking on how well Kaye's face looked and repeating news she'd already relayed in a letter or on the phone.

"I couldn't believe all the people pouring out of Arrivals earlier," she said. "I was dizzy from looking at the doors sliding back and forth. One time, when someone went to America, you never saw them again."

Oh no, that would be unthinkable. Not to see the rolling yellow sands of Sandymount, the two chimneys rising from the mist in

Ringsend, the Dublin mountains, Howth Head jutting out like an enormous sea mammal. From swerve of shore to bend of bay, James Joyce had described it in Ulysses.

"When will the sun rise?" Kaye asked, as they rolled alongside the seafront.

"It might never," Mam said.

Kaye sucked in her breath when a double-decker bus approached, but her father cruised on regardless, bombarding her with questions. "What time is it in America now?" and "Is McDonald's the same over there?"

The sun did rise, eventually, over the Sugar Loaf, streaking the sky yellow and pink, then disappeared behind a clump of grey clouds scudding across the sky.

"There's a new song out," Mam was still rattling on. "By the Pogues, we're hopin' it'll make the Number One Christmas song."

Kaye smiled at the idea of her fifty-five-year-old mother still following the pop charts, and her father an avid fan of McDonald's, at his age. She wondered how he was feeling about having no work.

Only three cars waited for the DART to pass through the Merrion Gates. "There's no traffic," she exclaimed, "and it eight o'clock already."

"Sure, you'd want to be mad to be out at this hour," her mother said.

As Lucky rushed to greet them, Kaye stood at the kitchen door, to let everything sink in. Soda bread cooling on a wire tray. The radio sitting on the shelf. The small fridge under the counter. The armchair beside the mantlepiece. The sea between the trees at the end of the garden.

Her mother filled the kettle and her father got out the frying pan. Kaye tore off a crust of bread and smothered it with butter. Lucky licked her fingers, her face, her lips. She danced him around the linoleum floor, as he barked excitedly. The radio, the smell of sausages, and the whistling kettle soon filled the room.

"What's all the noise?" Trish arrived in, rubbing her eyes.

"Your sister is home from America." Kaye sang, still holding onto Lucky's paws.

After breakfast, she opened her suitcase and distributed the gifts.

Her father put on his leather jacket. "You shouldn't haven't spent so much on me."

"Why not? You were so good to us." She felt her face redden. "You deserve it."

"Do I?" His eyes filled with wonder.

"Ah, would ya look." Her mother held up the tea towels, placemats, and napkins; the Christmas tree earrings and snowman ties; the doggie dish for Lucky and the boxes of red-and-white candy canes and *Hershey's Kisses*, the tin of *Oreo* cookies.

"American chocolate is shite," said Gary, stuffing a handful of *Kisses* into his mouth, as Kaye headed off to bed.

No matter how many times her parents had decorated her bedroom over the years, Kaye wouldn't let them change the teddy-bear curtains, something she was glad of now, as she took in the small room with its single bed, narrow wardrobe, solitary bookshelf. She pulled back the duvet. Not only was an electric blanket toasting the bed, but a hot water bottle too.

It was hard to believe she was at last breathing the same air as Liam again, listening to the same voices on the radio, gazing up at the same sky. All the years she had lain there dreaming about him. She tried to recall the time she had first set eyes on him striding towards her on the teller line, the time he had kissed her out there in the car, the time she had forced herself on him in his new house in Greystones and he had reluctantly pushed her away. But each time she tried to relive these memories; Nick's face got in the way.

She turned on her side and drew her knees into her chest. The fake grandfather clock chimed that another hour had passed, nearly knocking her out of the bed with fright. She kicked off the covers and hopped out of bed, ran down the stairs and took out the battery.

Olivia was not that far away, oblivious to the fact that Kaye was home. She hadn't yet decided if she'd contact her – she'd have to consult Trish first – but, she didn't want to think about that now: she was home and that's all that mattered. Just to hold onto this … she drifted off to sleep… just to hold onto the perfection of this moment.

After her nap, she watched TV for the rest of the day, in her dressing gown, devouring her mother's cooking, staying awake until eleven o'clock, so her body clock could acclimatise.

She was relaxing in the bath, suds up to her shoulders, head resting on a rolled-up towel, eyes closed, when the doorbell rang. Lucky yelped, her mother roared from the kitchen and Trish pounced along the carpeted floor. Then, there was a murmur of voices.

"A golden Hail Mary; tell her to say a golden Hail Mary." Kaye's head shot up. It was Olivia. Her Ma always said golden Hail Marys for their exams, and things.

"I will, I will," Trish said. "She's asleep." She added. "Jetlag, you know. I'll tell her you were here, bye-eeh."

A towel wrapped around her, water dripping onto the landing, Kaye got to a window just in time to see the little red Mini pull away from the gate. At the bottom of the stairs, stood Trish, a smile frozen on her face.

"She heard you were home and wants to see you, has something to tell you, is praying for a special intention."

"A special intention? I thought they went out with the tide, along with novenas and plenary indulgences. Why did you lie to her?"

"Because there was no way I was letting her talk to you until we discuss whether or not you're going to talk to her at all." Trish returned to the sitting-room.

A special intention? Miss Brennan used have them pray for special intentions. When someone was sick or doing their Christmas tests. But the only thing that had ever brought Olivia inside a church was a man. She'd be lighting candles and imploring God to make everything turn out all right. Surely, she didn't want Kaye to pray for her and Liam.

"Did she not come in to say hello?" Her mother found her in the rocking chair, staring at the floor, a mug of cold tea in her fist. "Isn't that a caution?"

"It's a wonder all right." Her father snapped open the newspaper. "She hasn't darkened the door since Katie left." He held the paper up in front of him like a shield.

"Ah, she was in an awful hurry," said Trish. "She'll be up again."

"She was a dote when she was coming here years ago. What happened to her?"

"Nothing happened, Mam. People change, that's all."

How did she know Kaye was home?

CHAPTER THIRTY-FOUR

"I told her," Bren said.

"When?"

"The other day in town. I told her you'd be home for Christmas. Is that a song?"

"I'm here a whole hour and you never thought to mention it?"

"As the bishop said to actress, it never came up."

She gave him a thump, knocking him sideways off his stool. It was Christmas Eve and Begnet's was packed. There were people home from England, Australia, and Spain. Kaye was the only one home from America.

"Is this yer apartment building?" The young barboy pointed at a picture of Manhattan she'd snapped from the Circle Line cruiser.

"Eh, no, that's the World Trade Center."

"D'yis live in something like that?"

"Sorta," she said, not to disappoint him.

Haven't seen you in a while, people shouted on their way by, *where have ya been?*

Over in America.

How did ya get on?

Did ya like it over there?

Are ya goin' back?

"Is this the boat you went over on?" The barboy pointed at another photograph.

"Eh, no, that's the Circle Line, a Cruise around Manhattan, for tourists. I flew over, on an aeroplane, you know?"

She rolled her eyes at Bren, who asked her, "Are ya goin' back?"

"No."

"Why not?" He eyed her. "Oh, don't tell me, don't tell me." He slurped his drink. "Don't ya still have that visa?"

"Yeah. It's valid for five years."

"Is it not an awful waste not to use it? And what about your ticket?"

"It is round-trip." She admitted. "But refundable."

"Return ticket, Katie, it's a return ticket. That's what we call it over here. And didn't ya have one of them goin' over and ya didn't come back. That was the longest summer ever." He clinked her glass with his.

"A Bronx summer." She raised her vodka and lime, a proper one, at last.

Every time the door opened her heart jumped. Here she was at last, sitting at Begnet's bar, with her new hairdo, new dress, new body, waiting for Liam to come in.

People kept to their round; she'd forgotten that; no one buying a drink out of turn. She sent a pint over to one of the older men, and regretted it, when he sent her one back.

"The returned Yank." Bren teased her. "Splashing yer money about, buying for the bar. Old Joe has to go home now, because he's no money left. You've upset his whole routine." She gave him another thump; swore to herself she wouldn't buy any more rounds out of turn.

The door swung open again. Kaye took a sip of her drink, trying to look blasé, but it was Mo, who came straight over and flashed a diamond on her finger; Jim behind her, looking uncomfortable, but proud. He wasn't that unlike Seanie, with his John Lennon specs.

"He proposed before we left the airport," Mo whispered.

He did?

"We picked the ring today."

"Imagine?" said Kaye, even though she couldn't. "Well, congratulations, I'm delighted for ye."

Mo handed her a bag full of *Taytos*, and chocolate bars, as well as a Christmas pudding, and a slab of smoked salmon.

"To bring back with you. You can get the rashers and sausages and the batch bread yourself."

"But I'm not going back."

"Sure."

"Thanks anyway."

"Do they not have shops over there?" The barboy asked her when Mo had gone.

"Oh, they do." Kaye opened a packet of the crisps. "The food isn't as nice as it is here."

"I often think about that kiss," Bren said, when they were alone.

"Feck off." She glanced at the clock; it was nearly midnight.

Still no sign of Liam.

"We'd better get goin' or the priest will be on the altar."

She'd love to have left the boy a tip, but God knows what Bren would say to that.

As she was shrugging on her tan leather coat from TJ Maxx, the door burst open, and in rushed Olivia, Liam behind her, their faces glittering from the cold.

Kaye looked away. For a moment, she found herself bizarrely hoping they wouldn't see her. But, when she turned back again, there they were, the man she loved and her best friend, standing in front of her.

"How's it goin'?" Liam held out his hand.

"Eh, fine." She tried to stop hers from shaking.

"We knew we'd find you here." Olivia gushed.

"Oh, yeah? Hi." Kaye gave her a watery smile.

Bren said nothing at all.

"You look great," said Olivia.

"Yeah, you look great," said Liam.

"I called up the other night," said Olivia.

"I know, I heard." Kaye looked at Bren and tilted her head at the door.

"We're going to Mass," he said. "Some of us have to pray, you know."

A choir on the TV was singing, *I'll be home for Christmas*, as Bren took Kaye by the arm and linked her into the hallway.

"I'll give you a ring some night." Olivia called after her.

"Yeah, do," said Kaye.

A sharp wind whipped around the side of the clubhouse, pushing the main door open, banging it against the wall. She pulled up her coat collar and sank her hands into its deep pockets. Fell into a trot alongside Bren. Bells chimed through the town, cold pins pricked their cheeks, rain drizzled on their heads. As they progressed up the street, people welcomed her home, asked where she'd been hiding, wished her a happy Christmas.

"It must be great, all the same," Bren said. "Comin' home. Ya'd nearly go away, just for that."

When they got to the church gate, she heard a voice behind her call her name.

"Katherine."

She spun around, and there was Liam in the red Fiesta, his blue eyes sparkling.

"We need to talk," he said.

"How about now?" She stood still, smiling at him.

"Not here." He lifted his shoulders, arms, eyebrows, his hands remaining on the steering wheel.

"We'll go somewhere else, then." She opened the car door and sat in beside him without looking at Bren.

This was it, she thought, she couldn't contain herself, as they drove up Bray Head. This was surely it. Beside him again, so close in the car, she could touch him, if she wanted. But she didn't want to. It must be the shock, she told herself, from finally being with him again. Instead, she rattled on about New York, Manhattan, the Bronx, South Bronx.

Halfway up the hill, he pulled over, turned the engine off.

They sat in silence, overlooking the basin of black sea and sky.

"I think I'm gay."

Gay?

Like Rock Hudson?

And those Englishmen she and Olivia had met in Mykonos?

"You knew, didn't you, you suspected something?"

No.

"I often wondered, if maybe, deep down?"

No.

"I've known since I was fourteen." His voice was monotone. "Since boarding school when the brothers used to hang my wet sheets over the railings, all the lads laughing. When we were allowed watch *Top of the Pops* on a Thursday. The lads couldn't wait to see the girls in their miniskirts. I found myself looking at the lads instead of Legs & Co."

She remembered then a picture he had shown her of when he was fourteen, in his football gear, his straight blond hair reaching his shoulders. Like a girl's, she had thought at the time. Beautiful.

She rummaged in her new *Guess* clutch bag for a cigarette.

Raindrops started to dimple the windshield. A dog barked in the distances, and bushes rustled at the foot of the giant cross.

"I put an ad in that magazine, *In Dublin*." He couldn't stop talking. "You should see all the replies I got. Married men even, and one from a priest, with a picture. Then I met Danny."

Oh yeah, Danny.

"He's not, you know, my ..." He shrugged. "I just ..." he sighed again. "Wanted someone to talk to, someone like me, who'd understand."

Kaye opened her window, flicked out the ash. The air rushed at her. She rolled it up again.

"Say something, Kaye." He rubbed his face with his hands. "Please say something."

She wanted to say she didn't mind, didn't disapprove, didn't think any less of him. She wanted to grip the sleeve of his jacket. To plead 'let's pretend, be boyfriend, girlfriend, not say a word to anyone.'

So why didn't she then?

Why, all of a sudden, did it not seem such a good idea?

In the darkness out there was the house she grew up in, the Tech, the church spire, the piers east, and west in Dun Laoghaire. Dad had brought them up here the day the church went on fire and the smoke filled the sky, obliterating Howth for the first time, racing towards them in clumps of black cloud.

"Danny and I have been exploring the scene."

Scene?

"We've been going to the Cage regularly, as well as the George and the Viking. We got to know a few of the other fellas. They make me feel like I belong. Danny and I made a promise we'd tell at least one more person over the Christmas."

One more?

"And I chose you."

He chose her.

"One more?" She finally found her voice.

"Yes." He was staring ahead again. "I told Olivia last year."

"You told her before you told me?"

"Well, yes. As I said before, it was easier because she wasn't involved. I did try to tell you that night at the Royal. Then."

"Then she and Bren disturbed us."

"Yes."

"So, she's known a whole year and never –"

"I made her promise not to. I wanted to tell you myself. Then you were going away for the summer, so we said we'd leave it until September. Then you decided to stay, so we thought it best to let you get on with your life. Everything seemed to be going so well for you, we didn't want –"

We, we, we.

"And it never dawned on either of you what you were putting me through?"

"Like I said, I was too taken up with my own problems."

Another quote from his letter that she now kept carefully among her class notes.

"So what are you going to do now?" She asked.

Go away, to America maybe. No, not New York. California. Australia even? Anywhere he could be free, be himself. Not have to constantly look over his shoulder. Afraid to lose his job. Bring shame on his family. He can't keep going into the Town Hall every day, Fridays in the Harbour Bar. He had to get away. Seems some people didn't immigrate for the money, after all. But what about AIDS, Kaye wanted to say.

"I'm sorry." He sighed.

"Me too." The ground squelched under her feet when she stepped out of the red Fiesta halfway up Bray Head.

All the times she'd blamed herself. Blaming, blaming herself.

"Get back in," he pleaded. "Please! I'll take you home."

"Just take me back into town."

They drove in silence again, one tiny part of her feeling really, really, sorry for him.

"You probably should have told me at the very beginning," she got out of the car. "But I'm glad you told me in the end." She turned on the heels of her Steve Madden boots – twenty percent off with her Macy's coupons – and trekked towards the telephone kiosk.

"Hello."

"I'm on Main Street," she said.

"You should've told me." Kaye pulled open the door of the approaching Mini and jumped in.

"I didn't know what to do." Olivia drove on. "He was so upset and in a state; afraid he'd lose his job if anyone had found out; afraid he'd end up in jail."

"Jail?"

"It is against the law here, you know. It is illegal to be gay."

Illegal?

"And ye thought I'd report him?"

"Well, not really, but you were so annoyed with him, you were capable of doing anything. We were afraid."

'We' again.

They turned into Seafield, lights twinkling like diamonds in the windows.

"The days I spent here." Olivia looked towards Butler's. "Were the happiest of my life. People used to ask was it not worse being with a real family, a happy family, then having to go back to the Home again, and I said, no, it was great to get out. I had something to aspire to. I wanted that for myself one day, a nice house and a nice family, and children with proper childhoods. I wanted a curly little head like yours; the kind grown-ups liked to pat. I wanted your voice, to read out stories in class, I wanted your brain, Kaye, your brain."

"And you wanted my boyfriend too?"

"He wasn't your boyfriend."

"I was in love with him," said Kaye. "Same thing."

"Oh, I'm sorry, so sorry." Olivia pulled at Kaye's sleeve. "Liam was a friend, a good friend. It's a pity you fancied him so much, because you missed out on a really good friend."

"You should've told me nothin' was goin' on. You more than anyone knew how much he meant to me, knew how much it would've hurt to be left out."

"I'm sorry." Olivia was snuffling now. "I hope we can still be friends."

Everyone wanted to be her friend. Nothing wrong with that, Oprah would say. It doesn't mean you have to invite them over for chicken salad. Olivia's face looked so girlish and vulnerable, just like when they'd first met, Kaye's heart started to soften. She probably would've done the very same thing, had she been in Olivia's shoes. Someone on Oprah had once said that a true friend reflects your truest self.

"Of course," she said. "We'll meet up soon."

She walked slowly to the front door, opened it quietly and was about to quench the candle on the hall table, which had been lit earlier by Trish, the youngest in the family, when she remembered it was also Trish who would blow it out the next day. Tradition.

She lay in bed, staring at the teddy bears and regretted taking the battery out of the grandfather clock. The sound had been consoling sometimes when she was the only one awake. The clown's tears on her *Pierrot* duvet cover were mocking her, mocking her.

But, for Kaye, no tears came. This time.

CHAPTER THIRTY-FIVE

Light slowly started to peep through the window, and movement could be heard in the adjoining rooms, creaks on the stairs. Eventually, it was hunger, and the smell of the cocktail sausages that drew her down. At least, she hoped they were cocktail, another tradition. She forced a smile before opening the kitchen door.

Her mother's cheeks were pink, from the heat.

"Hello love," she said, as she turned off the gas under the frying-pan and checked the toast under the grill.

"Happy Christmas, Katie." Dad was polishing his shoes. She still hadn't asked him how he was finding retirement. Felt shy broaching the subject, felt it was her fault. He seemed in good form though and he and Mam were off to Majorca in January; Gary heading to England were there was loads of engineering work. Would they not be lonely? Kaye had wanted to know. 'Not at all,' Mam had said. 'Won't it be nice to have some time on our own, after all these years.' That had never occurred to Kaye.

And now, despite all the changes, her ordinary parents were still doing ordinary things on an ordinary Christmas morning.

"Hi." She sounded cheerful. "Happy Christmas."

Trish and Gary were shrieking in the sitting-room, as they opened their presents and Kaye joined them before any ordinary questions about the night before were asked. She made appropriate oohs and aahs at her father's gift, *Nora* by Brenda Maddox, and the Claddagh ring from Mam. Trish gave her striped knee socks with individual toes. Her feet swelled just looking at them. A giant slab of *Whole Nut* chocolate was Gary's contribution.

"Because you're a nutter," he said, making her laugh.

"Ah Gawd, the poor thing," Trish said when Kaye told her. They were on their way over to Bren's house for Christmas drinks. "It makes sense thought, doesn't it?"

"Then, how come it never dawned on us before?"

"Because we'd never heard of such a thing. A girl falling in love with a gay lad? We'd never seen it in a film or read it in a book."

"True."

"It must've been a shock though. Are you alright?"

Kaye thought about it for a moment. "I am, yeah."

"Are you sure?"

"Yeah? Yeah, I am. There was a sense of loss, I suppose, for all the dreams I once had. But I feel fine now. It was more a shock than anything else. And worry, for him."

"Well, that's good. Now you can just forget about him."

"Well, I don't know about that." Kaye was surprised too. Why weren't there more tears? More heartache? "Maybe I'll have a delayed reaction," she said.

"Oh, let's hope not," said Trish doubtfully. "Now, no more talking about him."

"Ok. Oh, just one more thing," Kaye said after another while. "Olivia. Do you think she was right not to tell me?"

"No, she wasn't." Trish was insistent. "She should've assured you that there was nothing going on."

Good girl, Trish. That was exactly the answer Kaye had wanted.

"And at least you know now it wasn't you." Trish said. "There's nothing you can do about it. There has to be some freedom in that."

They turned the corner onto the road Liam's family lived on, which they had to pass through to get to Bren's, and there, outside his house was Olivia's red Mini Minor, parked alongside Liam's red Fiesta. The blow landed in her gut again. Remaining friends with Olivia was going to be harder than she had thought.

"She's in his house on Christmas Day, like one of the family. Where I had always longed to be."

"Are you okay, or is this your delayed reaction?"

Kaye didn't know what to say.

"Sure, we never went outside the door on Christmas Day, anyway." Trish insisted. "Tradition!" She sang the word like yer man in *Fiddler on the Roof.*

"It's because I was never asked, that's why. And tradition can be broken."

"No, it can't."

"Well, we're breaking it now."

Bren's house was jam-packed. There were people on the stairs, in the kitchen, in the lounge. How could a Christmas dinner be prepared with this lot in the way? But Bren's mother seemed serene, offering trays of *Ritz* crackers and cheese, not a hair out of place. There was a whiff of cooking, but nothing like there'd be in Butler's house. Kaye nodded 'yes' at the bottle of purple vodka in Bren's hand and proceeded to smile at everyone and answer questions about America.

Did they drink Coca Cola for breakfast?

Did she live in a skyscraper?

Had she served anyone famous?

"Yeah," she lied, "John F. Kennedy, Jnr." She held out her glass for Bren to refill. "He had apple pie and cream and left me two dollars."

The purple vodka was soon going to her head, making her dizzy. During the Queen's speech, she jumped up and started singing *A Nation Once Again*. Trish tried to clamp her hand over her mouth, but Kaye kept pushing it away. Next thing, everyone joined in. Then, she had them all up dancing for *Top of the Pops*; saying she was great gas, she hadn't changed a bit, wasn't it great she was home and not going back to that place?

"It's actually a very nice place." Kaye heard herself saying.

And even though the Pogues only made it to Number Two, she sang along with them, at the top of her voice, *Fairy Tale of New York*, until her heart near burst.

"Everything OK?" Bren drained the vodka bottle into her glass when he found her out in the back garden, smoking a cigarette.

"Grand," she said.

His look was disbelieving, so she told him all about the night before.

"Sure I knew that all along, it was sticking out a mile. Oh, sorry." He ducked her fist. "Look, if that's the way he is, that's the way he his. There's nothing you can do about it. You can dye your hair blue and lose two stone and it won't make a difference."

"Gee thanks," she said, sitting on her hunkers, holding onto her tummy.

"What a story though, Katie. Eh? What would Winnie Oprey make of this one?"

Kaye hadn't a clue. Oprah had never discussed this topic on her show.

Trish opened the door. "C'mon, we have to go." She tugged Kaye upright. "Great party, Bren." She guided her sister around the side of the house, to the gate.

"Bye." Bren shouted after them. "And Katie . . ."

"Yeah?"

"Happy Christmas."

When they passed Liam's house, she searched the downstairs windows for shadows, strained her ears for voices, but the windows were blank. There was no sound of a singsong, no sign of dancing, no talking or laughing. She swayed from side to side the whole way home.

The candle was still glowing in the glass door. Trish had forgotten to quench it that morning, and to place Baby Jesus in the crib. Another tradition broken.

On the dining-room table was a red tablecloth; a holly and candy-cane centrepiece; green-and-gold napkins; colourful crackers and party hats. The turkey carved, and the ham sliced, surrounded by platters of vegetables and stuffing and a gravy boat of brown gravy that Kaye would drink straight from the jug, if she was let.

"I'm sorry, Mammy," she said, crumpling into a chair.

"You haven't called me that since you were a child." Mam enveloped her in a hug.

After dinner, they delayed dessert and played *Pictionary*, pulled crackers and laughed at the jokes. She hadn't enjoyed a Christmas like it in years. This time last year, she'd been staring out the window at Howth, with nothing to look forward to.

Things can change if you want them to.

Now, she could be a teacher of English literature in a High School in New York. She could have an apartment in the Bronx. She could do a Masters' degree at Hunter College in Manhattan. And all of this she had created for herself. She was going to start practicing her affirmations in earnest, and create love, because she was worth loving. *Love is coming to me* … Her mother placed the plum pudding on the table. *Love is coming to me easily and effortlessly.*

The phone rang in the hall.

Mam went out to answer it.

"It's a lad," she returned, "for you."

Kaye hadn't been expecting such instant results.

"Hello?" she said.

"Hi there!"

Behind the familiar voice came the sound of Spanish music, Spanish voices laughing and singing, glasses clinking.

"Nick?"

"Hey, Kaye, how you doin'?"

"Great, how's everything?"

"Awesome, just awesome!"

"It's all sorted then?" She felt a twinge of disappointment, which made no sense at all.

"Yes, they're coming back to America in a few months."

"Oh." Oh no, it couldn't be. Not again.

"She's getting married. Wants a divorce And I get to see my daughter. It's all good."

"Oh, that is good," was all Kaye could say, because now all she felt was relief.

"Let me know when you're flying in," Nick continued. "I'll pick you up at the airport."

"Well," she said, about to explain to him, as she had done to everyone else, that she wasn't going back.

"Yeah?"

"Well, em. Well … yes. I'll … I'll let you know."

"Cool! So, see you then?"

"Yeah," she said, not knowing what else to say.

"Merry Christmas K, for Katherine." He didn't give her time to think.

"Merry Christmas, Nick the Trick!"

They both laughed.

She returned to the dining-room, where Trish peeked at her from under a pencilled eyebrow. "What was that all about?"

"I dunno." Kaye shrugged, looked around at them all. "Maybe I will go back?"

Gary and Dad regarded her, non-committal.

"Give it a go," Mam said. "Even if it doesn't work out, he'll get you over this hump."

Trish looked at Kaye and Kaye looked at Trish, lifting their shoulders to their ears.

"Everyone deserves a second chance." Mam blushed at Dad. "Love comes for a reason, a season, or a lifetime."

Chrissie and Billy; Mo and Jim; Tim and Izzy; Lou and Matt; Melissa and Jill - all the different couples she knew. None of them perfect, but perfect for them.

She will return to America, away from the pitying eyes, who'd assume she had been dropped, and possibly replaced by another, the age-old story, told and retold a million times. But she knew the truth and would harbour it in her heart. There will be other stories, not yet dreamed of.

Mam sprinkled the pudding with whiskey and set a match to it. Their faces glowed in the blue flame. The present is a gift, Kaye realised. Now was all that mattered, here and now with her family, in the house they had come to when she was seven, frightened and alone and pining for Kilcoughlan.

"Welcome home, Katie Daly." Her father raised his glass of *Mi-Wadi* orange squash.

"Welcome home, Kaye." The others chorused.

Bren was right. It was worth going away, for this.

About the Author

Frances Browner grew up in Dublin, and now resides in Greystones, County Wicklow. A creative writing tutor with Dun Laoghaire/Dublin ETB and Greystones Cancer Support Centre, she is very active in local arts, and received Person of the Year for culture in 2022.

Her fiction/memoirs have featured in *Woman's Way, Ireland's Own, Montauk Pioneer, East Hampton Star, Southampton Review, HCE Review, Blue Nib,* and a short story was highly commended for the Costa Book Awards 2020. She has been broadcast on RTE's *Living Word* and *Sunday Miscellany;* for the Francis McManus award, and in Scariff radio's *Flow of Words.*

Poems were published in journals/anthologies, including *Ogham Stone, Skylight 47, Boyne Berries, Pendemic, Not the Time to be Silent.* A haiku, 'Lockdown' won 1st prize in Dun Laoghaire Local Voices, 2020.

A collection of her work, *You Should've Been Someone* was released in 2015. A Micro chapbook, *SELFIES,* was part of Ghost City Press, Summer Series 2019 in Syracuse, NY, and her poetry collection, *Roots & Wings,* was launched by Revival Press in 2019.

About The Limerick Writers' Centre

The Limerick Writers' Centre, now based at The Umbrella Project, 78 O'Connell Street in Limerick City, is a non-profit organisation established in 2008 and is one of the most active literary organisations in the country. We endeavour to bring ideas about books, literature and writing to as wide an audience as possible, and especially to people who do not feel comfortable in the more traditional arts/literature venues and settings.

At the Centre we share a belief that writing and publishing should be made both available and accessible to all; we encourage everyone to engage actively with the city's literary community. We actively encourage all writers and aspiring writers, including those who write for pleasure, for poetic expression, for healing, for personal growth, for insight or just to inform.

Over the years, we have produced a broad range of writing, including poetry, history, memoir and general prose. Through our readings, workshops and writer groups, our aim is to spread a consciousness of literature. Through public performances we bring together groups of people who value literature, and we provide them with a space for expression.

We are, importantly, also dedicated to publishing short run, high quality produced titles that are accessible to readers. At our monthly public reading the 'On the Nail' Literary Gathering, we provide an opportunity for those writers to read their work in public and get valuable feedback.

The centre can be contacted through its website:
www.limerickwriterscentre.com